SERIAL LOVE

SAINTS PROTECTION & INVESTIGATIONS

MARYANN JORDAN

Serial Love

Saints
Protection & Investigations Series

By
Maryann Jordan

Cover design: Cosmic Letterz

ISBN ebook: 978-0-9968010-1-0

ISBN print: 978-0-9968010-2-7

❀ Created with Vellum

I dedicate this book to my mother, who taught me to love, to live, to explore, to create. She was educated in a time when many women did not pursue education. She taught both kindergarten and college classes. She often greeted me home from school with homemade chocolate-chip oatmeal cookies. She listened when no one else would and understood me better than anyone. She was my first best friend, and still is. Alzheimer's has taken her memory and wit, but cannot take her love.

1

PROLOGUE

Eight-year old Jack Bryant walked along the gravel drive, shuffling his feet as he kicked at the red dirt. The school bus had already discharged the other children living in the big houses in town before making the long journey into the country to his parent's farm. He could hear his father's tractor in the field next to the driveway, but did not look over. The events of the school day, fresh on his mind, diverted his attention away from everything except his anger.

By the time he entered the kitchen in the large farmhouse, even the sight of his mother pulling out a tray of cookies did not make him happy.

"Jacques," she said, warmly. "You look like you could use a cookie."

He tossed his backpack onto the table and slumped into a chair. The aroma of chocolate chip cookies fresh from the oven made it difficult to maintain his pout, but he attempted it nonetheless.

"Fine, I'll have one," he grumbled.

She poured a tall glass of milk and placed the drink on the table along with a saucer filled with several cookies. Eyeing her son, she sat down at the table and helped herself to a cookie as well.

"Hey," he complained, watching his mom eat the chewy goodness. "That was mine."

They sat in silence for a few minutes while he quickly ate the other cookies and drank the milk. The snack had the desired effect—he relaxed slightly in his seat, his stomach now satisfied.

"So, do you want to tell me what had you in such a bad mood when you came home?" his mother asked. Her kind eyes crinkled at the corners as she smiled at her only child.

"I hate being teased," he blurted, feeling embarrassed at the admission.

Her son was tall for his age, often mistaken for being at least ten years old already. "Teased? Who's teasing you?" she asked.

"Some of the kids."

"And what are they saying?"

"It's my name. It's a stupid name," he confessed. "No one else is named Jacques. Tommy Perks says so."

"Who is Tommy Perks compared to God?" she asked, her expression full of compassion.

Jack sat quietly, knowing there was no answer to that question. Sighing heavily he nodded, dejection still on his face.

"My father was named Jacques," she said, telling the story he had heard many times. "In the little village where your grandfather was born, the boys were named for saints. Your name…and his were no different."

Jack had lifted his gaze from the empty plate to his mother's smiling face before she plucked another cookie off the platter to serve him. Munching slowly, he focused on her words.

"St. James the Greater knew Jesus. He was one of his first followers. Do you understand how important that is?"

"Then why couldn't my name be James? That sounds cooler," Jack complained.

His mother's laughter rang out in the kitchen as she nodded. "Yes, I suppose that does sound *cooler* to you." Sobering, she continued, "When your grandparents escaped the Great War and moved to the United States, they brought with them the traditions of their beloved country. And in France, boys were often named Jacques for the Saint. He is also known as St. Jacobus."

Jack did not remember his grandfather, but his grandmother had lived with them until she passed away last year. Just like now, she would sit in the kitchen and listen to how his day at school had been. She would tell him stories of her life in France when she was a little girl and the handsome village soldier she had married.

Jack's mother added, "Since Jacques was your grandfather's name…well, my son, it became your name."

He sat, finished the last of the cookies offered to him, his full stomach taking the sting out of Tommy Perk's words. "Yeah, I know," he admitted. "At least I can be called Jack."

"Yes, you can be called Jack," she agreed, patting his

hand. "You know, St. James was considered to be a very impulsive and self-centered man before developing an understanding of holiness." She peered at her son carefully before adding, "You may follow in his footsteps."

Sliding down from the chair, he turned to walk out of the door knowing his chores on the farm needed to be finished before dinner. With his hand on the doorknob, he looked over his shoulder at his mom still sitting at the table, her face gentled with a smile for him. Impulsively, he ran back throwing his body into hers as his arms wrapped around her middle. She held her only child tightly as mother's tears slid from her eyes.

Then with the exuberance of a little boy, he was running outside ready to face the world once more.

Twelve Years Later

Jack Bryant stood proudly at the bus stop as he waited to board. With an associate's degree under his belt, he was prepared for the next phase of his career—the Army. The Greyhound bus rumbled down the street as he turned one last time toward his parents waiting with him.

His father, face lined and worn with years in the hot sun working on the farm, stood stoically as he lifted his hand to the son who was now a man. Jack glanced down at the hand offered, but pulled his father into a hug instead.

"Dad, I'll make you proud," Jack promised, noting the sting of tears in the back of his eyes as he embraced his father. A large man, not often given to outward signs of affection, surprised Jack as he returned his son's hug.

As his father pulled away, he looked up at his son's eager expression and replied, "Already have, boy. You already have."

Jack turned to his mother now openly crying, and lifted his arms, allowing her to rush in as well. Trying to make light of the situation, he said, "Mom, I'll miss you, but I'll miss your cookies the most."

She laughed through her tears as she hugged him tighter. As the squeal of the bus' brakes interrupted their moment, she moved out of his arms, reaching into her pocket. He looked down at her outstretched hand, a silver pendant glistening in the sunlight.

Pressing it into his hands, she said, "It's a St. James medallion. It was your grandfather's. I know you can't wear it in the Army, but he is the patron saint of soldiers. I…I just want you to have it. May he keep you safe."

Clearing his throat loudly to choke back the emotion, he clenched the pendant in his fist. Lifting his eyes to her face, he offered a smile. Nodding to both, he snatched his bag off the sidewalk and turned to walk to the bus.

With a glance over his shoulder, he said, "I love you mom. You too, dad." As he settled into the seat looking out of the window, he noticed his father placing his arm around his mother in a show of affection and support. Realizing his hand still clenched the pendant, he opened his fingers. He rubbed his thumb over the silver, feeling the indentations, thinking of his name. St. Jacques. St. James.

Sucking in a huge breath and letting it out slowly, he shoved the pendant into his jean's pocket. With a last wave goodbye, he headed toward his future. Army. Special Forces. Then? Jack was not sure, but with the medallion in his pocket, he breathed easier.

2

TEN YEARS LATER

The three girls left the bar, clinging to each other as they teetered on their high heels. Tipsy giggles were heard as they walked across the campus. Celebrating her twenty-first birthday getting drunk was so cliché, but Tonya Perkins loved it. She was the last of her friends to turn twenty-one, so they decided to go all out. Their short skirts and low tops left little to the imagination, but what the hell, it was a celebration. Starting with dinner where the servers sang *Happy Birthday* and ending with visiting several bars, each one offering the birthday girl free drinks, the trio now staggered back toward their apartment.

It was after midnight and the clicking of their heels resounded loudly, although the campus was hardly empty. Tonya loved Montwood College and recognized many of the faces passing by. Sybil and Alice had been her roommates since freshman year and while many college students did not get along with their first roommates, the three had been inseparable. Graduation was only a few months away and then real life would hit all of them. But for now? Continuing to celebrate was all she wanted to do.

Pounding footsteps came from behind and the three girls turned, still teetering on their heels as they saw two of the men they had been dancing with at the bar running toward them. Holding hands and giggling, they stopped as they waited.

"Damn, they're one man short," Alice said, recognizing the blond she had been tangled with on the dance floor.

Tonya saw that the two men approaching were the two that had been dancing with her friends. The blond-haired man that had been buying her continuous birthday drinks was not with them. The two men halted in front of the trio, eyeing Sybil and Alice.

"We thought you'd like to extend the evening," one of them said, sauntering up to Sybil. The other threw his arm around Alice, slurring his words as he invited her back to his apartment.

"Guys," Alice whined. "What happened to the guy all over Tonya? We can't just leave her."

The men looked confused for a second before one spoke, "He wasn't with us. We thought he was her boyfriend."

Tonya laughed and gave her friends a slight push toward the men. "Go on, bitches. I'm almost at the apartment and I'll be fine. You two have fun and don't do anything I wouldn't do."

"Well, then hell boys, you're outta luck," Sybil joked, "because she never does anything."

Offering goodbyes, Tonya watched the foursome turn and walk in the opposite direction. She pulled her keys out of her purse and headed down the block to their place. The area was illuminated with streetlights and the security light at the front of their apartment building. The only dark spot was near the trashcans. Passing the alcove where the garbage dumpster sat back from the road, she gasped as hands reached out to grab her. A foul smelling cloth was placed over her nose and as her body slumped backward, the stars in the sky were the last sight she viewed before blackness descended.

He stood outside the room where the girl was still sleeping, her restraints would keep her from escaping. Taking a deep breath and letting it out slowly, he reveled in the feeling of rightness. *The right time, the right place, the right girl. They were all sluts afterall...all of them. That's what mama always said.*

He looked down at the camera hanging around his neck. This part had gotten easier. In the old days, he had to develop his own film. But now? Digital and his computer made it simple.

Straightening, he sucked in another fortifying breath. With the long thin knife in his hand, he was ready. Entering the room, he smiled.

3

The early morning fog draped the woods creating shapes and patterns as Jack Bryant ran along the path. Late spring in Virginia was cool, but sweat dripped off of him as he continued to follow the trail around the perimeter of his property. It wound through a dense copse of trees, their protruding roots caused him to note their locations, but gave him no difficulty.

The years spent in Special Forces had him well trained to run through all types of terrain, his focus clear as his feet found their purchase wherever he was. This trail? Easy. Pounding along the route, he remembered his time in the Army with pride…and fondness. Earning a place in Captain Tony Alvarez's squad had been the ultimate goal. Those tours and missions made this run seem like a stroll in the park.

The back of his acreage sat at the base of the Blue Ridge Mountains and he began to climb slightly. The oak and maple trees created a complete canopy overhead while the redbud and occasional dogwood gave the hint of blooms in the sea of green leaves. Moss and fern grew beside a small stream he jumped over before turning and heading back to his cabin.

He loved the early morning runs. A time to plan his day. Work through problems. And running the perimeter of his land gave him a chance to make sure the fence was secure. He had bought the secluded property for its privacy and had researched his neighbors carefully before purchasing. The back of his land bordered on the Parkway and the north side owned by a small vineyard, floundering in its first years of growing the vines necessary to make wine. The owner, from another state, only occasionally made forays to the property, probably creating a tax write-off. The vineyard manager on site checked out fine when Jack completed an assessment of him. The manager kept to himself and was dedicated to making the farm productive, leaving little time for anything else.

A small cabin rental facility bordered his land on the south side. Owned and operated by an older widow, the vacation destination was also quiet and well run. Jack had initially been concerned about the constant comings and goings from tourists staying in the cabins, but that had not been an issue. The land between their two properties was thick in underbrush and trees, with no walking trails between. The entrance to her facility was nowhere near his, so he never noticed curious passers-by.

Privacy was important to him. He shook his head as he continued to run. *Important? Hell, most of my friends consider me to be a loner!* And that was fine by him. He spent a lot of money to create his working retreat, not to mention the amount of expensive, top-line equipment his company required. Nosy neighbors, curiosity seekers, random hikers...*not dealing with them!* While his company's location was not secret, it was also not broadcast. The ones who requested his services... private individuals or companies needing his help or the government agencies that wanted complete secrecy and discretion, never needed to come calling.

Jack had erected a defensible barrier around his acreage, using state of the art technology. Not only did he use old-fashioned barbed-wire fencing, but wired it to trigger his alarm system when breached. Security cameras maintained the area, making it virtually impossible for someone to be on his land without him knowing about it ahead of time.

He continued his run, satisfied with the security of his perimeter. Only the babbling of a nearby creek broke the quiet of the morning. The birds were waking, their myriad of calls beginning to fill the woods. Blue jays and cardinals dotted the cedar trees, providing a splash of color amongst the green.

As he rounded another curve in the trail, his house came into view. Made of dark wood logs, a stone fireplace and windows overlooking the mountains on one side gave the large building the look of a luxury cabin. The construction had taken a full year to build the structure and another three months to secure the property.

He slowed his pace to a walk, allowing the breeze to cool his body. The wide front porch beckoned him from his run, but he bypassed the chairs. Jogging up the steps of his house, he took a few minutes to stretch his warm muscles on the porch. His sharp eyes glanced around, a small smile curving the corners of his mouth as he appreciated all he surveyed.

Walking into the front room, he immediately went past the two-story living room on the left through the open dining room on the right and to the kitchen behind it. The large space, appointed with stainless appliances, was organized and airy. Grabbing a water bottle out of the refrigerator, he drank thirstily before moving down the hall to the staircase.

Taking the stairs two at a time, he stalked through into the master suite, heading straight toward the bathroom. He reached over to turn on the water in the glass block enclosed space. Stripping while the water warmed, he then stepped under the spray. Jack was a large man, and the bathroom was something he built especially for someone of his size. The oversized shower, with its multiple showerheads, sent water sluicing over his body. It did not take long to wash the sweat from the morning run off his body and he stepped out, wrapping the towel around his hips.

Not the type of man to spend any time in front of the mirror, he quickly combed his hair and stalked out into his utilitarian bedroom. Simple, but comfortable furnishings, the bed linens and walls in muted blue and grey colors. The room, like the man, oozed casual masculinity. Tossing on a dark t-shirt and slightly worn jeans, he sat on the edge of the bed to pull on his boots.

He made his way back down the stairs toward the

hall leading into the kitchen. Before reaching the front of his house, he stopped at a closet door and pulled it open. With a few taps of his fingers on a hidden security pad, he entered the code and the back wall swung open, exposing another set of stairs leading down.

Descending the steps, he moved through the door at the bottom, walking into a spacious open room filled with computer stations and monitor screens on the walls.

He entered the hub of his company. Saints Protection & Investigations. One he had built from the ground up, filling the space with the latest equipment and the best men he could find. His dream…now a reality.

A large conference table sat in the center, several folders open in front of a man flipping through the papers.

"Morning," Jack called out. "You hungry? The others will be here soon."

Marc Jenkins looked up at his boss and nodded. "Yeah, I'm coming." He stood, stretched his tall, lean frame and walked toward the stairs. Following Jack, he turned and secured the closet panel behind him. The opposite wall held another door, this one leading to the three-car garage built at the back of his home.

The two men efficiently prepared a quick breakfast as they waited for the others to arrive. Jack's gaze glanced to the security gate as the code was entered.

"Bart and Monty are here," he said, watching as the dark SUV moved through the gate and up the drive toward the cabin.

Jack continued to watch as the passenger alighted

from the vehicle first, twisting and turning his huge, muscular body from side to side. Jack smiled, knowing even in the full-sized SUV Bart would have felt constrained. As Bart stretched out the kinks from the trip, Monty moved toward the front door. Physically the two men appeared very different. Bart Taggart, bulky muscles from his years as a SEAL. Monty Lytton, tall and lean, but powerful. Deceptively powerful. Bart looked comfortable on the football field and Monty could have entered any boardroom taking command. But both equally dedicated to Jack and the company he had built.

A few minutes later, the two men strode into the kitchen, offering head jerks as early morning greetings as they made their way to the coffee pot. The four men were soon joined by the other four members of Jack's team. The group hung around the kitchen for a while, drinking coffee and conversing easily. To an outsider, the scene would appear they were friends gathering before heading out to a sporting event. But underneath the effortless banter, were men serious about their careers.

The seven followed Jack down to the basement control center and settled into the chairs around the table. They had worked together for about two years, helping Jack establish his business. A business that was growing in reputation.

Most of Jack's duty tours with the Army's Special Forces were spent as the Chief Warrant Officer for Tony Alvarez's squad. The twelve-member squad was known as the best, securing their missions with expert efficiency. Tony had been the consummate leader and Jack was honored to be his second in command. After Tony had retired, he began a security business in the state capitol city of Richmond and several of his former squad members had joined him.

Jack had another year of his Army commitment and had been called to work with an inter-disciplinary team, tracking down some of the most wanted insurgents. Unsure how the team would function as a unit, he had been amazed. Consisting of a Navy SEAL, CIA contact, weapons and explosive experts, and several Special Forces, they quickly acclimated to their assignments, each bringing their particular skills to the table.

And Jack knew then what he wanted to do when his tour of duty was over. Replicate in the civilian world what he had accomplished with that group. The business had taken almost four years to create, but with his contacts, he was able to lure these men to him, each from a variety of backgrounds. With the blessings of their representative agencies, Saints Protection & Investigations functioned as one unit. More importantly, flew under the radar, using whatever means necessary to accomplish their contracts.

The men focused their attention on Jack as he clicked on his laptop, projecting images on the wall screen. "The governor has requested our assistance. In the past several years, there have been a number of murders of young women on college campuses. The FBI have only recently begun linking them as a possible serial killer, and the killing spree may have been going on for years prior. The governor is now concerned because the FBI have been unable to solve the cases and they're asking for our assistance."

"Why the governor?" Bart asked.

"It appears the murders only occur at the numerous Virginia colleges. Now that the press is starting to get ahold of the possibility of a serial killer, the governor wants to cut down on the negative connection with the colleges."

Each man's computer tablet contained the information they began to decipher, as Jack continued his dissertation.

"Here's what we know. There's no particular physical type of woman. They've been blonde, brunette, and redhead. Their body types have also varied from very petite to a full, figured woman. Their ages are similar, but that would be due to the university setting. All have been between eighteen and twenty-three."

Blaise asked, "Why weren't they tied together earlier?"

"It appears, like with most serial killers, he stepped up his operation. There have been reports of missing girls for several years, but with no bodies or evidence of foul play, they were not considered linked. Eight months ago, the body of Helena Rorton was found dumped on the outskirts of Rasland College. She had been raped and mutilated. Evidence supported that a long knife had been used to cut patterns into her skin. It was also determined she had been alive when the torture began."

As the image of the murdered young woman flashed

on the screen, each man cursed at the damage and pain inflicted.

"At the time, there was no reason to think the murder was anything but an isolated event and the local Rasland police handled the case. And there's one other thing," Jack said, gaining the attention of the group. "She was missing her right index finger."

The men absorbed that information before Monty prodded, "Others?"

"Four months ago, Sheila Carlson, a freshman at Richmond Community College was missing for eight days before her body was found. Also naked, sexually assaulted, and tortured with a long knife. That was the first time the state police linked the two murders, but there was no other evidence to be found and there were such dissimilarities between the two. Different age, race, body types, and even the knife marks were not alike. But she, like Helena, was missing her right index finger."

"No forensic evidence?" asked Blaise, his eyes scanning the report on his tablet.

"Practically nothing. No DNA left. It was surmised the knife was the same. The bastard's careful, I'll give him that," Jack answered. "Now, two weeks ago, Tonya Perkins, of Montwood College, was also found. She had gone missing three days prior and her body turned up in the woods near the edge of the campus."

"I'll assume her finger was missing as well?" Cam growled.

Jack nodded, sighing heavily. "Yeah. Since specific, detailed information was never made public, the FBI is assuming it's a serial killer. And because there have been multiple reports of missing girls from college campuses all over the state, they're now digging into those cold cases."

"The director has agreed for us to take the case and work with them," Monty added. The former FBI agent smiled, knowing it had been hard for the director to agree with the governor. Monty's political undercover operation had been compromised and instead of staying with the agency, he had been lured away to the enticement of continuing his career in an unfettered environment, where carte blanche was the name of the game. Sure, the successes they had would be claimed by the various agencies, but in the end the goal would have been met. A successful mission.

The other men had similar tales. Marc, who was skilled in interrogation, had been a pilot for both Homeland Security and CIA. Luke, another former CIA employee, was a software engineer genius. Bart, trained as a SEAL, had left the Navy and been employed with Border Patrol. Cam, a former undercover detective with the Richmond Police Department, came to work for Jack after meeting him through Tony Alvarez when his gang cover was compromised. Chad was a former ATF explosive expert, who had served on the bomb squad. Blaise was a veterinarian, one of many who worked for various government agencies, had left the DEA, tired of the red-tape and ready to learn more investigative skills. Until he met Blaise, Jack did not even realize that the government hired so many veterinarians, but his medical knowledge and extra training as a medic had been invaluable.

Jack continued, "On your tablets are the files on all the known possible cases. I need you to familiarize yourself with them and then we'll meet back here in two days to plan."

As he expected, the men did not move, each already immersed in the files. Smiling to himself, he looked back over the information although it had been committed to memory.

Suddenly the perimeter alarms sounded, causing each man to jump to alert. Luke immediately turned to the security computers and pulled up the location and visual onto the large screen. "South quadrant, no visual yet."

"You know what to do," Jack stated, grabbing his weapon as he rushed up the stairs. Closely following, the other six men did the same, leaving Luke to coordinate from the secure room.

Monty, Chad, and Cam raced toward the barn, jumping onto all-terrain vehicles and heading toward the north, separating to cover more ground as they ascertained the security of the entire area. Jack, Bart, Blaise, and Marc ran south toward the area of penetration. The landscape was dense with trees and underbrush, many with thorny protrusions just for the purpose of slowing the progress of an intruder. The men knew where they were heading and exactly how to maneuver through the property.

"No visual yet; appears to have breached the fence

near the stream," Luke said, the others hearing through their earpieces.

The six men were narrowing their focus when Blaise saw a movement to their right. Jack circled around quickly, shouting, "Stop! You're on private property." Out from the tangled bushes stumbled an elderly woman.

She stared at the men in front of her, confusion in her eyes. Her short gray hair framed a face that had several bleeding scratches, her thin arms abused by the thorns. She was wearing blue jeans and a short-sleeve blouse, certainly providing no protection for her arms from the brambles.

Stunned, Jack growled his warning once more, starting toward the woman, when the other three on ATVs came careening to a halt in the area. Bart quickly lowered his gun but stayed on high alert, not willing to take any chances considering he was trained to be ready for any contingency.

The men stopped, all watching the woman carefully, noting her confusion. Cam stepped forward, his hand up in front of him in a conciliatory gesture. "Ma'am?"

Blaise moved up beside Cam. "Can we help you? Are you lost?"

The woman twisted to gaze behind her at Jack and said, "When did you grow that beard, Charlie? Mama's not gonna like it."

Jack's gaze cut over to Blaise, who was closest, the look of confusion now in his eyes.

"Ma'am," Blaise tried again, moving one step closer. "We need to—"

The sound of someone else crashing through the underbrush from behind the elderly woman had the men once more on alert as a scream pierced the air.

"Gram! Gram!"

Bursting into the group of startled, armed men circling around, a young woman came flying into the clearing. Immediately she flung herself at the woman, screaming, "Get away from her!"

Being the closest, Jack snagged her around the middle, effectively halting her progress as he lifted her feet off of the ground. She struggled, kicking and clawing, as he held her effortlessly. "Don't hurt her," she pleaded.

"Settle," he barked into her ear, giving her a little shake. "No one's going to hurt her. But if you don't stop trying to kick me, I can't guarantee the same for you."

Bart, Monty, and Cam re-holstered their firearms, although they remained alert. Blaise moved another step closer to the older woman, reaching his hand out gently. Chad circled around nearer to Jack so they effectively blocked the two women in.

"Gram," the young woman called again, this time gaining the older woman's attention. "Gram, it's me, Bethany."

Jack's gaze cut back to the woman he held in his arms, noting her long blonde hair was tangled with a few leaves and twigs embedded. He pulled her slightly to the side, seeing her face clearly for the first time. She appeared to be in her twenties, with blue eyes that were wide with fear. *Or is that anger?* Her body, while easy to hold above the ground, was hidden in a large, baggy plaid shirt but with his arm underneath her breasts, the feel of her indicated she had a perfect figure.

"Please let me go. I have to get to her. Please," Bethany pleaded.

He released her slowly after setting her feet back on the ground and she rushed out of his arms over to the woman. His mind was filled with the sensation of loss as her body was no longer pressed against his. Shaking his head to clear those thoughts away, he turned his attention back to the pair of women. Although there was no threat, the problem still existed…the two women had made it through his security and he needed to deal with that.

"Gram," Bethany said, as she threw her arms around the older woman. She twisted to look at the seven fierce men surrounding them and ordered, "Get back. Get away from her."

"Oh, my goodness. I thought you were Helen," the elderly woman said.

"No, Gram. I'm your granddaughter. Helen was your sister."

"Well, where did Helen go? Did she run off with Charlie here?" she asked, nodding back toward Jack.

Bethany's gaze cut over for the first time to the man who had stopped her. She had not noticed him when she was captured other than his rock hard body against her back and his unyielding arm wrapped around her middle.

He was tall, built like a lumberjack with muscles bulging from his tight, black t-shirt. His worn jeans were loose enough to allow movement, but could not disguise the powerful thighs underneath. His dark brown hair, cut close on the sides, had a natural waviness. His jaw was covered in a thick, but neatly trimmed beard, completing the lumberjack appearance, but she instantly knew that was a façade. The man with the piercing, grey eyes gazing directly at her was dangerous. And if the weapon tucked in the back of his jeans and the similar men surrounding them was anything to go by, they were not enthusiastic about her and Gram's unplanned arrival.

The expression on his face did not look happy and the feeling was mutual.

"She wasn't trying to trespass, you jerk," she bit out, staring right at Jack. Turning back to Gram, she said, "He's not Charlie. You've just gotten confused."

The men shot a glance toward Jack, seeking his instructions. Not liking being caught off guard, he growled, "Blaise, check them out."

Blaise, a veterinarian who also been trained with EMTs, stepped toward them once again. Bethany moved instinctively in front of her grandmother protectively.

"We're fine. I'm very sorry for the trouble and inconvenience. I'll take her back now."

Before she could stop her, Gram moved toward Blaise with a smile on her face. "I'm Ann. Nice to meet you young man."

"Gram, this isn't social time. You wandered away and I need to get you back to the cabins, okay?" Bethany said, fatigue showing for the first time.

"Hi, Ann," Blaise said congenially. "You've got some cuts there. Let me take a look at them."

"Okay," Gram said at the same time Bethany said, "No."

"Yes," Jack stated firmly, ignoring the pointed glare on Bethany's face.

"We're fine. I can take care of her cuts and scratches when I get her back to the cabins."

"And just how do you propose to do that without getting more injuries? Go back the way you came through the brambles?" Jack asked, one eyebrow lifted in question.

Pursing her lips tightly, Bethany's eyes darted back toward the woods. *Oh, Gram, what have you gotten us into now?*

"Bethany? Let us take you and Ann back to the cabin and get you cleaned up and checked out. Then one of us will drive you back to your place," Cam said.

She nervously shook her head as the reality of the situation swept over her. Seven large men, all armed, guarding their property.

As though reading her mind, the men stepped back to give the women some room.

Jack's eyes had not left the young woman. As irritated as he was at her intrusion, he admired her spunk. "We can't stand out here all day," he groused. "Let's go." Turning to Bethany, he said, "We can go back to my cabin and we'll make sure you're patched up. Or we'll take you back to your place. What's it gonna be?"

"Charlie, you're being rude," Ann said sharply to him.

Sighing deeply, Bethany turned around. "Gram, he's not Charlie. Now let me take you back and we'll see if we can find him." Looking over her shoulder, she said, "Thank you for you offer, but I'd like to get her home."

Jack nodded, spoke into his radio and within a few minutes, Luke drove up in his SUV. Bethany settled her grandmother in the passenger seat and opened the back door. Before her foot could step up, she was hoisted from behind by a pair of large hands. Glancing back, she saw Jack right behind her, his hands spanning her waist.

With ease, he had her buckled and then rounded the vehicle and entered the back seat as well. The others nodded and headed back to the compound. They knew Jack wanted to see where the women lived and how his perimeter was breached.

"Where to ma'am?" Luke asked.

"Turn left here and we're the next property over," Bethany directed.

Jack turned and looked carefully at her. "Are you staying in the rental cabins?"

"No."

"Do you live there?"

Silence greeted him from his seat partner, but Ann turned around from the front and beamed, "I own Mountville Cabins."

"Gram," Bethany said, her voice low in warning. "We don't need to tell all of our business to strangers."

"Oh, stuff and nonsense," Ann said. Looking at Jack, she narrowed her eyes. "Do I know you, young man? I don't think I've seen you around here before and I've lived here all of my life."

Jack looked into Ann's clear eyes, seeing no confusion now. "No ma'am. I'm new here."

Nodding, Ann smiled. "Thought so. But if you're gonna be courtin' my Bethany here, then you need to make sure your folks come around for a visit."

"Gram! He's not courting me. You got lost and he's taking us home," Bethany exclaimed, trying hard not to let the exasperation show in her voice.

"Well, why wouldn't he be courtin' you? You're pretty, nice and a good girl to boot." Ann looked over at Luke and added, "Unless you're the one courtin' her. You know it's hard to find a good girl nowadays."

Luke, looking into the rear-view mirror at his boss, tried to hide his smile. "Yes, ma'am. I'm sure. But Jack'll be good to her."

Before Jack could respond, Ann speared him with a glare. "Jack? I thought your name was Charlie?" She twisted farther around to look at Bethany and said, "Helen, aren't you goin' out with Charlie?"

Bethany leaned her face into her hands, fatigue taking over. When she realized Gram had wandered away from the cabins, she tore through the woods after her. Finding a few pieces of ripped clothing on a barbed wire fence, she knew Gram had slipped through the neighbor's property line. With her heart in her throat, she raced on ignoring the thorns clawing at her arms. Finally seeing Gram standing in the clearing, her heart did not have a chance to slow down considering that seven huge men were around Gram, with weapons in their hands.

If the situation were not so dire, she probably would have laughed at the absurdity of it all. Luke's voice interrupted her thoughts as he asked, "Where to now?"

Lifting her head, she saw they had turned by the wooden sign post with the name **Mountville Cabins** burned into it. Her grandfather had made that sign when he and his bride first built the facility. Vacationers had been coming to rent the small cabins for over forty years.

"Keep going straight and you can drop us off at the welcome cabin."

"So you do own Mountville?" Jack asked.

Bethany sat straighter in the seat, answering, "Yes. Gram owns it. She and Gramps built the cabins when they first got married. She's been running the business since he died three years ago."

Luke stopped the SUV in the parking area of the large, two-story cabin with the sign **Registration and Welcome Center** on the door. Baskets of ferns hung on the porch that spread across the width of the lodge. The small gravel path leading to the front steps was lined with an array of flowers on either side. Jack could tell they were well tended while appearing to be naturally planted at the same time.

Bethany hopped out before Jack could get around to her, but his hand landed on her shoulder as she struggled with the door to assist Gram.

"Let me," he insisted, moving her gently back.

Opening the door, he helped Ann who just beamed at him.

"Oh, Charlie, you're such a sweetie."

"Gram, he's not Charlie," Bethany said once more, moving up to put her arms around Ann. "Let me get you inside and take care of those cuts."

As the two women walked to the door, Luke came around the front of the vehicle. Looking at their retreating backs, he said softly, "Well, that was unexpected."

"Right," Jack growled. "You get back and work with the others. I want to know how the hell an old woman managed to get through our property line and we couldn't get visuals on her."

"You sticking around?"

"Yeah, just to make sure they really are all right. Send someone back in about an hour. In the meantime, we need to take care of our borders. Get 'em all on that today."

Luke nodded and with one last glance at the old cabin, he headed back to the vehicle.

4

Bethany escorted Ann into the cabin and walked past the front desk to the back room. As they moved through the large gathering room, Jack's gaze quickly took in the space filled with old game tables, a worn sofa, and bookshelves crammed with paperbacks. They walked toward the miniscule bathroom on the first floor.

Seating Ann, she wet a washcloth and turned to wipe her grandmother's face. Hearing a noise next to her, she startled seeing Jack standing in the doorway. "What are you still doing here?" she asked, stepping in front of Ann again.

"If I wanted to harm you two, I would have already done so," he responded.

Licking her lips, she nodded. "Yes, I suppose that's right." Wiping Ann's face with the warm, wet cloth, she glanced back over her shoulder. "I...I should apologize. She hasn't wandered in a while and well, I...I lost her."

Ann patted her hand, "Did I do something wrong, Bethany?"

Her granddaughter looked sharply at her, then smiled. "No Gram." Turning her head back to Jack, she whispered, "She remembers me now."

She gifted him with a smile, and this time he startled. Her blue eyes pierced his and her beauty astonished him. Not that he was unused to beautiful women, but he had spent so much time building his business that his base needs were met with the occasional consenting woman. But he always made sure they understood the rules—no attachments. His lifestyle and business did not accommodate entanglements. The women he had been with were certainly attractive, but not like this. Her face, bare of makeup, was perfection... only marred by the few scratches from the thorny bushes.

Shaking his head to clear the musing, he stepped back. The last thing he needed was a neighbor getting too nosy. Preferring to keep his life simple, he looked down at her sternly again. "Here, let me help," he said gruffly, gently pushing by Bethany, taking the antibiotic ointment out of her hands. "How long was she out there?"

Bethany, stinging from the obvious disapproval, snapped, "Only about twenty minutes. Why? Do you think I just let her wander for hours?"

"No, I was wondering if she needed fluids. She may be dehydrated."

"Oh." Embarrassed she had not thought of that

possibility, she stared at the man who spoke so roughly and yet his hands were so gentle with Gram. Deciding she could trust him, she left the room, moving to the small refrigerator in the office. Snagging a water bottle, she glanced at the mirror on the wall, its old wooden frame built by her grandfather from barn wood.

Her reflection dismayed her. Long blonde hair, mostly falling out of her braid and tangled around her face. A scratch was on her forehead, dried blood crusting around the edges. Leaning closer, she saw a few twigs nestled in her hair as well. *Wow, you're a real stunner,* she said to herself. *No wonder he looked at me in disgust.* Her mind went back to the other men on his property. Now that the adrenaline rush of finding her Gram was over, she was able to more clearly see what had been in front of her. All seven were tall, well built. Some were huge, others leaner, but all looked more than powerful enough to take on whatever might have come across that fence. *Armed for bear and only caught Gram and me.* She had to giggle at the thought.

Then there was the man that drove them back…an eighth handsome man.

So why did I only fixate on the one holding me? Sighing deeply, she chastised herself as she looked in the mirror again. *Whatever. I don't care what he thinks of me!*

She turned and walked back to the bathroom, wondering how a man so large could squat in such a small space with Gram. He was speaking softly to Ann and had her face and arms cleaned and medicated.

"I think you're going to be fine," he said as he

assisted her up from the seat. Ann looked up and patted his arm.

"You're a good man, Charlie," she said with a smile. Seeing Bethany behind him, she walked over and took the water bottle held out for her.

"Come on, Gram, let me get you upstairs. You should have a little rest," Bethany said, glad when Ann did not protest.

Having to lean back to keep her gaze on Jack's face, she said, "I should thank you. I know I reacted badly…I was just scared for her—"

"No need to apologize," he replied, not able to take his eyes off of her.

Licking her lips nervously, she self-consciously ran her hand over her messy braid. "Well, okay then. Thank you…um?"

"Jack. Jack Bryant."

Nodding, she offered a small smile. "Thank you, Jack. Goodbye then."

He stepped closer, his feet moving on their own, and peered down into her eyes. She was a head shorter than he was. *If she were in my arms, her head would be tucked under my chin and her cheek would be against my heartbeat.*

"Make sure you take care of those scratches," he said, his hand lifting to her forehead brushing the strands of blonde to the side, exposing her own injuries.

Unable to find her voice, she swallowed deeply and nodded. Then, holding Ann's hand, she led the older woman to the staircase on the side of the room.

A small sign at the bottom of the stairs read **Private – no guests allowed upstairs.** He shook his head, incredulous that those two defenseless women thought the sign would keep someone from going up to where they lived to possibly harm them if they wanted.

Walking back out to the porch, he looked around carefully as he waited for his ride back. The gravel lot in front of the main lodge meandered off to the right and he could see the first A-frame cabin in sight amongst the trees. Having studied the area before he purchased his property, he knew the gravel drive circled a small lake covering several acres and had ten A-frame cabins along the way. The road came back into the main lot from the left. The water had a few canoes and paddle-boats, now tied to a dock. The place looked neat and well-kept, but the years had taken its toll on the buildings.

The Saint's SUV pulled in front of the lodge and he hauled himself into the passenger side, nodding to Luke, who was driving again.

"They okay?" Luke asked.

Jack nodded slowly, his eyes still sharply looking around. "You all get anything yet?"

"Yeah, thought you'd want a debriefing when we got back."

"Good. I hate like hell that woman got through, but she exposed a weakness in our facility that we can learn from."

A few minutes later, he and Luke joined the rest of the men in the basement command center of his house.

Chad began, "We went back to the fence where Mrs. Bridwell crossed. We need to increase the security cameras to focus on that wooded area, near where the creek is. Almost the entire perimeter is on camera and yet she managed to find the one area that was more out of sight."

"Gonna take care of fixing the problem tomorrow, boss," Cam said with Bart nodding.

Luke, looking up from his computer screen asked, "You want to know what I found out?"

Jack nodded and turned his attention to his computer expert, knowing Luke would be able to ferret out all information.

"Ann Bridwell, widow of Martin Bridwell. They married in 1957 and bought the land in 1958 with his Army savings. Loans were easy for military personnel to get housing and property back then. They built the lodge to live in and then the other cabins. Did most of the work themselves and hired local help with the more difficult construction. As soon as they got one cabin built, they rented it as a private honeymoon location. Actually did really well for the times. Ended up with ten cabins to rent and have continued to be a steady cabin rental locality since they are close to the mountains for hikers, campers, fishermen, and then skiers in the winter. Martin died about three years ago and his wife has run the place by herself with part-time help from her granddaughter, Bethany, when she wasn't in college."

Luke stopped and Jack looked over at him. "That's it? That's all you got?"

"Not much there, Jack. They pay their bills, the mortgage is paid off, they pay their taxes. The cops have only been called a few times when someone partied too hard, but other than that, there's nothing."

Blaise spoke up, "You figure Alzheimer's? Is that what we saw today with Mrs. Bridwell's confusion?"

With a few more clicks, Luke said, "Nothing yet on her medical record although her insurance claims indicate she's been to the doctor several times in the past couple of months."

"What about the granddaughter, Bethany?" Monty added. "She's a real firecracker."

Bart laughed, "Fuck Jack, you should have seen your face when she came tearing out of the woods like a mama bear."

"And you caught her in mid-air," Marc said, joining in the laughter.

Jack grinned at the memory before his body reminded him of the way she felt in his arms. Even as she struggled, his body reacted to hers.

"You got more on the granddaughter?" Monty asked. "I'd like to know what her deal is."

"No," Jack said firmly, causing the other seven men to focus on him. Shifting uncomfortably in his seat, he was aware of their perusal. "No one looks into her. Except me."

The men eyed each other and grins spread among the group. In the couple of years they had been working together, Jack rarely went home with one of the women from a bar when they had all gone out. While most of them worked hard and played hard, Jack had been the one to go home early wanting to make sure he was doing all he could to build his business.

Luke shut his computer down, said, "Yes, sir."

"I hate to bring up unpleasant news, but before all this was happening, we were looking into the murders," Blaise said.

"Exactly," Jack agreed. "Thank you for helping with this morning and with securing the perimeter again, but Blaise is right. I still need you on task for our next briefing tomorrow morning about the possible serial killer."

With that, the men dispersed for the day leaving Jack alone.

That evening as the sun descended over the mountains in the background, Bethany settled Ann in one of the rockers before joining her. The Welcome Center officially closed at five p.m., but the renters knew that she lived above the main common area and could be found if needed. Thankfully, it appeared to be a slow evening.

She glanced to the side, watching Gram's face beaming in the sunset.

"This was your grandfather's favorite time," Gram said. "We would sit here and watch the sun set over the mountains and see the colors flash across the lake." Sighing heavily, she admitted, "I miss him."

"I know you do, Gram," Bethany acknowledged, her heart aching for her grandmother's sadness when the past was remembered and for the loss of her grandmother as the insidious disease was creeping in.

Alzheimer's. That was what the doctor had said. Early

stages of Alzheimer's like dementia. Bethany had sat numbly as the doctor explained what was happening and what to expect. She had taken Gram in for a checkup when it seemed as though Gram was forgetting the simplest of things. Running tests and a full exam, the Geriatric Specialist finally gave her the diagnosis and began Gram on medication to slow down the progression of the disease.

Some days were better than others and, thank God, most days were better than this one. Usually, Gram just forgot where she put the vacuum or someone's receipt. She recognized their returning customers' faces but began to forget their names. *And sometimes she thinks I'm her sister who's been dead for years. And Charlie? She was calling Jack by the name of Charlie. I'm pretty sure that was Helen's teenage sweetheart.* Shaking her head, she focused on the memory of the tall, handsome man they met today and she chuckled. *I'll bet we weren't what he was expecting!*

Sighing deeply, she thought about Jack sitting quietly washing Gram's cuts. *How could such a gruff man be so gentle?* Her reflections continued as she remembered the way his body felt against hers. *I was captured by him, but with ease, not pain.* It had been a long time since she had been held by a man. College certainly had its romantic encounters but once Gram needed more help, she decided to put her business degree to use here at Mountville.

And who has a security fence around their property? What does he do? Jack's face continued to fill her thoughts until Gram cut in.

"I'm sorry, Bethany."

Jerking her head to the side, she reached over to clasp her grandmother's hand. "Oh, Gram. Don't apologize. Please, it's okay."

"I just can't seem to remember things like I used to. I get so frustrated sometimes."

Bethany squeezed her grandmother's hand, fighting the tears prickling her eyes. "I know Gram. The doctor said to give the new medicine several weeks to help and you've just started taking it."

A few vacationers walked by on their way back to the cabins for the evening, calling out greetings as they went.

"Evenin', beautiful ladies," Mr. Taylor called, his arm around his wife as his two sons trailed behind.

Bethany waved and acknowledged the family that came to rent from them several times a year. It was nice having returning guests. It not only helped with the finances but gave her a sense that what they were doing must be right.

Mr. Taylor was always so friendly and once he found out Bethany had been in advertising, he would corner her and talk business. The company he worked for was based out of Richmond as well. His wife did not seem to like talking shop, so Bethany and Mr. Taylor would chat when they would visit.

A truck with a couple of men who had been out fishing for the day drove in, stopping in front of the women as Bethany waved them over.

"Have any luck?" she called out.

"Some," one of them replied with a smile. "Went to

Lake Abrell toward the end of the day and had better luck there."

"Good. Just remember gentlemen, we have a strict nine p.m. quiet time."

Nodding, the passenger grinned. "Yes, ma'am. You'll have no trouble from us."

Giving them a goodbye wave, she watched as their truck continued over the gravel road toward their cabin. The sun had made its final descent and the fireflies were out in number. Offering Gram a hand, she assisted the woman from her chair and ushered her inside.

It did not take long to settle her grandmother into her bed for the night, making sure she had everything she needed. Downstairs, she locked all of the doors after checking the security lights. She went through the motions automatically, her thoughts on the handsome neighbor. Gruff, yet gentle. Powerful, yet held her safely.

Who is he and what does he do? she wondered. *Who guards their land with armed men ready to strike?* Shaking her head, trying to erase the path her mind was taking, she forced herself to think about work. Sitting at the desk, she ran through the website checking for updated reservations.

Horace Malinski. *Oh, he's coming back. Of course, it's been about two months.* Mr. Malinski had been staying at Mountville for almost four years. He would stay for a week, always keeping to himself. Painfully shy. *Or kind of creepy,* Bethany had to admit. He would hole up in the cabin, rarely coming out. But he was quiet. Paid in full when making the reservation. And when he drove away, she knew his cabin would be scrubbed clean. In fact Sally, the cabins' housekeeper, would come away saying that his cabin was cleaner than she could have ever made it.

Continuing to check the reservations, she grimaced. Eight men sharing two cabins next month. *Great. Just great. A bachelor party.* Knowing how loud a group of drunk men could become, she clicked *confirmed* while planning on making them pay a security deposit as well as signing the lease agreement early.

Taking care of the reservations, she moved to the open lodge room. Sally had tidied the room before leaving and there was little for Bethany to do. She walked to the bookcase, filled with paperbacks that residents would read and leave, often adding to the pile with ones they brought from their homes. Finding a romance she had not seen before, she took the book upstairs as she headed to bed.

Once settled, she opened the book and was pleased to discover that it was good. Reading until her eyes began to close, she tossed it on her nightstand and turned off the lamp. As she drifted off to sleep, her dreams were filled with the handsome hero coming to rescue her. Unlike the Viking image on the cover of the book, her dream man was tall, broad, with dark brown hair and a beard. And she could feel his hard, strong body pressed against hers.

Jack sat at his table, his laptop open in front of him. *Nothing. Nothing but the basic information.* He did not know what he hoped to find, but Bethany Bridwell was still a mystery. His searches came up with a few campus articles printed by her when she worked on the university newspaper. She had a Facebook page that had been posted to rarely since leaving college. Other than a few likes on some friend's pictures, there was no activity.

He flipped through some of her last posted photos and saw a few of her with Ann and her grandfather from about five years earlier. Her tan face was beaming as she stood between them, arms around each one.

She had a business degree with a minor in marketing. Having been hired by an advertising company once she graduated, she quit her decent paying job six months ago to move in with her grandmother to help run Mountville. *Did she want to? Did she come willingly? Can she handle that on her own?*

He dug into her finances, knowing she had taken a serious cut in pay when coming to Mountville. It appeared she had been frugal, having built up a bit in savings but that would quickly be gone if she put her money back into the business. *And from the looks of a few of the buildings, they seemed fine but some upgrading would be needed soon.*

Giving himself a mental shake, Jack forced his thoughts back to the activity at hand. Her motives do not matter. All that matters is how she and her grandmother are as neighbors. *Can't have snooping on my property.*

But as soon as the dismissive thoughts flew through

his mind, he was forced to admit she intrigued him. The women he dated, if an occasional dinner and fuck afterward could be called dating, had been educated and in careers that offered them stability and financial success. While there had not been many, he could not think of one that would give it all up to take care of an elderly relative and certainly not for the difficult labor of running a wooded cabin rental facility. In fact, the last date had ended after dinner, as the woman's conversation became a list of the financial attributes she expected in a man and then devolved into her diatribe against men unwilling to commit. *No thank you, ma'am!*

Bethany's parents, Ed and Susan Bridwell, were professors at a small university in Arizona, but it appeared they kept up with their daughter and Ann. *So they offer emotional support, but not able to assist with the daily needs that Bethany has taken on.*

After a few more detailed, yet unproductive, searches, he closed his laptop. Checking the security of his property, he headed to bed. Taking a shower, he could not get the thoughts of her off of his mind. The way his body responded to being held against hers. The protective stance she assumed when guarding Ann. The fierce glare in her eyes that could change to one of affection when aimed at her grandmother. *What would it be like to have those eyes turned to me? To harness that courage and passion.*

His dick jumped to life at the thought of having her under him, and he knew his control was not going to make it better. Grasping his cock in his hand, he jerked off under the shower to the idea of making love to

Bethany. *Making love? Nope, just fucking for me. No time for anything else!*

But as he came hard, the hot cum shooting out against the tiled wall, he could not help but know that anything with the beautiful Ms. Bridwell would never be just a fuck.

5

Walking across the Montwood College campus, Jack felt ill at ease. Blaise at his side appeared to be embarrassed by the attention he garnered. Giggles and winks followed them, as the girls strolling by looked at the tall, muscular blond.

Jack, glancing at his investigative partner, noticed that while Blaise smiled back, he was not encouraging the behavior.

"Fuck, it's like being back in time," Blaise said. "Hell, I almost failed out of my first year of college due to spending more time with pussy than I did studying."

Lifting an eyebrow, Jack commented sardonically, "That's a shocker."

Chuckling, Blaise continued, "Hey, I got my shit together. Started hitting the books instead of the bars and once in Vet school I had no choice but to spend all my time studying." Looking around at the young girls, he added, "Jesus, they look young. Were we ever that young?"

"About a thousand years ago," Jack replied, knowing Blaise's years being sent to shit-hole areas of the world as he worked against bioterrorism had hardened him.

Coming to the campus center, they saw two girls standing outside watching them warily. Jack, aware of his and Blaise's size, stopped several feet away. "Sybil? Alice?"

The two girls nodded and he introduced him and Blaise.

"We know you have been interviewed by the police but thank you for agreeing to meet with us. Any information you can give us will help in finding your friend's killer. Shall we go inside?" he asked, nodding toward the building behind them.

Once settled, he began with the basic questions he knew they had been asked before. Having read their police and FBI report, he knew what they had said and wanted to see what they could add.

After gaining the preliminary information, he asked, "What was she wearing?" Seeing the girls immediately stiffen, he explained, "I'm not suggesting anything inappropriate on her part. We're looking into any similarity between the victims and it can be the smallest thing."

Sybil nodded as she said, "She loved purple. She hated dressing up, but it was her birthday and we were going to a club. So she wore my purple top and a black skirt. She never wore heels, but she borrowed those as well."

"She looked so pretty," Alice added.

"What did she normally wear?" Blaise asked, noting the wistful look on the young woman's face.

"She was always pretty," Sybil stated defensively, looking at Alice.

"I know. I didn't mean she wasn't," Alice defended. "But she normally wore longer skirts and she always had shirts that didn't show her boobs."

"Her parents were kind of strict," Sybil added.

"Any special religious affiliation?"

The two girls pondered the question for a moment before Alice answered. "No, not that I can think of."

"But," Sybil added, "we were often hungover on Sunday mornings, so I can't really tell you what she did. She wasn't a drinker. Well, until the last night." At that, her eyes teared up and Alice grabbed her hand.

"This was our fault, wasn't it?" Sybil whispered, looking into the hard faces of the two men sitting in front of her. "We took her out. We took her to a bar. We left her alone."

"Girls," Jack's voice softened. "The fault lies with the person who took her life. That's where the blame lies. Squarely on their shoulders…not yours."

"Tell us more about the man that was buying her drinks," Blaise prodded, following Jack's lead of having them focus on the killer.

Sucking in a huge breath, Alice said, "He was blond." Looking up at Blaise's hair, she added, "Not as blond as you. Kind of a sandy blond color."

"And he had a mustache," Sybil added.

"Did the hair and mustache seem the same? Were there any inconsistencies?"

Perplexed, both girls just stared, so Blaise continued. "Did the color look the same? Did the hair color match his face or did it appear dyed? Were the roots the same color as the rest of the hair? Was there white or gray mixed into the blond? Did he have wrinkles that seemed out of place with the blond hair?"

Sybil's face scrunched expressively as she thought about her answer. Alice's eyes glanced to the side in reflection. She was the first to speak.

"I admit that by the end, we were fairly drunk, but when he first came over..."

"Yes, go on," prodded Jack.

"There was no gray nor the different colors you usually see in hair."

"Different colors?"

Alice reached over to Sybil's light brown hair and held a handful out to the men. "See. Look closely. There's brown, a little red, and even some blonde." The men eyed the strands with interest. "Most natural hair is like that," she added. At the men's silent question, she explained, "My mom's a hair stylist. I grew up knowing about hair and coloring."

Offering an appreciative glance, Blaise nodded for her to continue. "His hair was just all the same from root to tip. His mustache was exactly the same as well. I assume that it was freshly dyed."

"Could he have been wearing a wig?"

Slowly Alice nodded. "Yeah. Now that I think back, it could have been. I just didn't think of it at the time."

"He was older," Sybil added. The men's attention jerked over to her as she continued. "When he laughed, he had little crinkles at his eyes."

Alice looked at her friend. "Everyone's eyes crinkle

when they laugh. See?" she said while smiling large, showing the lines around her eyes.

"Yes, but when you're young, they come right out when you stop smiling," Sybil noted as she pointed to Alice's face, no longer smiling. Gazing back at the men in front of her, she said, "When he was leaning over Tonya one time, I noticed the wrinkles around his eyes did not go away."

Both girls appeared perplexed and Sybil said, "Why didn't we think of these things right away? Why are we just noticing them now?"

Jack answered smoothly, "Most witnesses are upset, traumatized. The mind can blank out little details that later are able to be brought to the surface."

After continuing their questions for a while longer, they stood, thanking the girls for their cooperation. Jack handed them a business card, saying, "If you think of anything else, here is the email where you can reach me."

Alice took the card from his proffered hand, glancing down at the simplistic design. A saint's symbol, along with an email address, were the only items on the card.

The two women started to walk away when Alice turned back. Lifting her gaze to Jack's, she held it courageously. "You will find him, won't you?" she pleaded.

Nodding, he promised, "Yeah. We'll get him."

With his confident assurance, Alice linked her arm through Sybil's and the two walked out of the campus center.

Blaise looked at his friend and boss, asking, "You

reckon we can keep that promise?"

Jack speared him with a glance. "Yeah. This fucker's hiding and he'll strike again, but we'll get him."

With the interview complete, the two drove back to the company compound outside of Charlestown to meet with the others.

The next morning, the eight-member team of Saints met in the basement conference room to debrief. While Jack and Blaise had been at Montwood College, Bart and Marcus had gone to Rasland College to interview the friends and possible witnesses of Helena Rorton. Chad and Cam had also been on the road, driving to Richmond Community College to investigate Sheila Carlson's murder.

Luke had stayed behind, continuing to research the similarities as the team sent in their information. Monty had been busy with his contacts with the FBI. Monty reported, "Shirley Kerstig, an FBI profiler will join us by secure conference later." Luke had arranged for the team to have video conferencing with others, but only the group would be able to see the person speaking to them. The Saints Protection & Investigations would not be seen by the others, nor would their location be compromised. Working with the law while not playing by their rules, had Jack cautious about keeping his compound out of sight.

The men sat, laptops in front of them, as they compared their findings. Luke had taken their notes but wanted to verify the information before continuing his analytical investigations.

Jack began, "Tonya was in the company of a man at a bar before her disappearance. Blond with a mustache, but witnesses said it could have been a wig. She did not normally visit bars, so this was an anomaly for her. Helena had been to a campus church service and was seen praying with a redheaded man, according to her roommate who attended with her. He had a beard, but the witness could not identify if it were real; she also said the man was not college age. Sheila worked as a waitress in a coffee shop near the campus and so she was in contact with a great many people. No one could determine if there had been anyone in particular and the coffee shop has numerous repeat customers so there's a possible dead end there."

"Helena came from wealthy parents. She could have gone anywhere on daddy's money, but chose a state college to follow a high school boyfriend. He flunked out, but she stayed and was doing well," Bart reported.

Chad added, "Sheila was from a poor background; deadbeat dad and a mom working two jobs. She'd worked in high school and continued while in college. I see Tonya's parents are typical middle-class America."

Heaving a heavy sigh, Cam added, "One's blonde, another's redhead, and another's brunette. They were different ages, different body types, different backgrounds. So where's the connection?"

Jack turned to Luke, watching as his fingers flew across the keyboard of his computer. "You got anything for us?"

Luke shook his head, shooting a glare at Jack. "You know this shit doesn't just pop up like on TV. It takes time to get hits off of all this data."

"So what are we looking at?" Jack asked.

"Okay, I've loaded the bank records, school information which," he looked up at them and added, "goes all the way back to pre-school. Doctor's info, right down to when they got their shots and braces."

Cam could not hold back a slight grin, knowing that as quiet as Luke was, when he got going on an investigation, he was meticulous in detail. A glance around the table exposed the same expressions on the others' faces.

Luke continued, "I've loaded in the descriptions of their bodies, habits, classes, jobs, majors, activities..." He paused, perusing his co-workers faces. "If you've given the data to me or I've read it in the police files, it's in here. And it's not going to fucking pop out an answer in case you're wondering."

Blaise could not hold in his chuckle anymore. Luke was a data-mining genius, but testy when pushed.

"What about the cold cases of missing girls?" Bart asked.

Luke smiled, answering, "Already on it. I'm entering what information I've received, but that will take more time."

"How many are we talking about?" Marc asked.

"Hard to say," Jack answered. "On a college campus, you can have students drop out, go missing, go back home, or hell, just move to Montana if they want. The campus does not keep records on all of the students that just leave. But we do have the missing persons from the police. There are six women in the past five years that were attending college, went missing and their families filed missing person's reports."

"All from Virginia colleges?" Cam asked.

Jack nodded, glancing over at Luke still banging away on his keyboard. "You got their info?"

Luke jerked his eyes over to Jack, acknowledging, "Yeah. I'm on it."

Just then, Monty's laptop sounded and he quickly signaled for everyone to be silent. Connecting to his secure conference line, he spoke into the screen. "Ms. Kerstig? Glad you could join us." With a few taps, he projected her image on the wall screen but while the team could see her, she was unable to see any of them.

A middle-aged woman, short dark hair stylishly coiffed, sat at a table wearing the typical FBI uniform of bland, navy blazer and light blue blouse. She smiled from the screen, greeting, "Damn, Monty. Wish I could see your ugly face again."

The others laughed as Monty said, "Well, Shirley, it's good to see your sense of humor hasn't changed."

After quick introductions, she began. "I won't bore you with the details of the case since I'm sure you all are as thorough as Monty was when he was with the agency. And of course, my report is in there as well. With the additional information about the possible missing girls, I haven't changed my initial impressions, but Monty asked if I would give them to you here."

"We appreciate any assistance you can offer, Ms. Kerstig," Jack acknowledged, respecting the agent's efficiency.

"First, let me debunk a few myths concerning serial killers. First of all, contrary to popular belief, not all serial killers are loners. Some are...others are not. They are also not all white males. They are not only motivated by sex, although they can be. There is also a myth that they travel the highways and kill all over the country. Actually, most operate in a localized comfort zone."

"Comfort zone?" Cam interrupted.

"Yes," she confirmed. "There are transient individuals who kill in a much wider range, but some kill within a certain area. And contrary to the Hollywood version of serial killers, they are not insane or evil geniuses. They test from borderline to above average in intelligence."

"So what you're saying is there's no one profile of a serial killer," Bart clarified, heaving a sigh.

"Exactly. Now here is what we do know," she stated. "Serial killers gain confidence and while they do not want to get caught, they begin to make mistakes. They start feeling as though they will never be identified and they will take shortcuts in either the actual murder or in disposing of the bodies."

"With the increase in our ability to investigate and forensic developments, why is it still so hard to identify them?" Luke asked.

"In the case of these killings, they took place in Virginia but in different locations. Different law enforcement agencies were investigating, collecting evidence, sending evidence to different labs. It wasn't until Helena's murder with the similarities that the FBI became involved. Then with Tonya's murder being linked, it was determined to be the act of a serial killer."

Bart asked, "Three is significant?"

"Yes, it takes three murders that have common characteristics to suggest the reasonable possibility the same person committed the crimes to be considered a serial murder."

"Anything specific you can give us?" Jack prodded, his frustration showing.

Shirley smiled indulgently, hearing the irritation in his voice even though she could not see him. "Profiling is an inexact science you know? But yes, this is what I can surmise. The three girls whose bodies were found were sexually assaulted so that does give us a clue into the killer's motivation. While it does not mean he was motivated by sex, it does indicate a high probability he was not motivated by money or just a thrill. He could be sexually impotent or sexually angry. But not necessarily. Because the three girls were mutilated with what appears to be the same knife, it's as though he is trying to mark them, or change them, if you will."

"Change them?" Monty asked.

"Yes. Some serial killers hate something about their victims and in mutilating them, they see the act as erasing whatever is bothering them."

"So that could be a tie-in—something all three have in common that is upsetting to the killer?" Jack surmised.

Shirley nodded her acquiescence. "Absolutely. And it's not usually something simple like body type, although it could be. With the viciousness in which he violates the bodies, I would also surmise that not only is the killer sexually motivated, but anger is also a motivation. Perhaps there was neglect or abuse in their childhood. Considering we have at least one witness identifying a possible suspect in the bar chatting up Tonya, I would even consider psychopathy as a very probable diagnosis. This is using charm, manipulation, and then violence to satisfy their needs."

"Goddamn," Marc cursed before quickly apologizing.

"No need to apologize on my account," Shirley stated. "In closing, gentlemen, I would say we are looking for a male, thirty to fifty years old, who may have poor behavior control, early childhood behavior problems, possible juvenile delinquency, and exhibits a complete lack of remorse concerning their actions."

Shirley was quiet for a moment before continuing. "Mr. Bryant, I don't know much about your organization, but I do know Monty. He was one of our best, but I know the Bureau's sometimes cumbersome hierarchy was the tipping point that finally had him leave and join your company. It's my understanding that you…um… fly under the regulation radar…if that is a good way of putting it?"

Jack chuckled. "That would be a perfectly good description."

She nodded. "Please don't be offended by this. You have a great deal of latitude in your investigations which will make it easier for you to ascertain information. But the special information also gives you a great responsibility. The killer will strike again and while the

Bureau is placing the highest priority on this case, we know he may kill again before we can catch him. Make sure whatever you find, is shared. None of us wants the killer to get away due to faulty information gathering."

"Understood, Ms. Kerstig," he agreed.

The conference continued on for several more minutes before they ended the call with the profiler. Monty looked around the room, stating, "Shirley knows her shit, but I swear this is about as clear as mud, as my momma used to say."

The others agreed. No discernable personality trait of the killer they could pinpoint at this time.

Jack said, "While Luke is still collating the evidence, the rest of you will be assigned to continue the investigation and we need to make sure our location is secure. Chad, I'd like you and Cam to stay with me to work on the perimeter. I also need to file an initial report with the Governor. Bart and Blaise, you head to Tech and Eastburg campuses to see what you can dig up on the missing girls from there. Monty and Marc, you take Western VA community college and Blue Ridge. You know the drill—get whatever information you can, however you need to get it." Giving them a little grin, he added, "Just don't get caught."

The others chuckled, knowing Bart especially enjoyed breaking into wherever he needed to and so far...his luck had held out.

Jack finished by saying, "Now with added information and a little more idea of what we may be looking for let's see what we can find even though the trail may be cold."

6

Sally, an old friend of Bethany's mother, came into the lodge on Saturday morning, gathering clean linens to put on the cabins' beds. Her brown hair, streaked with gray, was efficiently pulled back as she stooped and bent to handle the laundry. A medical receptionist, she retired early at fiftly-five when her last child left for college, but loved to stay busy helping out at the cabins where she and Bethany's mother had played as children.

Mountville's weekly rentals ran from Saturday to Saturday, although if space was available Bethany would accommodate other days. Sometimes guests came on Friday for the weekend and would check out on Sunday. During the summer months, most of her cabins were filled with renters who stayed for the entire week but occasionally she would have room for a weekend visitor.

Tossing the soiled linens into the bin, Sally walked to the closet to grab the clean ones before heading back to the cabins. Since Bethany was out and about, Sally had Ann with her. It seemed to spark Ann's memories when she was helping in the cabins. While Sally cleaned, Ann would help a little and reminisce about the guests she remembered over the years.

"Come on, Ann. We're heading to cabin four now," Sally said. Ann smiled and followed the woman to the golf cart they used to drive around the area. Sally buckled Ann in, not sure if she would stay on her own.

"Oh, I remember cabin four," Ann exclaimed, joy written on her face. "We finished this one in 1963. Martin fell off the roof when trying to put the shingles on. I was pregnant at the time and as soon as I heard him yell, I skedaddled right up here."

"Was he hurt bad?" Sally asked.

"Oh no. Mostly his pride, I expect," Ann answered, still chuckling at the memory. "I haven't seen him today."

Sally, knowing that Martin had passed away three years ago, just said, "I saw him earlier. He'll be around later." It seemed strange to lie to the older woman, but Bethany had attended a seminar on Alzheimer's and Dementia and it was emphasized that instead of insisting the person was wrong, it was better to give them a simple answer that would placate them.

The two women passed Bethany as she was heading to the dock. Giving a wave to the young woman, they continued on to the cabins. Ann's clarity returned as she said wistfully, "I wish my granddaughter could find someone to take care of her. She works too hard."

Sally glanced to the side, saying nothing but agreeing with her friend.

Bethany finished tying the paddle boats to the dock, making sure the rules were clearly posted. Stubbing her shoe on a raised nail, she pulled out the hammer she kept in the tool chest that she carried around with her. A few pounds and the nail was once again flush with the wood. Glancing around, she found a few more that needed to be hammered into place. *Maybe next year we can replace the dock and use screws instead of nails.*

The summer storm that had passed by a couple of days ago left a few tree branches hanging down over the path. She strolled along the trail toward the lodge to get a saw when she saw Horace pulling up in his old car.

Changing directions she walked over, meeting him at the bottom of the steps leading to the front door. He looked the same as always—pale skin and light grey eyes that darted around. His hair was thin on top and his glasses slid down his nose. He always stayed in his cabin when visiting, never participating in any of the activities. She had visions of him as a vampire only coming out at night. Stifling a grin she greeted him.

"Mr. Malinski, good to see you again."

He nodded nervously, bobbing his head. "Ms. Bridwell." He followed her up the steps and over to the counter. She checked him in, then printed off the rental agreement. He did not read it, having been there many times.

"I've got you in cabin nine, same as you had last time if that's okay," she commented.

"Yes ma'am," he agreed. "I like things to be the same."

"I know you prefer to not be too close to the other cabins and a group just checked into cabin two."

He smiled, nervously fiddling with the papers she handed him before reaching out to take the key from her hand.

"Sally has already been there, so the clean linens will be on the bed and in the bathroom. You know the drill so let me know if you need anything."

Bobbing his head once again, he turned and headed back to his car. She followed him as far as the front porch and watched him drive down the gravel road toward the cabins on the farther side of the small lake. *What does he do?* The vampire thought flashed through her mind again, this time allowing the giggle to erupt. *He must sleep all day and then fly around at night.*

Jerking herself out of her musings, she stepped off the porch and headed to the right toward the shed at the back of the lodge to get the saw.

Using the sharp tool, she managed to get the tree limbs down but with some difficulty. She grasped them in her gloved hands and dragged them to the edge of the woods. By the time she finished, she was sweating and her arms ached from the strenuous activity. Spying her depleted pile of winter wood, she decided she would chop some of it after lunch.

Since Gram was with Sally, she fixed a sandwich upstairs in their apartment over the lodge. Eating quickly, she gulped some water before heading back out. Retracing her earlier steps to the shed, she retrieved the axe. As she locked the door, she turned, running into a body.

"Oh my goodness, I didn't mean to scare you," Mr. Taylor exclaimed, grabbing her arms as she stumbled.

"No, it's my fault," she said, smiling at the friendly guest. "I wasn't paying attention."

"Well, with a weapon like that," he said nodding to the axe, "you'd better be careful."

Laughing, she agreed. Looking down the path, she sighted his wife and two sons walking to the dock.

He followed her line of vision and said, "We're heading out on the paddle boats, but I saw you down on the dock earlier so I told my wife that we'd better check with you first."

"Oh, yes, you can use them. I was just making sure they were tied up. You can keep them out as long as you like since I haven't had anyone else asking for them today. The rules are posted and remember, it's at your own risk."

He smiled but made no effort to follow his wife right away. His gaze came back to the young woman running the small resort. "You're doing a good job here, you know. Running this place can't be easy but the help you're giving your grandmother...well, anyway I just wanted to say that I think you're doing a wonderful thing."

She returned his smile and shrugged. "I love living here and helping with Gram until..." her voice trailed off, sadness filling her expression.

He placed his hand on her shoulder, giving a little squeeze. "I understand. Well, I'd better join the family or they'll think I got lost along the way." With a nod, he moved toward the dock leaving Bethany standing outside the shed. Forcing the depressing thoughts from her mind, she swung the axe onto her shoulder and made her way to the woodpile at the edge of the woods.

Jack sat in his truck for ten minutes trying to decide what he was going to do. Earlier it had seemed so easy. *Saturday morning and I'll go over to the cabins next door to check on Bethany and Ann.* Simple. Easy. A neighborly act. *So why the hell am I still sitting in my truck in my driveway?* The answer was staring him in the face, but he did not want to have to admit it. *Because I fucking felt something when I was in her presence.*

I don't have time for this, he chastised himself. Running his hand over his beard, he thought of all of the reasons why he should not be considering seeing Bethany again. *Too complicated. My work. My privacy. Don't have the time that it takes for a woman to decide what they want.* Then her face came into his mind—her blonde hair blowing about her face as she fought to protect her grandmother.

Forcing that line of thinking from his mind, he backed out of the driveway. *Nope, she and Ann were hurt on my property, even though they were trespassing, and I'm just going to go check on them.*

Driving the short distance to the turn by the old wooden sign to Mountville, he controlled his thoughts. Barely. But by the time he made his way to the lodge, he knew; *Fuck that. I want to see her.*

Climbing down from his truck, he started toward the front steps when he heard voices coming from the side. A middle-aged woman with a pleasant smile was walking toward him with Ann in tow. He stopped, carefully observing that Ann seemed to be recovered from her ordeal, her facial scratches barely visible.

"Hi, I'm Sally. May I help you?"

"Morning ma'am," he replied. His eyes cut over to Ann, who was staring at him. "I was looking for Ms. Bridwell."

"I remember you," Ann pronounced, her face breaking into a wide smile. "You're courtin' my granddaughter."

Sally jerked her gaze to her friend then back again to Jack's. He saw her confusion and quickly said, "I own the property next door and was checking on—"

"Oh, yes!" Sally exclaimed, "Bethany told me what happened. Nice to meet you." She eyed him from head to toe and must have liked what she saw because she immediately said, "Bethany was over at the dock, but I think I saw her at the edge of the woods a few minutes ago. I'm taking Ann in for a bite of lunch or I'd show you myself."

Jack nodded and said, "Thank you, but I'm sure I can find it."

The two women walked into the lodge, leaving Jack striding determinedly toward the woods near the lake. The sounds of whacking and cursing soon met his ears.

Bethany stood next to a large stump where she had placed a smaller piece of wood that she was attempting to split. She had watched her grandfather split wood for years. He would always make her stand back for safety but with one swift slice he would have the pieces ready for her to scramble to gather for the woodpile.

Oh, Gramps. You made this seem so easy. She managed to slam the axe into the bottom stump, completely missing the wood she was trying to hit. Jerking hard to get the axe loose took all of her strength. "Damnit!" she huffed.

Finally dislodging the axe, she stumbled back a few steps. Pushing her hair away from her eyes, she stood in place once more, determined to chop the wood. With another swing, she was able to land the axe in the right place but without enough force to completely split the wood. Pleased that she had managed to improve her aim, she attempted to keep slamming the wood onto the stump to finish the task. Unfortunately, the effort of lifting the entire tool attached to the chunk only resulted in her slinging the axe around wildly.

"Aughhhh!" she screamed as she lifted the handle once more over her head, almost toppling backward in her efforts when suddenly the tool was snatched from her hands. Whirling around, she stared into the face of a large, visibly furious man. *Jack?*

"What the hell are you trying to do?" he growled, moving around her while completing the chop with one swift hack. The two pieces of wood fell to the side.

Lifting her gaze to his as he turned back around, she placed her hands on her hips, saying, "Obviously I was chopping wood."

"Waving a sharp axe around wildly, not able to hit

the side of a barn, is hardly chopping wood," he retorted. "You could've hurt yourself."

"It was heavy!" she shouted.

"All the more reason to not attempt something you can't handle," he argued back, taking two steps closer to her, forcing her to lean back to maintain eye contact. "The way you were swinging it around if that block fell off on the descent you could have chopped your leg off!"

"Who says I can't handle the axe? I was getting it if you hadn't jumped in to rescue the poor, little woman," she said sarcastically. Her hair had fallen toward her face again and as she pushed it out of the way, the realization that she was hot, sweaty, dirty, and disheveled once more when in his presence shot through her. She tried to tamp down those feelings but seeing him standing at the edge of the woods, his blue plaid shirt with the sleeves rolled up on his thick forearms and jeans that showed off his massive legs and...*Nope, not looking there.* She lifted her gaze once more, this time seeing him smile at having caught her ogling.

"Oh, never mind," she bit out, pulling her long hair back into a messy ponytail. "What are you here for anyway?" she asked as she turned to walk back up the path.

"I wanted to see you again," he pronounced with candor.

She stopped in her tracks before turning to peer into his face. What she saw was honesty staring back at her. Licking her lips nervously, she cocked her head to the side, waiting for his explanation.

Instead of answering, he placed another piece of wood on the stump and within a few minutes he had chopped several more before tossing them onto the woodpile. She watched his body as it moved in perfect harmony with the task. His muscles as they corded with strength and power. *What would it be like to have that power over me? His body moving into mine? His—blah, stop!*

Schooling her expression, she smiled as he turned back to her. "Thank you…again. It seems as though you have a habit of rescuing me. I'm sorry that I was so… um…unaccommodating."

He reared his head back in laughter, the muscles in his neck working as the sound reached her ears. Meeting her gaze again, he said, "Unaccommodating? Try downright angry, darlin'."

Pursing her lips, she agreed, "Okay, fine." She held out her hand for the axe, which he ignored.

Swinging it up on his shoulder he gave a nod toward the shed. "I've got it."

Refusing to argue anymore, she met his nod and turned to walk up the path. *The Paul Bunyan look is good on him*, she thought. Reaching the shed, she opened the door while stepping back to allow him entrance.

His eyes were riveted to her perfect ass showcased in the tight jeans. The tank top she was wearing was slightly stained with sweat and dirt, but looked as good as anything she could have had on as far as he was concerned. As she stopped at an old shed, he forced his eyes to go back to her face.

"Anywhere special?" he asked, looking around the orderly space.

She pointed to a hook on the wall and watched as he replaced the axe in its place. Closing the door behind him, she caught his incredulous expression. "What now?"

"You don't have a lock on that door?"

"Um, I think Gramps did, but I just haven't thought about it. Why?"

"Woman, you've got a shed full of tools that can be used as weapons, a constant changing group of guests that stay here that you don't know from shit, and you're wondering why the shed needs to be locked?" he growled.

Angry because she knew he was right but also because he had to point it out to her, she turned to stomp toward the lodge. He followed in her tracks, making a mental note that a lock was the next thing he planned on buying for her.

Bethany stopped stomping, realizing how childish it was when he was right. She should have a lock on the shed. Heaving a huge sigh, she glanced over her shoulder, seeing him right behind her. And caught him staring at her ass. Her hands immediately swiped at her bottom, fearing there was something she sat in. His eyes jumped up to hers, a twinkle in them letting her know he had been staring at her ass because he wanted to. A warm blush rose across her face as she turned back toward the lodge.

Reaching the shaded front porch, she nodded toward one of the chairs. "Make yourself comfortable and I'll get some lemonade." She opened the door then stopped suddenly. "Or would you rather have a beer?"

The crinkles at the corners of his eyes captured her attention as he answered, "Lemonade is fine." Nodding again, she walked inside. Once clear of the front room, she dashed up the stairs taking them two at a time.

Hurrying into the bathroom, she grabbed a brush and ran it quickly through her thick hair before twisting it up in a knot on top of her head. Wetting a washcloth, she swiped the cool towel over her face before eyeing herself in the mirror. *No makeup, no time.* Shaking her head at the absurdity of trying to impress a man like Jack, she jerked off her stained shirt and pulled on a clean white tank top.

Bounding down the stairs again, she poured two tall glasses of cold lemonade from the refrigerator before moving back to the porch. Her eyes met his immediately, the electricity crackling between them. Suddenly nervous, she simply reached her hand out with the drink.

His fingers slid across hers as he took the glass from her hand. "You gonna sit down too?" His voice was low...smooth. She offered a quick nod and she sat in the rocking chair next to his.

He watched her in silence for a few minutes as she made every attempt to avoid eye contact again. Her hair was pulled up, leaving a few blonde strands to blow in the breeze. Clear blue eyes, matching the cloudless sky. She had changed from the tank top to a clean t-shirt that was modest while still clinging to her curves. He had already perused her ass as she had walked in front of him. *Beautiful, pure fuckin' beautiful.*

"What?" she asked, her gaze jerking to his in confusion.

Hell, I said that aloud, he realized. "The view, darlin'. The view is beautiful."

She gifted him with a smile as she turned back toward the vista. From the porch, they could see the trees of the woods across the road with the Blue Ridge Mountains rising in the distance. She loved this view. The tranquility of this place. "It is beautiful here, isn't it? Do you have this kind of view at your place?"

He chuckled, realizing she thought he was talking about the mountains. "No darlin', I don't have this beauty on my land. At least not right now," he replied, his eyes still on her. *But maybe? Don't have a clue how that would work out, but just maybe.*

They sat in silence for a few more minutes allowing the breeze and shade to fight back the early summer heat.

"Why are you really here?" she finally asked softly, twisting to look at the handsome man sharing her porch.

He looked discomfited for a moment before shaking his head slightly. "Hell if I know," he replied under his breath. Turning to look at her, he said, "Actually I wanted to check on you and your grandmother to make sure you were all right."

She nodded, disappointed, but understood he felt a responsibility. "I appreciate that and we're fine. In fact, Gram's scratches are barely noticeable."

"Yeah, I saw her when I first came."

"Oh." Not able to think of anything else to say, she remained quiet.

"I also brought you something," he added, setting the glass onto the porch railing and reaching into his pocket. Her interest captured, she watched as he pulled out a sturdy, metal bracelet.

Turning toward her, he said, "This is for your grandmother."

"Gram? You're giving Gram a bracelet?" she asked in confusion.

He chuckled, "This is a tracking bracelet. We'll attach it around her ankle and she won't be able to take it off. It'll feel a little weird at first to her, but she'll soon become accustomed."

"Tracking?"

He pointed to the center of the bracelet where a flat disc was located. "There's a tiny electronic tracer inside. If she ever wanders away, then you call us. Luke has already programmed it into our system and we'd be able to pinpoint her anywhere. It's waterproof and won't need the battery changed for a long time."

She was speechless as she gazed at his outstretched hand, offering her a gift that was so much more than the bracelet. It was a gift of safety for Gram and peace of mind for her.

"I…I…don't know what to say," she said. Her eyes filled with tears as she blinked furiously to battle them back.

"Don't gotta say anything. You're doing a lot here and this'll take a worry off of your plate."

She turned the disk over in her hand and saw an

intricate inscription with SPI on the back. Lifting her questioning gaze back to his, he answered her silent question, "Saints Protection & Investigations. That's the name of my company."

Nodding slightly, she fingered the bracelet, tracing the engraved letters. "You said Luke could… um…track it?"

"I run a security operation," he replied, his eyes finding and holding hers. "I've got the equipment—"

"I can't afford the service," she said, handing the bracelet back to him as understanding dawned on her. It was not just a bracelet, but a continuing, expensive tracking system.

He swung his large body around so that he was facing her, taking her hand in his while pulling it toward him. Placing the bracelet in her palm, he continued, "I've got the equipment and the means. No cost to you. No cost to Ann. Just the satisfaction of knowing that you're not pounding the path through the woods some night looking for her."

And there is was again…the feeling that someone understood that what she needed was peace. Her fingers closed around the bracelet and she nodded as she wiped a lone tear with her other hand.

"Thank you. I...it's hard. Seeing someone you love stop being that person," she admitted quietly. "She's always been so spry. So vibrant. And smart…Jesus, she had a quick wit that kept us all in stitches."

Taking another sip of lemonade, she added, "But now, she lives mostly in the past, a little bit in the now, and sometimes in her own little world she has made up."

He leaned back in his seat, picking his lemonade up again. The quiet of the afternoon was occasionally broken by the laughter ringing from the lake where the Taylor family and others were enjoying the summer fun. Jack stayed silent, figuring if she wanted to talk, she would; and would do it easier if he was not filling the void with useless conversation. *Don't know what the hell I'm doing here, but come on girl. Trust me. Let me in, even if just a little.*

"My grandparents bought this land right after they got married with some of granddad's Army money," she said, her eyes still on the vista in front of her.

He knew this from the search Luke had done but kept that to himself. *Stories were better told by the persons involved anyway.*

"He knew carpentry and they built the first cabin and lived in it while working the next one. He wasn't trained in marketing, but Gramps understood people. Knew what they wanted and what they'd come for. He advertised it as a honeymoon getaway and by the time he had built five cabins, they were full most year 'round." She chuckled, adding, "He'd say that he didn't have to offer too many things to keep people busy if they were on their honeymoon."

Jack smiled, acknowledging her grandfather had been an intuitive man.

She saw his smile and felt the tingle straight through her. With her grandfather's small stature and Jack's huge presence, they could not have looked more different. And yet there was a strong similarity. Gramps knew what people needed and worked to provide it. Feeling the bracelet still clutched in her hand, she knew that Jack shared the same trait.

"After cabin five, he built this lodge with the apartment on the second floor and the office, reception, and lodge room below. They only had one son, my dad, so it was big enough for them. Then he finished through to cabin ten."

The silence was disturbed by the fishermen driving back in once more. She threw her hand up in a wave and watched it returned.

Jack spied it too, but with a completely different reaction. He saw the look on the men's faces—the same one he had when he looked at her. *Goddamn, she's a beauty and got no fucking clue how much of a beauty, which only made her more attractive.* A flash of something new, something different flew through him. Smart enough to recognize jealousy, he tamped that emotion down, struggling with wanting her and wanting her safe. And not sure how his lifestyle could accomplish both.

Bethany, unaware of the thoughts of the man sitting next to her, continued. "Gramps and Gram had a good life here. He died about three years ago and she's been doing okay on her own."

At this, he swung his gaze back to hers, knowing how much work she was putting into running the place now.

She saw his questioning expression and quickly added, "With some help of course. My parents were professors at Richmond State University until just this past year when they were offered a position with research capability in Arizona. Dad and mom helped out a lot. By then I was out of college with a business and marketing degree working for an ad agency in Richmond."

"You gave up your life?" he asked, already knowing the answer and that she quit a decent paying job.

She shrugged, "Yeah. I mean, I liked the job and the people, but…" She looked back at the mountains and sighed. "But look at that. I've always loved that. And Gram needed me. I couldn't let this place be sold or get run down."

"So you took all this on yourself?"

"I've got help. Sally does the cabin cleaning and Roscoe does the handiwork around."

The warm vibe changed once again to chilly as he stood, moving his large body to lean against the rail as he peered down at her. "You've got a man here to do handiwork?" Jack asked, his voice still low, but growling this time. Before she could answer, he continued, "So why the hell were you out with an axe today?"

"I'm not helpless," she protested. "He's off today and I saw a job that needed to be done so I did it."

He leaned back, letting his breath out slowly, as though counting. Frustration warred with anger inside of him.

"Jack, I'm not sure what's happening here," she whispered, her eyes meeting his. "We've only been around each other a couple of times and every time I find myself confused. You seem angry and then interested and then pull away."

He stared at her face, so full of pure honesty it almost hurt. Her beauty pulled him in—made him want the things in life that he had assumed were not for him. Relationships. Love. Family. He dealt in a world of missions, violence, and money being paid to get things done. Things that others could not get done. *And she's got no fuckin' place in that world.*

His thoughts warred with each other, then finally gave in to the darker side of his mind. Pushing away from the rail, he gave her a curt nod. "Just being neighborly," he lied. "Make sure you secure that bracelet around Ann's ankle 'cause we've already got it on our radar." With one last head jerk, he stalked down the steps and to his truck, leaving her sitting on the porch.

As his vehicle pulled out of sight, she stood sighing heavily, disappointment filling her soul. It had been so long since she was interested in a man. Someone more than an occasional date. His rugged handsome looks drew her in, but it was his intensity that had held her gaze. *As though he would stop at nothing to slay my dragons. And then...nothing.* Sighing again deeply, she looked down at the bracelet in her hand. It was a very nice gift. For a neighbor from a neighbor. A neighbor who was tying himself to her whether or not he realized it.

Snagging the two glasses off of the porch, she headed inside to find Gram and start dinner.

7

The humid night was dark and few stars shone with the impending storm. The campus was sparsely populated in the summer with fewer students taking in classes. The parking lot lights gave off very little illumination and it was easy to stand in the shadows and hide. The wind gust caught his coat, whipping it out for a second before he grabbed it back, buttoning the front securely.

Who have I seen here lately? Who comes to the library night after night? A dark haired girl pushed open the heavy doors. He watched her come out of the library and down the steps. *Yes, I recognize you from the other night. Studying. You've been studying. Such a good girl... always a good girl until they become sluts. And they all become sluts.*

He caught her giggle as she met a young man at the bottom of the steps and watched as they walked toward the dorm together. He palmed his crotch, but the urge was not there. He felt nothing. Turning, he climbed into his little, nondescript sedan, smiling to himself. *You're safe tonight, little girl. I don't need anyone now.*

Two weeks passed while Jack and his Saints were busy with combing the campuses and digging for more information. Jack moved to his porch with his morning cup of coffee, having already run the perimeter and taken a shower. He had attempted to force his mind to not think of Bethany every time he ran by the area where he had first seen her. *Or captured her, to be exact.* But he was unsuccessful. He thought of her anyway. Every. Single. Time.

His attention was diverted when Chad's SUV parked in the driveway, followed by Cam and Bart. Monty was still at the FBI headquarters, coordinating some shared information with them. Marc had pulled the all-nighter in the command center below and would soon be replaced by Blaise.

Giving head jerks in acknowledgment they met in the kitchen, all pouring coffee before moving downstairs. Assembled around the conference table, they once again shared information.

Cam spoke first. "Looked into a missing student from Washington College and talked to her roommate. The missing girl was Nola Talbot. From what I can find out, she was a really sweet girl but not the greatest student so when she just left school, everyone assumed she dropped out due to grades."

"But didn't she leave all her stuff behind?" Blaise

asked. "That doesn't make any sense."

"She had no family, so no parents to check with. The roommate did file a missing person's report but never heard anything back. And when the semester ended, the college, per policy, threw out all of her unclaimed possessions."

"So we got nothing on this girl at all," Jack growled.

"Well, she had been in the foster system in high school, so there are records if a body ever turns up."

Jack turned his gaze to Chad. "What've you got?"

"I checked on Laura Polinis from Bluefield College and Lisa Mullins from Tech. Laura went missing one weekend after a church revival. Her friends had gone to a huge musical festival which, of course, was synonymous with drugs and alcohol. She really wanted to go with her friends, but had promised to sing in a church revival first. She was going to meet her friends there later, but never made it to the festival, nor was heard from again. Her parents still hold out hope that she will surface. Lisa Mullins was quiet and very reserved. She came from a single parent home, who like the Polinis still hold out hope she'll be found. She worked at a pizza place and never made it home one night."

Each man studied the information on their laptops in frustration. "Except for a few descriptions, these girls, as a whole, have no fucking thing in common," Jack bit out once more.

Luke spoke up, "I'm adding all of this new data into the system to see if we can get any feedback at all on what another commonality might be."

"Meanwhile," Bart added, running his hand through

his shaggy blond hair, "This guy is probably already studying who his next victim is."

"So far the victims, including the missing girls, have been redheads, blondes, brunettes, green, blue, and brown eyes. They've been wealthy right down to the state paying tuition. Religious, not religious. Some worked, some played sports. Some lived in dorms and others in apartments," Cam reiterated.

"Were they just in the wrong place at the wrong time?" Chad asked.

Blaise glanced over. "Some guy gets the urge to kill and stalks whoever looks easy?"

Chad shrugged. "Just throwing it out there."

"So what do we have?" Jack asked the group.

Luke glanced up and said, "All victims were female, between the ages of eighteen and twenty-three. All were current college students here in Virginia. Monty's profiler said the killer usually did not travel too far, but when we pinpoint the victims' locations, we can see they are somewhat centrally located."

The team focused their attention on the large screen, seeing a map of Virginia and the locations pinpointed in red. "I've numbered them in terms of the approximate time that the student was missing or murdered. You can see it's as though a noose is getting tighter," Luke commented.

They stared at the map of Virginia with all of the colleges, universities, and community colleges marked. "The first missing girls were in schools that were about two hundred miles from the capitol. Then the first body that was found was about one hundred fifty miles away.

The next missing girl was about one hundred miles away and our final two bodies were within one hundred miles of Richmond," Blaise noted.

"Is this a specific pattern or is he purposefully moving closer to the capitol?" Cam wondered out loud.

"He's getting more comfortable," Jack stated firmly, causing the others to jerk their gazed from the map to their boss.

He continued, "He started farther away. That gives him time to make a get-away and if her body is found, he won't be anywhere near the scene. Remember what the profiler said? It's not that serial killers want to be found out but that they gain more confidence so they take more risks."

Mark interjected, "You think this guy was just getting warmed up with the first ones and he's now more comfortable staying closer to home?"

Jack nodded. "I'll bet my life this asshole lives in the Richmond area. Now of course that's a fucking big area but it's something to go on."

"I'll send this to Monty," Luke said, "and let him get it to his FBI contacts."

The room fell quiet for a moment, each man studying the reports.

"All the women were pretty," Bart added. Seeing the looks of the others, he shook his head. "Just sayin', guys. Look at the pictures...not a homely one up there."

The others had to agree that he was right and the fact was that Bart knew pretty. With his tall frame and bulky muscles, he usually walked away with the prettiest girl in the bar. He continued, "So for similarities, our killer likes them to be young women, with a certain education, and pretty. Other than that, he's not too discriminating."

"Shit," Cam bit out. "That doesn't exactly narrow the focus down too much."

"Okay," Jack said. "I want Bart, Cam, Monty, Blaise, and Luke to stay on this, continuing to sift through everything coming from the interviews, different police records, and what Monty brings back from the FBI."

Tossing two files down the table, he said, "Chad and Marc, we've got some security escorts to provide assisting Tony Alvarez's team back in Richmond." Marc grinned, having worked alongside Alvarez Security before.

Looking at his Saints, he continued, "Men, you've all worked hard and traveled a lot. Take a breather this weekend and we'll convene back on Monday morning here to see what information Monty can provide."

As the men stood from the table, stretching their tall frames, Jack added quietly, "Just as a reminder, a couple of weeks ago, I gave Ms. Bridwell a tracker bracelet for her grandmother to use. She's to call here if Ann wanders again."

The men nodded their approval, but could not hold back the grins.

Jack looked at the familiar faces of the men he trusted and saw the shared glances. Men that had his back and he had theirs. Men who now looked like they were in on a fuckin' secret. "Don't read more into it than what it is," he growled. "Nothing personal. Just watching out for them."

"You been back around to see her?" Chad asked. Seeing Jack's stoic expression, he pushed. "Why not, boss?"

"Jack, you marked her as yours when you told us to back off and didn't want any of us checking into her," Blaise reminded.

The men made their way to the kitchen, where Jack pulled beers out for them before they settled on his back porch with its own view of the Blue Ridge Mountains. Each taking a long pull from their bottles, the companionable silence was easy to take.

Finally, Jack spoke, "Spent my time in the military protecting people and taking care of the missions that came my way. Loved my brothers, but we had to do a lot of fucked up shit in a fucked up war to give people back home their peace. And some of you did a tour over there, or somewhere, in your former lives so you know what I mean. Spent the last years building up this business knowing what I wanted to do and how to go about doing it." Jack looked around at the men on his deck. "There's still a lot of fucked up shit in our own country, but I do this so most people can sleep in their beds at night and have pleasant dreams." He paused, turning his gaze back to the sun setting over the mountains. "But I also knew that this life wasn't leading to a white picket fence kind of a world for me." Then his voice softer, almost on an afterthought, he added, "And she deserves that kind of world."

No one said anything, the summer heat broken by the breeze that flowed down from the mountains. From the outside, it appeared just as it should—a group of men enjoying each other's company on a Friday evening on the porch of one of their nice houses with acres of unspoiled land surrounding it.

But inside this home was a command center that allowed them to utilize the equipment, resources, and contacts that Jack had built. His business. His world. The kind of world each of them committed to making safer was not pretty. And the little they had seen of Bethany Bridwell, Jack was right…she deserved pretty.

That still sucked. For their boss and friend. And for them, as they silently pondered what their lives would bring.

"You get me now," Jack said, his voice taking on its typical gruffness while he took another long pull on his beer. "I went over, gave her the bracelet, and confess that I stayed a bit, getting to know her. I liked what I saw and liked what I heard. But I need to keep this world separate from her and the only way I can do that is to not get personal."

Chad growled and Jack's eyes turned toward him. Jack watched him, the most selfless man he had ever met, finish his beer while standing next to the rail admiring the view. Chad had spent his early years in the military, working on a bomb squad. He did two tours and then left the military do work for ATF continuing to volunteer for bomb duty. Jack held his gaze when Chad turned around.

"Boss?" Chad started. "You giving it all up for the business means that you never really get to enjoy this world that you're making better. This is magnificent," he continued, his hand making a sweeping motion toward the mountains. "But this alone for the rest of your life...not so great."

Jack just stared at the men nodding in agreement, giving him head jerks as they finished their drinks and headed into the house. He did not walk them to the front door. He could hear them leave and he stayed on his porch. Alone. And wondered if there could be a place for a blue-eyed, blonde with a heart of gold in his world.

The noises in the next room irritated the man. Why did they have to be so loud? Finally, unable to stand the commotion, he went into the bathroom, shutting the door. Splashing cold water onto his face, he blinked as he looked into the mirror. Taking several deep breaths, he forced his mind to calm. With a glance at the door, making sure it was locked, he turned to the air conditioning vent. Carefully unscrewing the cover, he placed it on the toilet lid before reaching his hand into the duct. He curled his hand around the black handle of the long knife before sliding it from its concealment. The long, slim blade glistened under the bright florescent lights of the bathroom. Scrubbed clean and bleached, there was not a speck of dirt...or blood...on it.

Memories flooded back as they always did, calling to him from many years ago. He had never been what his father had wanted. And his mother? What a weak bitch. Watching his father use the knife with expert precision he yearned for the time when he could wield it himself.

He remembered the last one—how she had wept and begged. *Don't they understand that they have to die? It's not about them. It's about me. What I need to do? They don't matter.* He never liked talking to them, but the moment when they recognized him gave him such a rush. Sucking in a deep breath, he smiled slowly as the memories soothed over him. Their naked bodies, ripe for the taking. The precision of what he must do.

He ran his fingers lovingly along the flat edge of the knife, careful not to cut himself. *You're so pretty,* he thought while admiring the knife's perfection. *You want more don't you? You want to be used.* Heaving a sigh, he replaced the weapon into its exile and screwed the cover back on carefully. *Soon. Not now, but soon.*

Calmed, he left the bathroom able to face the commotion outside.

8

Bethany stepped off of the lodge porch into the early morning sunlight. Another hot, clear day in the Virginia summer and all of the cabins are rented. Smiling to herself, she heaved a sigh of relief. Leaving the advertising company had not been an easy decision, after all, the money had been excellent and the benefits were really good for a recent graduate. And there was a certain excitement living in the large city, where there was always something going on. She had been determined to enjoy life after college—concerts, plays, art shows, and even clubbing with a few friends had filled her time off. Until Gram became sick, then she withdrew to the country every weekend to help out.

Filling her lungs with the clear air, she then sipped the hot coffee that filled her travel mug. Beginning her early morning walk around, she liked to inspect the cabins and road before deciding what needed to be worked on for the day.

"Can I come too?" Gram said, walking out of the lodge.

Bethany smiled as she turned, seeing Gram in a pair of grey striped pants, a pink flowered top, and purple moccasins on her feet. "You got dressed by yourself this morning," she remarked with a giggle.

"Well of course I did! I'm not a child," Gram huffed as she made her way to Bethany, who gave her an affectionate hug.

"I know, Gram. And I'd love your company as I do my walk-around this morning."

Linking her arm through her grandmother's, they started up the road toward the first cabin. The guests had not risen yet and so the morning was quiet, other than for the sound of the birds gathering around the bird feeders she had set out.

As the two continued to walk, Bethany's mind was on the list of things that needed to be accomplished. The flower box on cabin three was sagging on one side and had to be refastened later before it fell. She had encouraged Gram to spend more money several years ago and have gutter guards installed so the leaves would not clog the gutters. The guards had been a good decision, but cabin four had a small branch down on its roof which could impact the gutters. Checking that out needed to go on the day's list as well.

"I've been here my whole adult life," Gram said, her voice breaking the morning silence. "Did you know that I was only eighteen years old when Martin and I married?"

Bethany jerked her gaze over to Gram, seeing her

clear-eyed and cognizant. Determined to make the most of the memory, knowing at any moment Gram could slip back into time, she said, "Tell me about him."

The smile on her grandmother's face was priceless. They had walked several steps in silence again before she began to speak.

"Martin was so handsome and I fell in love with him when I was only fourteen years old. He was two years older and I thought he was so grown up. My daddy wouldn't let us date until I was fifteen and for a year we were inseparable.

By this time, they had rounded the lake and were coming to the last two cabins. Bethany kept her attention on her grandmother, knowing that she could easily come back later to check on them. Gram was more important by far.

"He went off to the Army when I was only sixteen years old, but I wrote him every week. He was gone for almost two years and the night he got back, he came to my door." Gram giggled at the memory. "I nearly ran my daddy down trying to get to the door first." Bethany grinned, imagining the young Ann rushing to get to her love.

"He stepped in, shook my father's hand and before I could even kiss him, he turned to my father and asked for my hand in marriage. Daddy was stunned, but I knew he was impressed with Martin as a man." Gram sighed, saying, "We were married the day after I turned eighteen. Never apart for one night. Not one in all those years. Poor years. Hard years. Until we made this place work. But never a night apart."

The lodge in sight, the two women headed up the path by the lake. Bethany could hear the stirrings of the guests. Two cabins were full of fishermen spending the weekend and they were preparing to leave for the river nearby. The Taylors had left, only to be replaced by other families spending a week or weekend here in the cabins. A couple on their honeymoon had come in the night before and were in the farthest cabin. That was rare since most young couples prefer honeymoons in exotic locations, but occasionally they did come. For the beauty of the Blue Ridge Mountains and the peace of a little cabin in the woods.

If I ever get married, I'd like that too, Bethany thought. With that, her mind rolled to the handsome neighbor who she had tried not to think about. But his dark, brooding face crowded her dreams at night and images of his powerful body on top of hers caused her to wake in a lust-filled sweat.

She glanced down at Gram's ankle, the tracking bracelet gleaming in the sunlight. Gram had been concerned at first, not understanding why she had to wear jewelry on her ankle, but she soon became adjusted to it. *To give such a gift, and then turn around and leave so abruptly. And to be silent for weeks. If ever there was a brush off, I guess that was it.* She wished it did not sting...but it did.

Heaving a sigh as they climbed back up the lodge steps, she forced him out of her mind. *Lots to do today and might as well get going.* "Come on, Gram," she called. "I'll fix you breakfast."

Her grandmother looked up at her and smiled. "Sure Helen, and then we'll find Charlie."

Bethany just returned her smile, shaking her head. *Well, it was nice while it lasted.*

That evening, Bethany left the stew in the crockpot while she ran outside to investigate the noises she was hearing. At first she just thought it was one of the larger groups talking loudly but the increasingly raised voices were now shouting in anger. As she stepped out on the porch, she saw one pickup truck parked in front of the lodge, the occupants out in the gravel drive arguing with the men in the two other pick-up trucks behind them.

A quick glance down at the angry voices, some slurred with alcohol, caused her to stiffen in anger. Her eyes jerked to the side where two families were hustling their children from the lake back to their cabins. *Damnit!* Gram had followed her to the door and Bethany turned and yelled over her shoulder, "Gram, get back inside. Now." *Please God, let her do what I ask!*

"Gentlemen!" Turning back to the scene below, her voice broke through their ruckus. "I ask that you respect the other guests and keep your voices down."

One man staggered around looking up at her incredulously. "You wanna know what that son-of-a-bitch did? Cut my line. Had a goddamn winner and he cut my fuckin' line. He cost me the trophy and $250 in winnings!"

She remembered seeing one of the nearby lakes hosting a fishing contest this weekend and now knew why she had several cabins filled with fishermen.

"Whatever the reason is for your argument, you'll have to keep your voices down and settle it quietly." Spearing them with a glare, she continued, "And settling it non-violently. I suggest you all sleep it off."

"Fuck you," the man slurred turning back toward the man approaching him.

"I didn't cut your line, you asshole. It just snapped 'cause you're a fucking idiot who can't pull back when you should!" another man interjected, stepping forward.

Before he could continue to protest his innocence, his accuser swung a punch landing it on his jaw, sending him staggering backward onto the gravel.

Uncertain what to do, Bethany instinctively stepped down two steps, screaming, "STOP!" but it was apparent that her voice was ineffective with the ensuing melee. Turning she spied a broom on the front porch and she leaned over grabbing it, to what avail she had no idea.

The man on the ground jumped up and rushed the angry competitor, taking him down in a tackle, both landing hard on the gravel. Bethany watched in amazement as the one who had been drinking managed to straddle the other and began hitting him with his fists, cursing wildly.

"Do something!" she screamed at the other men standing around.

"Hell, they can fight it out themselves," one burly

man answered back. "They ain't hurtin' nobody but themselves."

"They're hurting my business!" she yelled as she bolted down the steps to the two men now rolling on the ground.

"Oh hell, George, get in there and break it up," one of the men whined to the burly one.

Bethany swung the broom over her head and brought it down with a whack on the back of the cursing man, seeing blood running from his nose.

"What the fuck?" he roared, swinging back with his arm and connecting with Bethany's shoulder. With his attention focused on her, the other man got another punch in, connecting with his jaw.

She staggered, raising the broom once more, when the burly man stepped in and grabbed her broom handle.

"Now missy, don't be getting' in the way of them two working out their disagreement."

Before she could react further, the sound of gravel crunching had her jerking her gaze to the road. Two large SUVs sped down the lane and skidded to a stop, sending the rocks flying. To her amazement, four men jumped out, immediately descending on the men fighting. Instantly, she recognized the leader. *Jack? And some of his men?*

Startled, she staggered back again, the broom still raised, as she witnessed them quell the fight with little difficulty. The large Hispanic man, *Cam? I think,* had one man pinned against the truck, his hand on the man's throat. The fisherman was attempting to struggle, but Cam seemed to be holding him in place without any effort.

The other two of Jack's men, whose names she could not remember, also had two of the fishermen on the ground, their knees planted in their backs as they grinned at each other.

Her body shook with adrenaline coursing through her veins and found it was hard to catch her breath.

Jack jerked the instigator to his feet and propelled him to the bottom of the steps. "You got something to say to the lady, asshole?"

The man's eyes, wide with fear, looked all around as his drunken mind slowly caught up to what had happened. "Huh?" he said. A shake brought the man's attention back to Jack's.

"You start a fight on someone else's property, in full view of families with small children that are trying to vacation. When asked nicely to stop, you get belligerent. And not only belligerent, but you also insult a lady. I don't give a shit how drunk you are, you're gonna apologize right fuckin' now." Jack's voice was low, but the growl was unmistakable.

The man lifted his eyes toward her and mumbled, "Sorry ma'am."

Bethany opened her mouth to tell them all to pack up and get out, unsure that the words would come out, but Jack handled it for her.

"You're all leaving and be assured your credit cards will be charged for the full amount of the weekend."

Several of the men not involved in the fight protested. "We didn't do anything," they whined. One look from Jack and they shut their mouths, their expressions changing from whining to fear.

"There're four of you pussies standing around letting these other assholes argue, cause a public disturbance, insult a woman, and get into a fight. That makes you equally culpable. So take your goddamn friends, pack your shit and get out. You got thirty minutes to do it."

Chastised, they grabbed their friends and pushed them into the two trucks before driving toward the cabins. Jack jerked his head toward the fishermen, and the other three Saints nodded toward Bethany before getting in one of their SUVs and following the pick-up trucks.

Jack turned his gaze back to the woman standing like a statue on the second step, the broom still clasped in her hands. Her khaki shorts were mid-thigh, but in his opinion they were way too short. His eyes moved to her light blue tank top, showcasing her heaving chest as he continued his gaze upwards to her face. Stalking up the stairs he stopped two below her and was still at eye level. His gaze then dropped to her white knuckles clutching her weapon.

"You want to tell me what the fuck you were doing with that broom?" he asked, his hand reaching out, pulling it away from her and tossing it behind her to the porch.

Her embarrassment was masked by her confusion. "How? How did you know to come?"

Not answering her question, he repeated, "You think that broom was going to do shit? You got a problem, you get inside the house, lock the goddamn door and call the fuckin' police!"

Her expression changed to irritation. "I wasn't going to get hurt. I just thought that I'd beat them apart. You know, like dogs fighting."

At that explanation, he found himself speechless… and furious, but before he could retort, she poked his chest with a finger and repeated, "How did you know something was happening here?"

Their attention was diverted by the sound of two pick-up trucks driving out of Mountville followed by the SUV that had stopped next to the first one that Jack drove in.

Cam lowered the driver's window, smiling, asked if they were all right.

She forced a smile on her face and said, "Yes, thank you for your assistance…again." She saw the three men inside wave and then drive away after giving Jack a head jerk.

He turned back to look at her, this time taking a step upward so that now he was looking down at her. She refused to remove her finger from his chest, then found her hand clasped in his.

Holding her gaze while rubbing her fingers, he repeated much gentler, "You have a problem, you get inside the house, lock the door and call the police."

Before she could argue back, the door opened and Gram walked out onto the porch. "It's quieter now out here. Oh, hello Charlie. You here courtin' again?"

"No," Bethany answered at the same time that Jack said, "Yes."

She whirled around, her eyes wide and hissed, "Don't confuse her." She tried to jerk her hand out of his but found his grip was as strong as it was gentle.

"Not planning on confusing her," he replied, the crinkles next to his eyes deepening as the corners of his mouth turned up.

"Well, the stew's ready, so ya'll come on in," Gram called, as she turned and went back inside.

"You're not staying," Bethany seethed.

"Of course I am. Wouldn't want to upset Ann and besides, I'd love more of your company," he said smoothly, a grin appearing taking his handsome looks straight to drop-dead-I-want-to-climb-on-top-of-you gorgeous.

"We're still going to talk about this," Bethany hissed again.

He nodded, smiling and said, "Count on it." Stepping around Bethany, his hand still holding hers, he tugged her along after him. Once inside, he saw little had changed in the few weeks since he had first set foot in the lodge. He followed Ann to the stairs on the left side of the main room, his fingers now linked with Bethany's.

At the top of the stairs, they rounded a corner and he could see the apartment that Bethany's grandparents had lived in their entire married lives. A small, but comfortable den was on the right, the walls of exposed logs with a fireplace at the end. A hall split the area, leading to the bedrooms. The open floor plan included a dining table at the other end, leading into the kitchen. The scent of homemade soup and bread filled the room.

Bethany managed to disentangle herself, stalking into the kitchen. Lifting the lid on the crock-pot, she stirred the stew before checking to make sure the bread had not burned. Her mind was a jumble of thoughts as she heard Gram chatting with Jack as they placed the dishes on the table.

She stood at the sink, looking out of the window overlooking the back of the property...the side where Jack lived. The sinking sun cast a myriad of colors over the evening sky, but for once she was not enjoying the view.

She could not remove the events of the previous half hour out of her mind—the guests arguing, the fight, the rescue. Grasping the counter tightly to keep her legs from buckling, she suddenly felt a presence behind her.

Jack's arms reached around the counter, planting his hands on her trembling ones. He stepped forward until his front was touching her back. He rested his chin on her head, wrapping her in his warmth.

She wanted to lean her head back into him but was afraid to move. Weeks ago, she told him all about herself when they sat on the porch. And he gave her nothing. *But now?*

He felt her reticence and knew he needed to breach the gap he had caused. Keeping one arm on hers, he lifted his other and wrapped it around her middle pulling her into his hard body. Leaning his head to the side, he whispered, "Come on, doll. Give it to me."

With his soft encouragement, she dropped her head back into his chest, taking a shuttering breath. "I...I don't know what's wrong with me."

"It's adrenaline. It hit you when you rushed out, but now your body has to deal with the overload. You'll be fine. It'll pass, I promise." Wrapping his other arm over her chest, he enveloped her as the trembling subsided.

He felt her shudder, then a few minutes later felt her body begin to relax as he willed her to take from his strength.

She closed her eyes, her mind utterly aware of every nuance. The power in his arms as they embraced her. The hard muscles of his pecs and abs as they were pressed against her back. The softness of his beard, as it tickled her ear when he leaned in and whispered. He could stand behind her and she fit snuggly underneath his chin as though meant just for his body. It had only been a minute but her body craved his presence.

"You shouldn't be kissing in the kitchen," Gram admonished, walking into the room. Bethany jumped and Jack released her slowly, his chuckle rumbling over her.

The dinner was simple but filling and Jack ate heartily while enjoying keeping up with Ann's conversations. Bethany had warned him that she was spending more and more time in the past, thinking that she was a young woman.

"Gram, I'm going to clean up and then I'll help you get ready for bed," Bethany volunteered.

"I've got this," Jack said, motioning for her to go on with Ann.

Offering him a small smile, she followed her grandmother down the hall. Jack quickly washed the dishes and wiped the counters. He moved into the den and wandered to the fireplace where the mantle was loaded with family pictures.

He could not help but grin at the sight of Bethany as a baby, a gap-tooth grinning child, a pretty teenager, and a gorgeous young woman in her cap and gown, standing with her parents and grandparents.

"She's in bed," Bethany whispered as she appeared in the room.

Jack turned and stared at the woman standing in front of him. Her long blonde hair, now out of its braid, lay waving down her back and spilling over her shoulders. The faded jeans, that became that way due to hard labor and not from some fancy clothing store that sold them already faded, cupped her ass perfectly. The baggy, baby-blue t-shirt that had also seen better days showcased her breasts. Her makeup-free face, porcelain complexion, and blue eyes completed the picture he had been unable to forget for weeks. For a second he faltered, *Do I take this chance?* Then he saw the fire in her eyes and knew exactly what he wanted.

Unable to hold back the grin, he stalked toward her grabbing her hand as he walked by, turning her so that she had to follow him. Across the room. Down the stairs. To the porch.

9

As Bethany allowed herself to be led to the porch, she had missed that he had two long-neck beers in the other hand, one of which he gave to her after she plopped down in the chair. Her thoughts whirled once again, which seemed to be her normal state of mind when he was around. She had never been around an alpha before, always considering caveman behavior to be boorish. After all, she was a modern woman. *So why do I need to clench my legs together to quell the desire for him to take me? Or want him to kiss me until the thoughts stop flying at me?*

Finding no answer to the questions in her mind, she stayed in the chair, crossed her legs…tightly…and then took a long drink from her beer. Looking up, she saw him smiling at her, as though he knew everything she was thinking. *Damn!*

Jack settled into a chair after moving it to a slight angle. He wanted to enjoy the view—both the evening sky and the woman sitting near him. Finding his dick was already answering the call of the wild, he shifted in his seat, searching for a more comfortable position.

After a few minutes of quiet, the crickets and bull-frogs mixed with the distant sounds of families settling their children for the night, she asked the question that she had already discerned the answer to. "You have this place watched, don't you?"

He looked over, seeing her calm face. No more anger, but the tension rolled off of her.

"Yeah, I do."

"Isn't that illegal?" she bit out.

He glanced at her, his eyebrow lifted and answered with nothing more than a cocky grin.

"I see." She paused, recognizing that whatever world he functioned in, playing by the rules did not seem to matter. "You don't consider those cameras to be an invasion of privacy?" her voice dripped with sarcasm.

"Nope."

Her gaze darted to his as she was unable to hide the incredulous expression on her face. "Nope? Nope?" she asked, her wide eyes locked onto his.

He twisted in his chair to face her as he answered, "First time I saw you, I knew you were special. Anyone who'd come crashing into the midst of a group of men with weapons to save your grandmother was someone I wanted to know. Then, I'm not ashamed to admit, when your body was held against mine, I felt something and I'm not just talking about my dick wanting to know you as well."

At this, her blue eyes grew even wider, but her only reaction was to take another drink of her beer.

"I came over here and saw how you and Ann lived. Saw how you work to keep something for your grandmother alive even though her mind can't really process it now." At this he saw those blue eyes that he had been staring into blink rapidly holding back the immediate reaction of tears, so he plunged on.

"I looked into this place when I bought my property three years ago, knew a widow owned it, but never knew you had come along to take over. But after meeting the two of you and acknowledging what I felt, I gave you the bracelet for her because I wanted to take something off of your plate, even if it was worry. And I also knew that two women living alone, running a business where a constant change of strangers practically camp right outside where you sleep, put you at a daily risk. So I had a few cameras installed just so we could keep an eye out. You may want to rail and protest, but doll, today proved that it was the right move."

"You could have asked," she bit out.

"Would you have accepted?" he bit back.

Pursing her lips in frustration, she said nothing.

"Thought so," he chuckled. Then he sobered, looking at her directly. "We sat right here and talked on this porch, Bethany. I'm telling you straight up, I felt something. Wanted something. And I know you wanted it too."

She opened her mouth to protest but shut it quickly. *He's right. I did want it. But then he turned on a dime, walked away, and I didn't see him for weeks.* "We didn't talk, Jack. I did. I talked. I gave you who I was and you gave me nothing of yourself. I let you in, but you just walked away."

"Yeah, I can see it in your eyes, doll. But I live a life that doesn't offer white picket fences and decided right here on this porch that I needed to leave." He leaned back in his chair, taking another drink from his beer.

Her eyes watched the muscles in his neck as he tipped his head back and drank. His beard was neatly trimmed and she fought the desire to reach over to touch it. Run her fingers through it as she ran her tongue along its edges. He set the bottle down and grinned, jerking her back to reality as she knew she had been caught ogling. Again.

"So you decided to invade my privacy?" she asked, warring between wanting to tell him to get off her property and desperately wanting to know why he was here, on her porch, explaining his life to her.

"Yep," came his reply.

Once again, they fell into silence. By now the families were settled and with the fishermen gone, the grounds were very quiet. She remembered the events of the afternoon. The anger...and fear...she felt at the drunken brawl right at her feet. *What would have happened if Jack hadn't shown up? Could I have stopped them? Would they have stopped? Would the fight have gotten more out of hand and someone gotten seriously hurt? Gram? Would the other guests have checked out in fear?*

"None of that shit happened, babe, so you can get it out of your mind," he said quietly.

Jerking her incredulous gaze back to him once more,

she cried, "How do you know what I'm thinking all the time?"

Chuckling, he said, "Girl, your face gives you away. Your thoughts and feelings are written all over it."

"Well, you must be an expert at reading faces because I don't think I'm that easy to read," she retorted.

He said nothing for a moment and she thought he was not going to reply until finally he quietly agreed, "I am."

Not understanding, she waited, already knowing he would speak when he wanted.

"I grew up on a farm in southwest Virginia. Good parents. Worked hard, but knew the farming life wasn't for me. Pop wanted me to go to college, but I wanted to join the military. So we compromised. Did two years, got my associates degree and then joined. Made it all the way to the Special Forces. Worked hard there and ended up on an elite squad. Best goddamn team a man could ever want to work with."

He became quiet again, so she asked, "You want another beer?"

"Wouldn't turn one down," he answered. He watched as she rose from her chair and walked inside. *Haven't told anyone these stories other than the men I work with.* The realization of what he was doing hit him, but never a man to back away from a challenge…he was ready.

She returned carrying another cold bottle, handing it to him. He dragged his fingers across hers before taking the beer, noting the spark between them and the pleasure of seeing that she noticed it also. As she settled back into her seat he took a drink before he began again.

"The squad's leader, Tony Alvarez, left the Army and within a few months, some of the others did as well. They had served several tours and were ready for the civilian life. He started a security business in Richmond and has three or four of my brothers-in-arms working with him."

"You didn't get out then?" she asked, wondering why he did not do the same.

He shook his head. "I was offered a chance to do another mission. A different kind of operation. Worked with a multi-agency group. It functioned well, better than I expected. No egos, just men with different backgrounds willing to pull resources together to get a job done." He turned his head out toward the star-filled sky. "Thought working for Tony was the greatest thing I could have done, but gotta confess even that came in a close second to leading my own team."

She nodded, not as much in understanding as wanting him to continue. She had to admit to herself that she was fascinated.

"So when I got out of the Special Forces, I decided to replicate that same multi-agency team, only in the civilian world. Some of them joined me, tired of the red tape tying their hands when they tried to investigate crimes. Built the business, hired more like-minded men, and now I've got a company I'm proud of, doing the work I love doing."

She took in what he was saying, trying to process it all the while knowing that her heart was warmed that there was a man like Jack who cared so much about protecting others that he would give her grandmother a tracker bracelet. With her beer now finished, she leaned forward setting it on the wooden deck. Twisting in her chair, she faced him full on.

"So everything you are telling me about your life now, is supposed to make me understand why there are no white-picket fences in your future?" she asked.

He said nothing, but his gaze watched her carefully.

"I'll be honest, Jack, I don't play games." She grunted in exasperation, continuing, "I don't even know the games to play. You tell me you felt something, you have my place wired for security, you give a tracer to Gram...and then you disappear for weeks. Hell, if the fight hadn't broken out today, I doubt you'd be on my porch now, telling me all of this." She stopped, twisting her head toward the dark woods, her face a mask of confusion. "Now you are giving me this, but still say there's no future. What am I supposed to do with that?"

"I was going to come anyway," he confessed softly. Watching her face swing back toward his, he nodded. "Yeah, doll. I'd decided I at least wanted to explain my life. I've got no idea if or how it can work, but I wanted you to know."

Sighing deeply, she leaned back in the chair but kept her gaze on him. "Then you're going to have to give me more."

Fireflies danced in the lane between the porch and the woods, creating an ever-changing pattern in the darkness. Bethany had strung Christmas lights in a few of the trees around the lodge, adding to the fairy-tale illusion.

"I work in a world of violence. Things that white-bread America has no idea about. I'm called in, by private contract or by the government to step in when the bureaucracy is so cumbersome that the feds can't solve the crimes or stop the shit from happening. My men are all highly trained but bring their own specialties and diverse backgrounds to the team. We're given... creative license to take care of the problems."

"Creative license?"

"Yeah, doll. We do whatever it takes to fulfill the mission. Whatever it takes to keep people safe."

Processing his words, she whispered into the darkness, "And that takes away your white-picket-fence?" There was no answer, so she whispered more. "It seems to me that for someone who does what you do, how you do it, the white-picket fence to come home to would look mighty good."

Her hushed voice flowed over him, filling the secret crevices in his soul, the places that he wondered if they had become so dark that no light would penetrate. But her words did. He closed his eyes, momentarily stunned at the beauty she was offering. Sucking in a deep breath, he let it out slowly. His eyes jerked open at the touch of her hand on his. Glancing down, he saw her slim fingers tracing patterns on the back of his hand. Turning his palm up, she easily entwined her fingers with his.

Giving her hand a gentle tug, he pulled her from her chair over to his. She came readily. Throwing one leg over his, she settled in his lap. His hands dug into her hips as her hands cupped his face.

Yeah, she thought. *His beard is as soft as I imagined.*

Her thoughts whirled, trying to wrap her mind around his world. Or at least the glimpse he offered of his world. The intensity of his gaze should have scared her. Frightened her away. But all she could think was how it pulled her in. She smoothed her hand over his brow, letting her fingertips gently press out the crinkles at the edges of his eyes.

She watched, fascinated, as he closed his eyes and ever so slightly leaned his face against her palm, allowing her to take a tiny part of his burden away. That imperceptible movement sealed her fate, as she knew she wanted to take a chance on this man willing to give her just a bit of himself.

Their eyes held, but he stayed perfectly still. She realized he was giving her the choice. The chance to say yes or no. She chose yes. Yes, to a very uncertain thing, but after all...*that's what a chance is.*

Leaning in the rest of the way, her hands still on his face, she touched her mouth to his. Just a touch, and then she leaned back to peer into his eyes. What she saw made her smile and move back in again.

This time the kiss she offered was no longer chaste. She moved her lips over his, feeling the softness and strength of his mouth. Wanting more, she licked his lips and as he opened on a groan, she took her opportunity, sliding her tongue into his mouth.

That was all the encouragement he needed. He took over the kiss. And he took over hard. Angling her head for deeper access, he plundered her mouth with his tongue. Sucking, pulling, exploring her warm depths. She tasted divine. More than he could have imagined and he had imagined a lot.

As her mouth was ravaged, she continued to caress his jaw then slid one hand down to his shoulder feeling the muscles bunch underneath her fingers. His hand wandered as well, moving up her back until his fingers tangled in the thick, blonde tresses that he had wanted to touch ever since she crashed through the woods and into his arms.

Pulling her closer, he crushed her breasts against his chest at the same time that he was painfully aware of her core nestled directly on his swollen dick. The image of her naked, in this same position riding his cock, had him thrusting his hips upwards.

She groaned at the contact, flexing her hips downward wanting to quench the desire for friction.

The kiss continued until Bethany wasn't sure where she ended and he began. His tongue had ravaged her senses leaving her wrecked for any other man. *All this from a kiss,* she thought before he moved from her mouth, his kisses trailing from her lips to her earlobe and then down her throat, where he sucked at the sensitive place where her pulse beat erratically.

No longer caring that they were in plain view on the front porch of the lodge, she squirmed again on his lap, seeking relief.

Her movement finally brought Jack back to his senses and he gently took her arms and pushed her away. Seeing the disappointment and rejection on her face had him ready to pull her back in, kiss her senseless and take her on the porch. But she deserved more. Much more.

Shaking his head, he said, "No, doll. Not saying no to this...just no to right now. We're in plain sight of anyone walking along the lane and I'm not taking advantage of your situation." He stood, holding her arms firmly so she would not fall as they moved together. Steadying her on her legs, he continued to hold her tightly.

"You gotta think about everything I said tonight. What I said, what you need, and what you feel. Then it's up to you. I want you and while my life is not easy, if you want in, baby, I'll work like hell to make it work for us. But I'm leaving that first step up to you."

"How will I let you know?" she asked, peering up into his eyes, wanting so much to see what she knew was in hers.

"Got a security gate. You drive up and I'll let you in."

Nodding, she drew a shaky breath, running her tongue over her tingling lips. He smiled, leaned down and kissed her once more. "Now go inside and let me hear the deadbolt lock."

He patted her ass as she turned, still in her kiss-induced stupor, and did as told. She went inside, turned the deadbolt, stood by the window looking out as he pulled himself up into his truck and drove away. Then she mounted the stairs, changed into pajamas, brushed her teeth, and climbed into bed. There she lay awake pondering all that he had told her, wondering if there really was a place for her in his life. Then she fell asleep, dreaming of the big, handsome man whose kisses stole her breath…and her heart.

Jack passed by the drive to his property and headed into the small town about ten miles down the road. Pulling into Chuck's Bar & Grill, he grinned as he recognized several of the vehicles in the parking lot. Chuck's had become a second meeting place for the Saints besides Jack's compound. A place where they could relax, shoot pool, drink beer, meet up with some women always on the prowl, and if they were daring? Chow down on some of Chuck's greasy hamburgers and French fries.

Walking into the dim interior, his eyes quickly adjusted as he walked over to the bar. Sliding onto one of the mismatched stools next to the clean, but well-worn bar, he gave a chin lift to Chuck, standing at the other end. Chuck walked over, a beer already in his hand to give to Jack.

"Yo, big man. What's happenin'?" Chuck called out.

Jack took a pull on his beer and just smiled. "Not much, Chuck. Was heading home and decided to pop in and have a beer with some friends."

A tall, middle-aged blonde, with big curves and even bigger hair grinned over at Jack. "Lordy me, if it ain't the boss-man himself. How ya' doin' honey?" she called out.

"Life's not bad, Trudie," he replied.

Walking over, she eyed him suspiciously. "You're smiling," she accused. "Well, not much, but I can see it kinda twinklin' in your eyes." Rearing back, she slapped her hand down on the well-worn bar and exclaimed, "You got yourself a woman?"

Chuck whipped his head around at this and watched as Jack threw up his hands in defeat. "Now Trudie, you know you're the only woman for me," he said.

Just then Marc and Cam came from the back pool area to get new beers and saw their boss trying to defend himself from Trudie's glare.

"A woman?" Cam asked.

Trudie tapped a long fingernail on the beer she was handing to Marc and said, "Yessir, I do believe our Jack may be smiling for a woman-reason."

After Cam and Marc got their beers, they headed back toward the pool tables, Jack following closely behind before Trudie became any more clairvoyant.

Blaise and Bart were at one table, a pretty red-head and a built brunette snuggling up close to them. Chuck's was known as a local hangout, but as the only bar in the area, it was not unusual to find visitors here as well; sportsmen, skiers in the winter, campers in the summer. Jack did not recognize the girls, but then Blaise and Bart were pussy-magnets. His eyes swept back over Cam, Marc, and Chad…hell, all his men were pussy-magnets.

Taking another pull from his beer, his mind wandered back to the beautiful woman he had left at her lodge and wondered if she would take the chance. For him…he was ready.

10

Jack stood on his deck, morning coffee in his hand, attempting to review the notes Luke left for him on the latest information concerning the victims. But his mind was on her. The way her silky hair slid through his fingers. Her breasts crushed against his chest. Her hips involuntarily grinding against his cock, seeking what they both wanted. Needed.

Using the discipline forged during his tours with the Special Forces, he shook his head and refocused on the words in front of him. He settled in one of his chairs, coffee cup on the wide arms and began perusing on his tablet.

The report indicated that when Luke went back further in time, there were reports of missing girls from college campuses in Virginia for the past fourteen years. Luke had already siphoned off the ones that occurred somewhere else and only listed the ones where loved ones had contacted the police as missing.

Once more, the list appeared inconclusive. Different

races, different backgrounds, different majors, jobs... anything to tie them together.

An hour later, he rubbed his hand over his face, finished his coffee and stood, stretching his tall frame, working the kinks out. He had called a meeting with his men for later in the afternoon so he moved inside to go through his secure emails and deal with the management end of his business.

As he placed his cup in the sink, the front gate alarm sounded. His heart pounded, a condition he was not used to, in anticipation of who might be there. He walked over to one of the control panels by the front door and looked at the screen. Bethany. The camera was angled so he could see her face perfectly as she sat in the driver's seat with the window down, nervously looking toward the security panel next to her car. *Beautiful. Fuckin' beautiful.*

He decided against speaking at the moment and simply released the gate, allowing it to swing open. Her confused expression showed indecision as she visibly debated driving through. *Come on, baby. Make that choice.*

Suddenly, her countenance changed, determination marking her features as she put the car in drive and moved through the gate. Jack exhaled, not realizing he had been holding his breath. With a smile, he walked through his front door to his porch.

Bethany drove slowly down the long drive, trees lining the way blocking the view of her destination. *When he said security gate, he really meant it,* she thought nervously. Glancing at the homemade cobbler sitting on the seat next to her, she wondered if she was doing the right thing. *His business. His life. His world. Can I fit into that?* All she knew was that when she woke up this morning, his face was the only thing she wanted to see. Breathing deeply to quell the nerves threatening to take over, she continued up the drive.

Through the trees, she was able to discern a huge, two-story log cabin, wide front porch made out of the same dark wood. Two chimneys, one on either end, stood as sentinels to the impressive structure. *Wow!* was the only thought that came to mind.

Then she saw him standing on the front porch. Waiting. For her. Heart pounding, she could not keep the smile from her face. Leaning against one of the log columns, one leg crossed in front of the other, arms crossed over his massive chest, and that face...that gorgeous face staring straight at her.

She stopped her car at the curve in front of the house, assuming a garage was around back. Before she could put her hand on the door, she found it opened for her. He reached in, taking her hand and gently pulled her out.

They stood, silently staring at each other for a moment. He peered into her eyes, finding what he searched for—trust.

"Hey, beautiful," he greeted, noting the long waves falling down her back and perfect complexion, tanned from working in the sun.

"Hey, yourself," she replied with a smile. She tilted

her face up to his, pleased when his lips found hers in a soft kiss.

"Come on in," he invited.

She suddenly started, saying, "I have a present for you. Well, actually it's from both Gram and me." She moved to the passenger side and pulled out a huge pan, covered with aluminum foil. Standing, she bumped the car door with her hip to close it. Turning back to him, she saw his eager expression.

Laughing, she said, "You don't even know what's in here."

Taking the heavy platter from her, he replied, "Baby, whatever you and Ann fixed is gonna be amazing." The scent of the fruit wafted from the dish and he lifted an eyebrow in question.

"It's peach cobbler, just out of the oven," she explained. "We made a lot. We had a ton of fresh peaches from the farmer's market down the street and," she gave a little shrug, "I wasn't sure if you wanted to share with...um...whoever comes and works here... um...with you." She suddenly realized that he might not be alone. He might be working and not have time for her now.

"If you're busy, I can come another time," she said, stepping back toward her car. "I don't want to interrupt anything."

His gaze caught hers and he could not hold the smile from his face. "Relax, beautiful. No one's here now except us. Yes, I've got some men who work for me who will be here later, but you're always welcome." Seeing the tension leave her body, he jerked his head toward the house. "Come on in."

With him carrying the cobbler, she walked beside him into his house. Once inside he moved toward the kitchen counter to place the dish there, while she stayed in the front foyer, unabashedly gawking.

The living room on the left was two-stories with a fireplace on the inside wall and large windows on the two walls facing the outside. The panoramic view of the mountains behind his woods was spectacular. The furniture was oversized, but considering the size of him and his friends, she was not surprised. The colors were neutral, browns, tans, and taupe, but there was nothing boring about the effect. Dark, exposed wood was everywhere and the few pieces of artwork on the walls were obviously expensive, but not ostentatious.

He was walking back into the room just as her eyes had wandered to the right, where a long, heavy wooden table sat in the dining area. That room was minimally furnished, but with the table large enough to hold at least ten people, the space did not appear bare. A quick glance behind him showed the kitchen, granite counter tops, and stainless appliances.

He glimpsed at her wide eyes and moved directly into her line of vision. "You okay, babe?"

She blinked slowly. Twice. Before becoming unglued. "Yes, yes," she said in a rush. "I'm sorry. I'm just overwhelmed at how beautiful your place is." Looking around, she giggled. "I guess I thought you had a little cabin in the woods."

"You've got the sweet, little cabins in the woods, darlin'. I built this for my comfort and to have my business here as well." He linked his fingers with hers and said, "Come on," leading her back into the kitchen. He turned and grasped her waist, noting how his hands spanned around her middle. With an effortless lift, he placed her on a tall kitchen stool as he rounded the counter.

She cocked her head at him in question and he chuckled. "You brought dessert, so I'll throw a couple of sandwiches together."

In a few minutes, he had fixed two huge sandwiches, leaving her to wonder how she would ever get her mouth around hers, and they made their way to his deck, which was just as large as the front porch and had even more spectacular views. A table was placed under a wooden arbor, with a sunscreen overhead, capturing the breeze while repelling the hot rays of the summer sun. Setting their plates down, she sat across from him and they began to eat.

A comfortable silence ensued as they enjoyed the meal, the warm summer day, and the majestic view in the background.

She looked down at her half-eaten sandwich and then at his clean plate. "I can't eat another bite," she groaned, then grinned as he slid the rest over to his plate and finished it off.

She spied a porch swing at the other end and while she loved it, she had to admit that it appeared to be misplaced here in his male bastion. He saw where her gaze landed and stood, taking her hand once more.

Leading her to the swing, they settled side by side, its slow rocking motion relaxing them both.

"Is Ann okay by herself?" he asked, realizing that he had been so focused on Bethany coming he had not thought of her grandmother.

"Sally's with her and Roscoe's working today," she replied with a smile. She looked down at their clasped hands. *This feels right. Like I'm taking a chance but it's not really a chance.*

Looking around at the beautiful vista in front of her, she cocked her head to the side and asked, "Why here, Jack? Why not some big building in Richmond?"

"Tony's got a place like that," he answered. "Nice building, not exactly downtown, but still in the city. Underground garage, a reception area with a nice lady that books his appointments. Behind the conference rooms for clients is a huge area where his team works."

"You didn't want to have that kind of setup?"

"I need space. Fresh air. Grew up on a farm in southwest Virginia and I find the city to be...I don't know... choking, I guess."

She nodded her understanding. "I lived and worked in the city but always loved coming to Mountville. And now, I can't imagine moving back."

"I also didn't want to live out here but have to drive for fuckin' ever to get to my office. So, I built everything I need right here. Got space, land, privacy. My men come out here to meet. I'm only about twenty minutes outside of Charlestown, so it works for all of us."

They sat in companionable silence for a few more

minutes, the gentle movement of the swing relaxing both of them.

"So..." he said, dragging out the word. "You came today." His statement was more of a question. An unspoken, *What does this mean?*

She lifted her gaze to his, unable to hold back the smile that escaped when she recognized the strong man's nervousness.

"Yeah," she whispered. "I came." Looking out over his neat yard for a moment, she turned back to him as she felt the squeeze on her fingers.

She had practiced what to say ever since she woke this morning after seeing his face in her dreams all night long. Licking her lips, she could not remember her speech so she blurted, "You say you don't have a white-picket fence in your future, Jack, but you came to me. You let me in. The bracelet...the coming to the rescue yesterday...all of that could be just being a good neighbor...granted a good neighbor who has the means to protect someone. But when I say you came to me, I mean you *came* to me. You talked. You let me in. Then you kissed me and said you wanted more. And you gave me the freedom to choose to come here if that was what I wanted. I came today because I want in. I want to know you. I'd like to see where we can go. But I've got no idea what I'm getting myself into if you still say there's no white fence."

He listened as her words rushed out, warmed by the fact that she had come...and understanding his words had made her feel lost.

"For so long, finding someone was not what was in

my future," he answered honestly. "I loved what I did in the Army with Special Forces and then on my team. I knew if I wanted to replicate it here, I needed money, dedication, and total commitment to building a business that would make a difference. It's taken several years and quite honestly, in a shorter period than I would have thought, it's booming and making money for me and my new team. But it's taken my one hundred percent to make it so."

She nodded, understanding that just like she had been committed to her job and now to Gram's care and business, he had done the same. *But what is he offering? I can't do casual.*

Gathering her thoughts, she plunged on. "I get that… I really do. But Jack, I can't be…um…an incidental… um…you know."

His brow furrowed, not following her train of thought. "Baby, you're gonna have to spell it out for me, 'cause I'm not sure what you mean. An incidental what?"

Blushing furiously, she felt her cheeks warm and not from the summer heat. Leaning in to whisper as though they were in a crowd instead of in the middle of nowhere with no one else around, she said, "You know. A…friend with benefits. A…um…fuck bud—"

Rearing back in dismay, he growled, "A fuck buddy? That's what you think I'm offering?"

"I don't know," she rushed. "You haven't really told me exactly what you're thinking." Blinking furiously, she knew her blush had deepened.

To her surprise, he pulled her over, sliding her entire

body until she was tucked into his. He wrapped his arms around her small frame, holding her tightly, praying she could feel his sincerity even if his words had not conveyed it.

"Okay, baby, here goes. You're right, I haven't made myself plain, which makes no fuckin' sense because I'm a man who usually puts it right out there." Pushing her back slightly so that he could hold her gaze while his arms continued to hold her body, he said, "I felt something for you from the first time we met. Started out as admiration, moved to concern, and now has shifted to you being someone I want to know. I can't promise you the dream future right now, but I want to spend time with you and see where this might take us. The rest, we'll figure out as we go. But you being an incidental, fuck-buddy is not what's on the table." He peered into her sky-blue eyes and asked, "Understand?"

A smile split her face and he had to admit, lit his heart. Reaching up his hand to cup her cheek, he rubbed his thumb over the soft skin. Leaning in, he stopped a whisper away. "I need to hear you say it, beautiful."

"I'm with you, Jack. I'm willing to see where this goes."

Hearing those words, he slammed his lips over hers, taking her mouth in a kiss that devastated any doubts she may have had. Plunging his tongue into her warmth, he explored her feel, her taste, drinking in her essence. He shifted her around so she was now sitting in his lap, her back to his arm still wrapped around her and her legs stretched over the seat of the swing.

He continued to cup her face as he took the kiss

deeper, swallowing her moans as he plundered her mouth. Sliding his hand from her jaw downward, he felt her pulse at the base of her neck before it barely skimmed over her breasts and down to her waist. Slipping under the bottom of her shirt, he promised himself he just wanted to touch her skin, but that was a mistake. The instant his fingers found the silky smoothness of her stomach, he had to force himself to move them to glide over her back instead of her breasts, where they wanted to be.

His cock was painfully pushing against his zipper, and her sweet ass wiggling in his lap was not helping. Shifting his right arm, he leaned her further back as he slid his hand to the front until her bra covered breasts filled his palms. Her nipples were discernable through the material and he gently pinched one as her head fell back against his arm.

Bethany tried to remember her last lover but it had been awhile and her body was now decrying that loss. She had not even used her battery operated boyfriend in so long she was not sure where it was located. The electricity jolting from her nipples to her core had her already climbing the peak, wanting to throw herself off into the abyss.

Throwing caution to the wind, she reached down to lift her shirt up over her bra and as his eyes sought hers quickly, a lust-filled smile was all she could offer. His smile matched hers as his fingers pulled the cups of her bra down exposing her rosy-tipped nipples, already pebbled as they beckoned his mouth.

He answered their call, kissing his way down to her

breasts, his mouth latched onto one extended nipple, tugging and pulling as he sucked it deeply. She involuntarily reached her hand down, touching herself through her jean shorts, but he moved her hand away and replaced it with his.

She assisted him with the zipper and he slid his fingers down the front of her shorts, dragging them through her wet folds. That elicited another moan from her, zinging straight to his dick, which was ready to explode.

With his mouth sucking her breasts and his fingers plunging inside her sex, she forgot all time and space, only concentrating on the amazing way her body was responding to his touch. She pushed her hips up toward his hand, urging him to continue as she felt her orgasm impending.

He chuckled at the movement of her hips, knowing his fingers needed no encouragement to continue their deep exploration of her warm channel. He pressed his thumb on her clit and that sent her over the edge.

She suddenly reared back, her orgasm rushing over her sending electric sparks outward in all directions as her slick inner walls grabbed his fingers.

"Ride it out, baby," he whispered, allowing her body to respond and then slowly come down off her orgasmic high.

Her eyes fluttered open to find his staring straight into hers as he slipped his fingers out of her wetness and brought them to his mouth, sucking deeply on them. She could not have looked away if her life depended on it. The sight of this gorgeous man sucking her juices off his fingers, after giving her the best orgasm of her life, had her mesmerized. And they had not even gotten to using his dick yet, which made her wonder if she would die from orgasmic overload when that happened.

He then leaned in and kissed her, soft and gentle, but allowing her to taste her essence on his lips. Pulling back slightly, he said, "I want to take you out. On a real date."

"I'd like that. Very much," she breathed.

"You say when, 'cause you need to have Sally with Ann."

"She can come whenever," Bethany answered with a smile.

"Tomorrow too soon?" he asked.

Giggling, she replied, "No, I'd love to see you then."

The sound of an alarm rang and she startled. Trying to move off of his lap quickly she became a tangled mess of arms and legs waving in the process.

"Babe, it's okay," he assured, standing and placing her feet on the deck. He assisted her in zipping her shorts back up while she jerked her bra and shirt into place.

"What was that?" she asked, looking around.

"I'm afraid I let time get away from me and my team is coming in for our scheduled meeting."

"Oh my God," she exclaimed. "I have to get out of here. I can't let them see me."

"Babe, slow down. You're fine. They've already met you. They're gonna know you're here when they see your car in front of the house. Plus they're the ones who wanted me to pull my head outta my ass about you anyway."

"But I look a mess," she said, her hands worrying over her hair trying to smooth it down. "We look like we've been messing around and oh—" she cut off, her wide eyes searching his with fright.

"What, baby?"

"Can they tell that I've just…um…you know?"

He threw his head back, laughing. "I promise you the only thing they'll be thinking is how beautiful you are and how I've claimed you so that none of them had better be flirting."

He adjusted his cock, willing it to behave and snagged her hand to head back inside just as the others were on the front porch. He threw open the door, seeing them all standing around instead of entering. With a questioning expression on his face, he said, "You all usually just come in."

Cam came in first, spying a very nervous Bethany standing by the kitchen counter. After one look, it was clear that their boss had definitely been getting busy with the pretty neighbor. *Good. 'Bout time!*

He walked over to her, throwing out his hand in greeting. "Hey. I'm Cam."

Luke walked by Jack and said, "Saw you had company. Didn't want to…um—"

"Got it," Jack bit out, wanting to spare Bethany any embarrassment.

Luke introduced himself to her as well. She looked shocked as five other men came in, each greeting her with smiles.

Bart, Marc, Chad, Monty, and Blaise. *I know I saw them when Gram wandered over here, but I must not have been paying attention. Jesus, they're all gorgeous!* Her eyes nervously sought Jack's and she smiled when she saw them latched onto hers. The other men were stunners, but only Jack made her heart race.

"God, what smells so good?" Bart asked, sniffing the air. Cam, standing closest to the kitchen counter, lifted up the aluminum foil.

"Peach cobbler!" he exclaimed. Their eyes all turned toward Bethany.

"I…made…I mean, Gram and I made some…for all of you…to um…thank you for helping. And for last night…the um…fight." Suddenly nervous again, she relaxed when she felt Jack's arm around her shoulder pulling her in tight.

"Men, make yourselves at home like you normally do while I walk Bethany to her car." He stopped and glared back at them, "And if I come back and the cobbler's gone? There'll be hell to pay."

The men all laughed and watched as Jack started toward the door with her.

"Beautiful, remember to get Sally to watch Ann tomorrow night."

Taking Jack's hand, they walked out to her little car, now dwarfed between four other large SUVs and pickup trucks. He opened the door for her but stopped her from entering. He pressed her between his body and her car, leaning down to capture her lips.

Giving into the pleasure once more, she groaned and

he wanted nothing more than to toss the guys out, forget the mission, and carry her up to his bed.

"It's fine," her voice broke into his thoughts.

He leaned down and touched his forehead to hers. "I'm sorry, babe. I so wish I didn't have this meeting right now."

"Jack, it's not forever. It's just for now. You call me when you can and I'll let you make it up to me, big boy," she teased, pressing her hips into his crotch.

Eyes wide, he said, "Oh baby, you're gonna pay for that."

"Promise?" she whispered, kissing his throat.

"Guaranteed."

With that, he swatted her ass as she climbed into her car and watched her drive away, determined to find a way to make his life work with a white-picket fence.

11

After polishing off the cobbler, each pleased that she had made enough to feed eight large men, they relocated down to the command center.

"Glad to see you changed your mind about the lovely Ms. Bridwell," Blaise commented, patting Jack on the shoulder.

"Gotta say, I'm nervous as hell, but...well...I'm glad too," he responded with a nod to his men.

Settling around the table with their tablets once again in front of them and Luke at the controls for the information presented on the screen, they began their reports.

Bart stated, "Cam and I checked on the autopsy reports and interviewed the people who found the last three girls. Got some details on the cuts on the bodies."

Luke flashed the gruesome photographs on the screen, as Bart continued. "No one's made any identifications with the lacerations. They appear to be random slicing of skin, in no particular order and no obvious message. But when we interviewed the first doctor who did the autopsy on Sheila Carlson, he mentioned he had been standing at her side while his assistant was at her head looking down on the body and in toward her feet. He said the assistant made the comment that it almost looked like arrows in the direction of her genitals toward her throat."

Cam continued, "The doc said that they'd already taken pictures so he wasn't all that interested in his assistant's comments, but it was something that stuck in his mind. Later he looked at the photographs, but he didn't get that feeling at all. He mentioned it to the FBI who also have not seen anything obvious in the cuts."

Monty said, "Even though the FBI haven't latched onto that, I brought it to the attention of Shirley. She said it could be significant. We know the victims were alive when first tortured and were raped. If the killer obsesses over the genitals first, then makes his way up the body, with a throat slash last to actually kill, that would support a killer who's driven by sex."

"I thought most killers motivated by sex would go for hookers or hitchhikers or something like that," Blaise commented.

"Not necessarily. Some do go for prostitutes," Marc answered, "but they can also spend time scoping out their victims."

"So, the ones who go for prostitutes may just be prowling around looking for an easy victim. This guy seems to be stalking his victims first," Chad added.

"Right, so who's got the time and access to move around like this? Granted his field of operation is narrowing, but this takes some organization," Jack surmised.

"Salesmen, anyone who travels for business."

"College recruiters," Cam added quickly. "They travel around to high schools and work on college campuses."

Luke began to put in more information, saying, "That's good. Keep going."

"Yeah, but college recruiters only work for one college and they're limited by geographical caseloads," Chad remarked.

"Keep brainstorming," Jack ordered. "We can eliminate later."

The group continued to throw out ideas as the meeting went on. They added truck drivers, pilots, athletes, sportsmen, retail buyers, photographers, consultants, and the list kept going.

"Fuck, this is never-ending," Bart growled.

Jack's emergency number lit up and he took the call. The others watched carefully as his face grew hard. "Right. We'll be there."

Looking over his group, he reported, "A decomposed body has been found in the woods about a mile from Washington College. Preliminary says it could be Nola Talbot."

"Who do you want on it, boss?" Marc asked.

"I'm going," Jack replied. "Monty you coordinate with the FBI on this and I'll take Chad and Blaise."

"Boss," Cam said softly. "Let one of us take the lead. You've got a date tomorrow night."

Jack shook his head, a flash of regret in his eyes, before he growled, "No. I've got this. I need you, Bart and Marc to get to the other medical examiners and interview them personally. I want to know if anyone else had impressions about the cuts. None of the other girls' cuts seemed to be in a pattern but find out if the sex to throat kill was something anyone else thought. Luke?"

"I know, boss. I'm working it."

The group dispersed, each moving out to take care of business until they were ready to travel. Jack watched them leave and then made his way to the kitchen where he washed the cobbler dish. Sighing heavily, he made his call.

That evening as he, Chad and Blaise drove out, his thoughts were on the beautiful blonde. She had assured him that she understood and to call her when he got back into town. She even promised she would dress up for the occasion and get out of her jeans. He joked that he would not mind her being out of her jeans. Laughing, they hung up, but his heart was heavy.

As the night road passed them by, he forced his thoughts to the task tomorrow. Dealing with the decomposed body of another young woman.

He watched her leave the library again. The last time, she had gone straight to the dorm, but tonight she met with a small group and they were walking in the opposite direction. *Where are you going, my pretty?* Following at a distance, his lip curled in disgust as they entered a bar. Adjusting his mustache, he paid the cover fee and walked into the dimly lit atmosphere. It was crowded and the loud, live music irritated him. To add to his agitation, he lost her in the crowd. Seeing stairs to the side, he made his way up and found an opening at the rail looking down. *Yes, there you are.* Her hands were raised above her head, her hips grinding to the beat of the music. *And that man, his dick pressed into your ass. I knew it. You all turn into sluts at some time.* He slid his hand discreetly down to his crotch, pressing his palm against his cock until it hurt. *You're making me hurt, you little bitch.* He smiled slowly, continuing to massage himself to erection. *But your time's coming. Then I'll make you hurt.*

Jack, Chad, and Blaise watched as the medical examiner began his work on the body. There was little left after animals had devoured and dragged off several bones. Her right skeletal arm was intact and it was obvious—her right index finger was missing.

With little flesh left on the body, the medical examiner was unable to discern weapon of death, but the missing finger tied this into the same pattern as their killer. Jack, as the doctor was comparing the dental records to the teeth, stared at the remains. *No family. No parents to check with. Foster placement in high school.* Rage at a lone, young women whom life had already abandoned, in college trying to make something of herself only to end up on a slab in a medical examiner's office —*Fuck!*

"She's Nola Talbot. Positive identification based on dental records," the examiner stated definitively.

Nodding to his men, Jack turned to walk outside. At the door, he turned back around, staring at the remains one last time. Lifting his eyes to the examiner, he said, "When you're all done with her, contact me. I'll pay for her burial."

If the doctor was surprised, he did not show it. He had paid for a few burials himself over the years. He just nodded and turned back to his duties.

Chad and Blaise shared a look, unsurprised as well.

Back in the SUV driving home, the three were silent for the first part of the trip, each lost in their own thoughts.

"Call the others. We meet when we get in," Jack ordered and both men immediately began texting.

Blaise added, "Boss, if you wanted to take an evening off to go ou—"

"Nope. Meeting."

The two men nodded, knowing their boss' mind was not going to change about the evening. They just hoped that it would not change about Bethany.

The men had just met back at Jack's and had begun to process the new information when Monty called.

"Hate to dump this on you, but there's been another one."

Jack had him on speaker and growled, "Damn, go ahead."

"Just got a call from my FBI contact who hasn't even called the Governor yet. Virginia University in Charlestown. Same MO. I'm heading there now. Figured you'd want to be there as well."

"Yep," Jack answered. Looking around, he said, "Luke, what do you want to do on this one?"

"Same as always. You interview and feed me info. I've got an angle I've been looking at, but I'll take whatever data you can send to me."

"Chad, Blaise. You two just drove through the night. You up for more?"

"Absolutely," both replied at the same time.

"All right, Monty. The six of us will roll out of here. We should be there in about thirty minutes. We'll rendezvous and you can get us inside where the FBI is investigating. I want all of you on this and use whatever means you need to. We've got to stop this fucker."

Once more, the men left Jack's place to prepare to hit the road. He stood by his kitchen counter looking down at the empty, washed cobbler dish and his mind turned to the beautiful blonde with the heart of gold. *How the hell can I give you what you need when I can't be home regular hours? And how the hell can I keep my world from tainting yours?* Locking up and leaving his house, he felt more desolate than he ever had going on a mission.

He was beginning to see the handwriting on the wall

telling him there was no way a white-picket fence would fit in his life. And Bethany deserved nothing less.

The men effectively spread out, each knowing what needed to be done. Cam, Blaise, and Bart went to interview the girl's roommates, classmates, and friends to gather as much information as they could. Hacking into student records, Marc delved into her classes, grades, loans, and accounts. Luke was back at the compound digging into her Facebook and social media. Monty was with the FBI at the scene where the body was found.

And once again, Jack was in the medical examiner's room, this time staring at the mutilated body of Karen Solter. Blonde, blue eyes, medium build. *Fuck. Looks too fuckin' much like—Stop...don't go there.*

Forcing his mind to the task at hand, he discreetly moved from the side to the head of the victim, looking down her body. While the cameras had taken pictures from multiple angles, he was stunned to see what the other medical examiner's assistant had said. At this angle, it did appear as though the random mess of cuts did point like arrows from the girl's pubic region toward the throat slice. *Doesn't give us much, but could confirm the sexual motivation of the actual killings.*

Moving back around to the side and out of the way, he admired the professionalism of the medical examiner, who combined clinical precision with a profound respect for the murdered girl.

"Weapon of death?" he quietly asked as the doctor

took meticulous measurements of the length and depth of the wounds.

"Very long, thin blade. These lacerations are almost surgical in exactitude."

"You think a scalpel?" he prodded.

"No, no. A scalpel wouldn't be long enough."

The examiner walked over to a computer and quickly began searching. "Here," he said. "I would have to take more measurements, but something like this."

Jack walked over and stared at a long, filet knife. The one on the screen called it a fishing filet knife. *Fishing?* His thoughts raced to the fishermen he ejected from Bethany's place days earlier. Once again, forcing her from his mind, he asked, "This would be a common knife, wouldn't it?"

The doctor gave a derisive snort, "Oh yeah. Got two of them at home myself. Take the grandson fishing when he comes to visit. Hell, in Virginia, with our beaches, rivers, and lakes, you'd find one of these in over half the homes here."

Nodding, Jack left soon after, meeting some of the men in their hotel room. Marc reported what was becoming a familiar tune as they were finally starting to connect some dots in the backgrounds of the victims.

"She was a solid student, not brilliant, but studied a lot and studied hard. Her professors have mostly been here a while and I've already checked with Luke, none of them had been at any of the other colleges when one of the girls went missing."

Cam, Blaise, and Bart had preliminary reports and would continue interviewing the next day.

"She was considered a good girl," Cam said. "No partying, no boyfriends, no booze."

"Her roommates appeared genuinely upset. Liked her and said she had no enemies. Usually kept to herself and studied in the library most evenings. They had recently met with some friends and they were surprised when she had come along to a bar for dancing. That was unusual for her, but they were thrilled she came with them," Blaise reported, looking down at his notes.

Bart took over from there. "I checked out the bar they went to. Live music and a friend of theirs was playing so that appeared to be the reason she went. They said she had a great time dancing. She didn't drink so no one could have spiked it. There was a guy she was dancing with for a long time, but he left earlier than her group did and he left alone. He has an alibi; he met up with his girlfriend later."

"Now there was one piece of information I followed up on but it led to a dead-end. The roommates said the bar was crowded and they lost track of each other, but one said she looked up at one time and saw Karen standing on the stairs leading to the loft chatting with a man there. Later, when she looked up, neither Karen nor the man was there."

"She leave with him?" Jack asked.

"Roommates say no way. She was not about to pick up a guy in a bar; it just wasn't her."

"Cameras in the bar?"

"Only in the bar area so the owner can keep track of his bartenders' handling of money."

"Get it," Jack growled. "Send it to Luke."

Bart nodded and immediately headed out into the night. An hour later he was back, a grin on his face. "Easiest bar to break into I've ever done." Seeing Jack's face, he added, "Already sent to Luke."

Finishing their meeting for the night, they planned the next couple of days. And Jack knew they were going to be long ones.

He taped the latest pictures up on his wall, adding them to his collection. "I told you that you should have stayed a good girl. But no, you had to become a slut. So now, you join the others." Standing back admiring his wallpaper, his eyes roamed over the macabre collage.

His fingers trailed along the wall, touching the photographs almost lovingly. Reverently. The memories of each one flooding his mind. He was at peace. The urge had been assuaged, leaving only satisfaction in its wake.

His cell phone vibrated and he grimaced at the interruption. Pulling it out, he read the text, sighing.

Collecting his things, he readied himself to go back home. Using a large bucket filled with water and bleach, he quickly wiped down the tabletop and splashed the remaining liquid on the floor. With an old broom, he gave a few sweeps to send the bloody water out of the door.

He never spent too much time on cleaning the room...it was just a place to make the sluts pay. But the knife was different. Carefully washing, bleaching, and then drying the instrument, he tucked it back into his case.

With a last glance around, he stepped out into the night air and locked the door behind him. He smiled, humming a tune as he drove away.

12

"What do you think?" Bethany asked, twirling around breathlessly, allowing the jewel-blue jersey dress to flare out around her. "Do you like it better than the green one?"

Sally and Gram clapped in approval for each dress she had tried on, deciding to plan ahead for the date with Jack. When he left, he had said to be prepared for this next Saturday. He had been gone for almost a week, with no contact, but she knew he was working. It stung a little that he had not called or texted, but she reminded herself that he said his work was unpredictable.

She had stayed busy and now was playing dress up with Sally and Gram helping her to choose her best date clothes.

"Oh, darling, they all look so pretty on you," Sally enthused. "Don't you think so Ann?"

Bethany looked over at her grandmother, knowing that she was slipping farther away from reality. Gram did not reply but offered a smile instead. It was all she could give and Bethany would take anything offered, wanting to hold on to every memory with her grandmother.

"Why haven't I seen you in any of these dresses before?" Sally asked. "Have you had them here all along?"

"Yes," laughed Bethany, "but there's hardly been a reason to wear them here. How can I chop wood in a dress and high heels?"

"Well, no matter which one you choose, you'll be beautiful," Sally remarked. She looked at Ann and said, "Let me help your grandmother to bed while you change."

Smiling, Bethany agreed, then moved back to her bedroom. A few minutes later, dressed in her pajamas, she checked in as Sally was just getting Ann into bed.

Leaning over, she whispered, "I love you, Gram," kissing her cheek.

Sally and Bethany quietly left the room. "She's getting worse, you know," Sally said.

Bethany sighed, "I know. I called mom and dad the other night and they were checking on the closest facility to here." Tears filled her eyes, but she dashed them away quickly.

But not quickly enough. Sally walked over, offering her a hug and said, "You're a good woman, Bethany."

Soon afterward Sally left and Bethany locked up the lodge. Climbing into bed, she looked at the dresses hanging on a hook on her closet door. Smiling, she thought of the date she and Jack would finally be able to go on. Saturday was only two days away and she had the perfect pampering day planned for tomorrow.

The next day, Bethany drove into the city for an early appointment at a spa and salon. Starting with a massage, she felt the kinks smoothed out of her work-tired muscles, followed by a hair trim and style. She loved the feel of someone else drying her hair while brushing it out. It reminded her of the times when she was a little girl and her mother would sit for a long time running the hair brush through Bethany's thick tresses. Then lastly, she sat getting a pedicure while reading a trashy magazine, checking out the latest Hollywood couples.

Laying the articles down in her lap, she leaned her head back against the chair. She heard about the new college girl's murder on the television and assumed that Jack was involved. *How does he do what he does?* Glad that someone like him was on the case, she still hated that he had been gone for days.

Her mind rolled back to the last time she was with him on his deck. The memory of his lips on hers before they moved to her breasts as his fingers had worked deep inside of her. She could still remember the tingles from the orgasm that had rushed over her body—

"You coming ma'am?"

Her eyes jerked open in surprise as she saw the small Asian pedicurist standing with his hand held out to her, waiting for her to step off of the chair. Jumping up, she could feel her blush heating her face as she placed her hand in his. "Yes, yes, I'm coming," she replied as she allowed him to assist her down so as not to mess with her pedicure.

Driving home, it was hard to contain her excitement as she sang along with the radio. *Jack calls me beautiful when I've been out chopping wood. I wonder what he'll say when he sees me all fixed up?* Smiling to herself, she pulled into Mountville and parked in front of the lodge.

Roscoe walked by, coming from the shed. "You look real purdy, Miss Bethany," he called out.

"Thank you. Was everything here all right?"

"Cabins and folks are fine. Sally's got Ms. Ann settled in for a nap and I'm just working on some of the little repairs. I noticed you got a lock on the tool shed now."

"Oh, my goodness, yes. I completely forgot to give you a key." He followed her into the lodge, where she went around the check-in counter and opened a drawer. "Here, you can just keep this one. Right now, you and I will have the only keys and I'll keep a spare in here in case you forget yours."

Fingering the key that she gave him, he nodded. "Sounds good miss." With that, he turned and headed back out to work.

She bounded up the stairs and saw Sally in the small kitchen. "Hey," she whispered. "How was everything?"

Sally returned her hug, answering, "We mostly stayed in and watched TV. She didn't seem to want to go outside and since it was humid, I didn't force a walk today."

She then held Bethany at arm's length and said, "I

don't have to ask you how your day was. You are gorgeous!"

Smiling, Bethany replied, "It felt so good to get pampered and know that at the end will be a hot date with a hot guy…that I already know likes me!"

"And what about you? Do you already know you like him?" Sally teased.

"Oh, yeah." The smile on Bethany's face had Sally laughing.

"Girl, you are so ready for this man to get back into town and I can't wait to hear what he says when he lays eyes on you."

"Well, come around tomorrow and you'll be able to do just that," she invited.

Saying goodbye, she closed the door behind Sally and checked in on her grandmother, still sleeping peacefully. Kneeling by the bed, she whispered, "Oh, Gram. You've always listened to my secrets and plans. I like him, Gram. Really, really like him. I haven't been around any man that actually made my heart beat faster. Or one who wants me protected. Or who makes me feel like our crazy lives could mesh."

Reaching out, she barely touched her grandmother's hand, not wanting to wake her, but needing that contact. "I wish you were still here with me, Gram. Not just in body, but here with me the way you always were."

Sighing deeply, she rose and tiptoed out of the room, closing the door behind her. Walking to her purse, she pulled out her cell phone. *Come on Jack, call me.*

The drive home from Charlestown was not long, but Jack's musings were filled with dark thoughts. The men in the back seat were beginning to joke, a natural defense mechanism when their jobs were stressful, but this time Jack was not joining in. His mind was on the case, how to stop a murderer that they could not find, and a beautiful blonde that would be home waiting for him.

Rubbing his hand over his face, he wondered how he was going to do this. Or not do this. *Damn!* Before he could ponder the situations anymore, they pulled into the driveway. As the men disembarked from the vehicles, he looked over at them.

Every one of them would volunteer to stay and keep working the case instead of going to their homes if he asked. But he knew they needed their down time. Just like he did.

"Go on home. We'll reconvene here eight a.m. Monday morning. We've got a lot of data to process and for the weekend, we'll let the FBI do their jobs. Monty, be ready to give us their info then. Luke, we need whatever you can data-mine for us at that time." He held their stares for a moment, then added, "We've got other contracts that I'm working on, to see what we can fulfill, but I don't need to tell you that we gotta stop this man."

The others nodded solemnly as they began to head to their trucks.

"Have a great weekend date with the beautiful Ms.

Bridwell," Cam called out. The others smiled and threw out their encouragements as well.

Throwing up a half-hearted wave, he just nodded and headed into his house. He watched them drive away before walking into his kitchen and pulling out a beer. He moved to his living room and stood in front of the bank of windows offering the majestic view. Taking a swig, he pulled out his phone. This was going to be a long-ass weekend.

Deep in a romance novel, Bethany jumped when her cell phone rang. Looking down, she could not keep the grin off her face. **Jack**. *Yes! Finally!*

"Hey, Jack," she answered. "How are you? I've been listening to the news and figured you've been super busy. Are you okay?"

There was a second of silence before his rough voice came through. "Yeah, I'm fine."

"I know you must be exhausted," she continued to blab. "Are you back home or still on the road?"

"I'm home now."

Pulling her lips in, she wondered at his straightforward answers and assumed he must be tired. "Well, I'm glad you're home. I hope you can rest tonight."

"Yeah, that's the plan."

Twisting the sheet in her hand, she was confused about his lack of enthusiasm. A hollow feeling developed in the pit of her stomach, and she felt her heart begin to beat a loud rhythm. Sucking in a deep breath, she plunged on.

"Are we still on for tomorrow night? I've got everything picked out for me to wear so I can totally wow you. You might not recognize me without my jeans or a t-shirt," she joked, hoping to get a reaction from him.

Silence greeted her. Licking her lips nervously, she added, "But Jack, I know you've been gone and you're tired and probably still working, aren't you? Uh…we can postpone our date…it doesn't have to be tomorrow."

Silence.

"In fact, I could maybe run by just to welcome you home. If you had a few minutes, that is. We could…uh… hang out on your porch…or…" Her heart began to pound at his lack of comments.

"Listen, about tomorrow night. I don't think that will be a very good idea. I'm sorry that you've gone to trouble for it," he said, hating his own lies.

"Sure," she replied, overly brightly. "That's fine. I'm sorry, Jack. I should have realized that you're still working and wouldn't have time. I could always bring you dinner and promise to not stay and bother you." Hope dripped from her words, but she was helpless to stop them.

"I think that we probably shouldn't plan anything at all. I thought this could be a good idea, but I'm really not what you need and…" he faltered, unaccustomed to not knowing what to say, "and I just don't have time in my life to try to make something work."

This time the silence came through loud and clear,

but it was him on the receiving end. Hoping to soften the blow, he added, "You need someone who can come home to peach cobbler."

Silence. No one spoke for a few seconds, the dead-air hanging between them.

"That's it, Jack? That's all? What happened to you wanting me in your life?"

He had no answer.

"What about you claiming me? Or wanting to see where this goes? You're just going to throw it all away before giving us a chance?" her voice rose in anger with each word.

"I'm sorry, Bethany. I just think we need to stop this before it goes anywhere."

"Goes anywhere? Well, pardon me for thinking that letting a man suck on me with his fingers inside of me, as going somewhere. I guess I'm not used to being the incidental that you claimed I wasn't!"

"You're taking this all wrong," he growled in frustration. "You were never casual. I can't deal with my job, my business, and my life and have you in it as well."

Her stomach churning, she blinked to keep the tears at bay. "Oh great, the old *it's not you, it's me* line. That's just an excuse and you know it. There are committed couples all over the world in jobs that require a lot of time and energy to make it all work. What you're really saying is that you don't consider me worth the trouble." She threw the words out, praying that he would at least deny them. He did not.

"Yeah, I guess you're right," he lied. "It's just not what I want or what I need."

A deathlike silence followed.

Jack's fist clenched at his side, the desire to pound it into the wall was overwhelming, but he forced himself to not move.

"I think you're lying," she said, her voice shaking. "I think we could be good together. Or I did. The man I was interested in was caring. The man talking to me right now is selfish. Yes, Jack, selfish. You're so determined to be a martyr to your business that you won't consider your own happiness...or mine."

Steeling himself for her anger, her words were like blows to his gut. It was on the tip of his tongue to apologize, tell her he was wrong, beg her to go out with him. But once again, he let the silence hang in the space between them.

"Well, I guess there's nothing left to say. I want your cameras turned off, Jack. I won't have my privacy invaded and if they're not, then I'll call the police." She hesitated a moment before adding, "I'd like to say that I'll get rid of Gram's bracelet, but honestly I need that. But I'll be sending you a check to pay for the cost."

He started to protest, but she cut him off. "No, you can't have it both ways. You can send me a bill or I'll look online to see what the costs would be."

Blinking again, this time unable to hold the tears at bay, she said, "Goodbye. I'm sure you're very good at your job and I do wish you success with that. But...well, I guess I don't have anything else to say. Goodbye." She tried to disconnect just before the sobs took over. Tossing the phone down on her nightstand, she fell over on the bed, her heart aching.

Why should it hurt so bad? It's not like I knew him for that long. The answers to her questions were staring her in the face. *I was already falling for him and what I thought we could be. And now...* She lay on her bed, sobs wracking her body, glad that Gram was fast asleep in the other room and could not hear her.

With Gram no longer able to be the companion she once was, her parents on the other side of the country, and the friends she had still back in Richmond, Bethany felt very alone. The sadness slid over her like a shroud threatening to suffocate her.

After crying until no more tears existed, she turned out the light, lying in bed knowing that sleep would elude her. She was right. For long hours, she thought of the dark and brooding man who had stolen her heart. And handed it back to her in shreds. *What an idiot, I am. He tried to tell me he had no place for me in his future when we first met. I should have listened to that man...not the one I was willing to give myself to!*

Jack heard the sob just before she disconnected. He threw his phone across the room, not caring if it shattered. "Goddamnit!" he yelled to the empty room. Hanging his head in frustration, he gritted his teeth until he thought they would crack. *She's wrong. I'm not selfish! I'm thinking of her and only her. She deserves more than a man that works all the time. In a world that's fucked up, dark, and full of terrors she can't even imagine.*

The vision of her smile filled his mind as he stared

out into the black night. Her laughter. Soft touch. Bringing dessert to him and his men. No other woman had ever tried to fit into his life and it had made it so easy in the past to realize that his life would not mesh with theirs. *But she was different. Giving. Ready to accept me for who I am...and what I do. Would it have worked? No fuckin' way to know, but at least she had been willing to try.*

Shaking his head, he forced his mind to think of the reasons why he was right. *Better to end it now before it hurts more. Better than to let something grow and then find out it can't work.*

But staring out his window into the blackness, her smiling face still filled his thoughts…taunting him with what he had just destroyed.

Stalking across the room he tossed the unfinished beer into the trash. Walking back to the liquor cabinet, he pulled out a whiskey bottle. Grabbing a glass he took them both to the living room and sat facing the windows again. Pouring a drink, he decided that getting shitfaced was the only way to make this nightmare disappear.

13

Two days later, Bethany was working in the flower beds just outside of the lodge. They did not need weeding, but she refused to have any down time. Two days of little sleep, little food, and a lot of work was taking its toll on her. Gram was staying in the lodge most of the time, not interested in walking around but preferring to putter around inside the house.

On her knees in the dirt, she could feel the urge to cry once more, but fought it off. *I was fine before Jack Bryant and I'll be fine now!*

Just then, a car pulled into the front of the lodge and she looked up in surprise as her parents waved excitedly at her.

"Mom! Dad!" she cried, jumping up to greet them as they alighted from their car. "You guys didn't tell me you were coming!"

Her mother moved toward her, arms extended. Blonde hair like Bethany's, now with a touch of gray, was pulled back away from her face with a clip. Her face was an older version of her daughter's, still smooth and beautiful. Dressed for comfort, she was in neat jeans and a short sleeve pink blouse.

Her father followed his wife and as Bethany noted, he was also dressed in jeans and a polo, looking ready to pile up on one of the rocking chairs on the front porch or down by the dock.

Hugging them both, she exclaimed, "Why didn't you call?" Grabbing the overnight case from her mom, she continued, "Come on in. Gram will be glad to see you." She halted suddenly and her face sobered. "Well, the truth is, she might not recognize you…but she'll be happy for the company anyway."

She noticed her parents shared a look, but she dismissed it in her excitement to have them there.

"Gram?" she called out, walking into the lodge's main room. "We have visitors."

Her dad looked over at his mother and noticed the change since he had seen her two months ago. "Mom?" he said, walking over to where she sat looking up with a smile. He kissed her cheek and she said, "You'll like it here. We got nice cabins."

Ed looked at his wife quickly and saw her sad expression. She walked over, greeting her mother-in-law with a kiss as well.

"Ann, it's so good to see you," Susan added. She blinked back the tears, knowing how hard this was for her husband, and then turned to peer at her daughter. Shocked that she had not noticed it in her eagerness to arrive, she realized Bethany looked...devastated.

Just then, Sally entered the lodge and greeted Ed and

Susan. She glanced at Bethany and asked, "You want me to take Ann up and fix her an early lunch?"

Bethany offered her a heartfelt smile of gratitude. The two of them had shared several tearful conversations about Jack in the past two days and it was clear Sally knew that she needed to talk to her parents. Confide in them. Draw strength from them.

"Yeah, that'd be great."

They watched as Sally assisted Gram upstairs, then heard her puttering in the kitchen while talking softly to Ann.

"We need to talk," her father began, but before he could say anything else, Susan interrupted.

"I think we need to listen first," she said, looking at her daughter as only a mother does. "You don't look happy and I want to know why."

The three settled in the comfortable chairs in front of the lodge's fireplace as they had done on so many trips to Mountville to visit her grandparents over the years.

"So what's going on that's put such a sad look in your eye, baby?" her mom asked. "And I know it's not all about Gram."

Shrugging while shaking her head, Bethany said, "A tale as old as time, mom."

Her father looked confused but wisely kept his mouth shut as he looked to his wife for guidance. Susan nodded in understanding and gently ordered, "Tell us about him."

"He owns the property next to us and we met under unusual circumstances when Gram wandered away one day. He owns some kind of a security business," she added, her nose scrunched in thought. "Kind of secret, with government contracts and…well anyway, he was very sweet and even set Gram up with a tracker bracelet so she could be tracked if she wandered again."

"That's right, I remember you telling us about that," her father commented.

"And…" her mother prodded.

"We…well I can't say we started seeing each other really…but we were together some and both had feelings for each other so we decided to follow through on them and see where they went. I guess I went overboard and…" her voice trailed off sadly.

"You were already falling," her mother finished for her.

"That sounds so lame," Bethany confessed. "I'm not some teenager who falls in love at the drop of a hat." Her parents gifted her with the time to finish her story without butting in.

"But, yeah," she admitted. "My heart was definitely already involved. He just didn't feel the same."

"What happened?" her mother asked.

"He had to leave for business, and I know it was bad. He couldn't tell me much, but I'm pretty sure that he was working on those college murders."

"We've been reading about those and you've no idea how glad we are that you're no longer in college!" her father added.

"I know his job is stressful and he sees horrible things. I just…I just foolishly allowed myself to believe him when he told me that I meant something to him."

Pulling herself up straight in her chair, she said, "But I've got responsibilities and a life to live so I'm not going to pine over him anymore." She knew the words were lies as soon as they left her mouth and one look at her mother told her that she knew they were lies also.

But like a good mom, she played along. "Well, just make sure to take care of yourself and don't work too hard."

Offering them what she hoped was a reassuring smile, she agreed. Forcing her mind out of her own troubles, she looked at them speculatively. "Okay, guys, enough about me. We talked last week and you never mentioned flying out here for a visit. What's the real reason behind this impromptu trip?"

Her parents shared a look again, further cementing her idea that something was happening. Cocking her head to the side, she waited.

Sighing deeply, her father said, "We wanted to be here to talk to you about Gram. There are some things in the works, but we need your input as well."

"Okaaaay," she said slowly, uneasy from the sound of his words.

"There's an opening at a memory care facility near where we live in Arizona—"

"No!" Bethany shouted. "You can't take her that far away. It makes no sense. She's fine here until an opening comes here." Jumping up, she paced the room, her mind working furiously. "You're not even permanent residents of Arizona. What happens when you transfer colleges?"

"Bethany, sit down, please," her mother begged.

"We've made no decision yet. That's why we're here—to get your input."

Chastised, she sat back down, putting her head in her hands. "I'm sorry. What other decision is there?"

"Well," her father started again, "there is an opening now in the facility that's close to here."

At that, Bethany's head snapped up. "That's perfect. That'll be great. Gram will get the safe care she needs and still be close to me." Looking at her parents' doubtful faces, she asked, "So what's to discuss?"

"Honey, what about you? Your needs? Your career? We don't want you locked into staying here just because Gram is nearby. You may want to move back to Richmond and continue with your job there."

Bethany sat, stunned, realizing she had not considered the possibility of leaving Mountville...and the neighbor next door...and returning to the city to live. She looked around the inside of the old lodge. The one that constantly needed work, compared to her apartment in the city with modern conveniences and was near shopping centers and restaurants. She glanced down at her dirty knees and fingernails, compared to her professional work clothes and weekly manicures. She thought of the loneliness of her social life here compared to the bustling city with co-workers, friends, bars, museums, and concerts...and the opportunity to meet someone who did want to spend time with her.

But she could not escape the glaring reality—this was what she wanted. Her gaze lifted to her parents as she confessed, "I want Gram near here. And I want to stay at Mountville. This is my life now."

Her father started to protest, but Susan's hand on his arm stopped him. She considered her daughter carefully and said, "I want you to sleep on it, sweetheart. The decision needs to be considered thoughtfully. This place is part of your history, but it doesn't have to be your future. Gram will be taken care of, no matter what. You need to think about you."

Nodding, she agreed as they rose from their seats for a family hug. Tears hit the back of her eyes as she blinked to keep them at bay. Too many changes in just a few days had her on edge. Pulling back, she plastered a bright smile and said, "Let's go have lunch with Gram."

He fingered the wig and mustache carefully before placing them back in the box. Glancing down, he lined them up—the blond, next to the black, next to the brown. *Which one next? Which one will it be?* He pondered purchasing another one, even considered one with long hair. *Perhaps pulled back in a ponytail. Young women like the wild, youthful look. Yes, maybe a new one is needed. But not now.* The urge was gone, once more replaced with calm. Breathing deeply, he smiled as he closed the suitcase, placing it back in his hiding place.

He had several hiding places—all carefully planned. He knew he would not get caught even though the newspapers were beginning to talk. Shaking his head, he thought *Don't they get it? I'm taking care of the sluts. That needs to be done.*

Hearing noises from inside of his house, he locked

the garage and made his way back into his kitchen. Smiling.

Jack once more stood with his coffee mug in his hand, hoping the effects of drinking himself into a stupor two nights ago were no longer noticeable. His men were due soon and he was regretting his stupid decision…all of his stupid decisions.

Friday night into Saturday, he thought of all of the reasons his decision to not start a relationship with Bethany made sense. His life was too unpredictable. Too full of violence. Too hard to separate the business with the personal. The more he had tried to convince himself he was right, the more he drank. He had been right at the beginning—she deserved the white-picket fence. Kids, dog, and a husband that did not see death and destruction when he went to work.

By Saturday night, when he should have been picking up the beautiful woman for their date, the one who had told him she had a perfect dress for him, he sat, sobering alone in his house. All of the reasons from the night before were less clear.

The fact was that it was too late to *not* start a relationship. He started one from the moment he held her to his body when they were attempting to help her grandmother. He continued the relationship when he brought the bracelet for Ann.And stayed for dinner. And talked on her front porch. And had her place wired for security. And when he raced over there when he had seen there was trouble. And when he first kissed her. And when she came to him with that fuckin' fantastic cobbler and gave herself and her trust to him.

Rubbing his hand over his face, he saw the first of his men's vehicles coming down the drive. *At least I spent most of yesterday focusing on the case.* Stepping inside of his house, he moved to start the business day.

Once more, the eight men sat around the conference table in the SPI command center. While the men had the weekend to recuperate, they all had the hardened expressions of anger that the case was not yet solved.

Monty had been the last to arrive, but his news was the best. "The FBI showed the pictures of the man on the bar stairs with Karen to the friends of Tonya." Luke projected the pictures to each of their tablets as Monty continued. "They have positively identified him as the person with Tonya, even though his mustache is now brown."

"Any ID?" Jack asked, but Monty just shook his head. "We'll get on it," Jack confirmed. "Who's up for travel?"

Every man volunteered and, not for the first time, was Jack aware his team was the best he could have assembled. "Right. Cam, you and Blaise hit the witnesses on the western part of the state. Marc and Chad, take the Richmond area. Bart and Monty, take the southern campuses. Show that to any roommates, friends, especially anyone who was with the victims at their last known locations. Luke and I'll coordinate with the FBI in Richmond and see what identification magic Luke can perform."

The others chuckled, knowing Luke's software could

outperform any of the government's highest security programs.

"Boss, I saw something this weekend that may have no significance, but it hit me weird."

"Go on," Jack responded as the others turned to Cam.

"I was at a bar Saturday night just chillin' and was watching a scene in front of me 'cause I thought I was going to have to intervene. A guy was hittin' on a girl, but she wasn't falling for his pick-up lines and told him politely several times to leave her alone. Just when I was about to step in, she whirled around and poked him in the chest while telling him in no uncertain terms to get away from her. The bouncer stepped in, removed the guy, show's over. But something about that kept gnawing at me."

Cam looked at everyone and held up his right index. "She was poking him in the chest with her right index finger to make her point. And he was pissed. Can't tell you he even heard her words, but he sure felt that finger and I got the feeling he wanted to snap it off."

A deathly silence descended on the group.

"Shit," Chad said. Immediately the others began to speak all at once.

Jack called the Saints back to order and he reiterated, "So this guy disguises himself. Follows a girl somewhere or maybe just finds someone, tries to pick her up. Remember Tonya's friends said he wasn't young. So he tries to pick up someone younger who's not interested, they blow him off or get mad and maybe resort to poking him to make their point. He snaps. After he captures them, subdues them somehow, tortures, rapes and kills them, then he cuts off the offensive finger."

"Were they already dead?" Blaise asked, scrolling through his notes.

Jack cursed. "Damn. No, you're right. The coroner's report on Tonya, Helena, and Sheila was that the digit was removed before death."

The silence once more hung about the group.

"The ultimate revenge. I can't get you interested, so I'll rape you. You insulted me by poking me with your finger, so I'll cut it off," Bart growled.

Blaise shook his head. "This is much more than a man who can't get a young woman interested. This fucker is sick and is going to keep killing."

"Spent the weekend at home with my family," Marc said, gaining the attention of the group. He looked around, his face a mask of frustration. "Gotta sister at Dominion College. Sophomore. Pretty. Nice. Decent student. And right-handed."

"Fuck man," Luke bit out.

"Spent the weekend with her and my parents and even though she's home for the summer, we talked about her not going back until this is over with."

"Some serial killers are not caught for years, Marc," Jack said.

Nodding, Marc agreed. "Yep, but I'd rather her not be at risk than to take that chance."

"This is exactly why the governor gave us this task. We've got to find this fucker and shut him down."

As the agenda came to a close, the group made their way upstairs to head to their assignments.

"You have a good date with the beautiful Ms. Bridwell, boss?" Cam asked. "I meant to ask when we came in, but we got to the meeting so quickly."

Jack looked discomfited as he turned and stared out of the window. The men all shared glances, curious but not wanting to pry.

Finally, Jack spoke, "Decided to call it off."

"The date...or..." Cam ventured.

"Nope, all of it. Told her it wouldn't work. Not with my business. Figured I may as well let her down easy now than to have to her let down hard later."

"So you took that choice away from her?" Blaise asked.

Jack's eyes darted to Blaise's quickly, his eyebrow raised in question.

"You made the decision for her that your life won't be good enough. You made the decision for her that she can do better. You never gave her the chance to decide for herself if what you have to offer is enough."

Before the others chimed in, Jack growled, "Appreciate what you're trying to do, but my personal life is off topic."

The other quieted, but it was obvious to Jack they were not happy. Sighing heavily, he rubbed his hand over his face, the weight of the unsolved case and his fucked-up, non-relationship with Bethany bearing down on him.

Shaking his head, he said, "Sorry guys. We're in this together and I've never pulled high-handed shit on you before. Not gonna start now." He looked around at the faces that were becoming as familiar to him as his brothers-in-arms while in the Special Forces. Ones that for the last two years had been joining with him, having his back as he had theirs.

"My love life...or lack of it...is not up for debate, but I will say I appreciate your concern."

The others stayed respectfully quiet, allowing him to gather his thoughts, each of them realizing that none of them were in a committed relationship. More than a few wondered if they, too, were giving up the chance of love by being in this profession.

"Right now," Jack continued, looking at them, "I have to give one hundred percent to this case. When it's over? Who knows, but for now I'm doing what I think is best."

The men nodded as they prepared to leave, each with their assignments. With head jerks as goodbyes, they headed out of the door.

Jack poured a cup of coffee and handed it to Luke before getting a second one for himself. "All right, let's do some identification magic," he said, as the two of them walked back downstairs.

14

Bethany sat on the front porch of the lodge in the pre-dawn morning, tears sliding down her face once more. *How much have I cried in the past week?* Her heart squeezed with pain as she took a deep breath. Her mind wandered back over the previous days, now all swimming together.

The morning after her parents arrived she knew that this lodge, this life was what she wanted. Convincing her parents had not been too difficult once they could see how much she loved the country over the city, using her degree for her own business rather than for someone else's.

But life at Mountville without Gram? *How will I bear it?*

Once the decision was made, her father had called Golden Arbor and accepted the place for Gram. Thankfully, Gram's descent into Alzheimer's meant she was not upset with the transition. In fact, other than some initial concern, she adapted immediately to the nursing staff and other residents. Roscoe pitched in with the use of his truck and they moved her bedroom furniture to her new room. Bethany and Sally fixed it up to look almost like the room she had occupied in Mountville for over fifty years.

Visiting every day allowed them to see her settled comfortably. She now referred to Bethany as Helen each time and once looked at Ed and called him by his father's name of Martin. Her mind was firmly in the past, but it appeared to give her peace.

Ed and Susan left two days later to fly back to Arizona after heartfelt hugs and promises for Bethany to take care of herself. She held her emotions together, throwing herself into hard work until yesterday. Having gone to check on Gram, she found her smiling in the common room. They chatted a few minutes, Gram continuing to think she was her sister Helen.

Suddenly Gram looked over and asked, "Helen, what happened to Charlie? I liked him."

Assuming that Gram was talking about the original man from fifty years ago who had been interested in Helen, she just replied, "I don't know."

Gram gazed at her for a long time, then said, "You know, he cared for my granddaughter."

Bethany's eyes grew wide, uncertain where her grandmother's mind was at the moment.

"He came around courtin' my granddaughter. Good lookin' man. Nice too. I was hopin' he'd stay with her."

Bethany's chin quivered as she blinked to hold the tears at bay once more. Leaning over, she patted her grandmother's hand and then watched as Gram closed her eyes to take a nap. Slipping out a few minutes later, she drove home, climbed the stairs, and finally allowed the emotions to pour out of her.

Now, days later, she was perched on the porch watching the sunrise over the trees to the east. The sky was cast in pale tints of blue as the night was slowly receding. Roscoe walked by, surprised to see her up so early.

"Ms. Bridwell," he greeted. "You doin' all right?"

Shaking her head slowly, she replied, "Nah, but I will be."

He wandered over to the bottom of the porch and admired the young woman in front of him. "Got a lotta respect for you. You're a good girl."

She just smiled her response, then asked, "What are you doing up so early?"

"Sometimes I go to the dock and do a little sunrise fishing before the guests get up. Never know what I'll catch. Sometimes nothin'. Sometimes enough for my dinner. If you're ever interested, let me know and I'll catch some fish for you."

"I haven't had fresh fish since Gramps fixed them," she said. "But you'd have to prepare them for me. I've got no idea how to cut them up."

"It ain't hard," Roscoe replied. "Just need a sharp knife and a little know-how." With a nod, he left her to her privacy and ambled over to the shed.

She sat for a few more minutes, letting the thoughts of her parents and Gram no longer being here drift away. Her mind flowed to the neighbor who refused to give them a chance. *We could have had a shot of making a relationship work, Jack,* she thought for the millionth time. *At least I was ready to fight for the chance to build something with you!*

Sucking in a lung full of fresh, early morning air, she let it out slowly as she rose to her feet. Wiping away her tears, she walked back inside. With a heavy heart, she readied to face the day's chores.

Jack sat alone in the command center, having had a video conference with the men. Each was reporting back from the interviews with witnesses looking at the photo of the mustachioed man. The results were encouraging. At least two of the victims' friends had seen someone who looked like him the last time they had seen the victim. Luke had scanned the photo through every known database he had and narrowed the field down considerably. There were still a great number of men in Virginia that made a similar match, but for once Jack felt as though the case was moving in the right direction.

Now, he sat alone in front of one of their security monitor screens. For the wealthy, they offered security cameras that were not monitored twenty-four seven, but could be viewed when needed. Except for one. He had one on continuously and he was riveted to it. One that he watched almost every day whenever he was alone and had the opportunity.

The one on Mountville. He had not disbanded the

cameras that gave him a view of the lodge. *Invasion of her privacy? Hell yeah. Gonna cut them off? Hell no.*

Something was not right. He saw Bethany wander around aimlessly, not with her usual purpose. Sally came but not as often. He watched early one morning and saw Bethany sitting alone on the front porch. *Ann. Where was Ann?* He knew that Ann was not walking alone anymore, but most days either Bethany or Sally would take Ann for a little walk.

Moving to his computer, he quickly did a secure search. Ann Bridwell was now a resident of Golden Arbor. *Damn! That's why the bracelet still showed her location at Mountville. They must have removed it before she moved.*

He scooted his chair back to the monitor and watched, hoping for a glimpse of Bethany, knowing now she would be devastated. Sure enough, she came out to greet some guests. He zoomed in on her face. Smiling...but the smile did not reach her eyes.

Jack leaned back in the chair, his eyes tightly shut remembering her smile when it was turned on him. *Glorious. Fuckin' glorious.* And, suddenly, he knew. If he could have that smile beamed on him every morning when he woke and waiting for him when he got home? It would be worth everything. *But would it be worth it to her?*

Remembering the words of Blaise over a week ago, he realized he never gave her the chance she was willing to take on them.

Not knowing if it was too late, he headed up the

stairs and out of the door. *Time to man up and convince her that I can be there for her.*

Pulling into Mountville's lane, Jack noted the gathering clouds above. Uncharacteristically nervous, he focused on the task at hand—groveling. Parking in front of the lodge, he unfolded his tall frame from his SUV and jogged up the steps. Entering the room he did not see Bethany, but called up the stairs to see if she was in her apartment. Receiving no answer, he walked through the main room to the back door and out onto the patio. The tool shed was to the left of the lodge and he was pleased to see the padlock securely on the door.

Roscoe and Sally came from around the front, the cleaning supply buckets in their hands. Both stopped suddenly at the sight of him and Jack immediately noted the unhappy expression on Sally's face.

Taking a deep breath, he called out, "I came by to see Bethany. Do you know where I would find her?"

Before Roscoe could answer, Sally bit out, "I don't know where Ms. Bridwell is. Perhaps you should call at a later time to see if she's available."

Moving toward them, he replied, "I deserve you bein' pissed at me. I made a mistake. Thought I knew what was best for both of us, but that's between her and me. I'm asking you to please tell me where she is."

Sally pursed her lips, staring at his face for a long time. Roscoe wisely kept still and his mouth shut. She must have seen something that she trusted because after a moment her stance relaxed. Slightly. "She's out at cabin seven, getting a little work done." Sally had stepped in front of Jack before he had a chance to move. "Young man, I've known Bethany since she was born. I know you must have had your reasons, but you gotta know you hurt her bad. And she might've been able to snap outta her sadness quicker if other things had not come toppling down on her."

"Ann," he said quietly.

"Ah, so you know. Then you also know that right now is not the time to play with that girl. She's too vulnerable and if you hurt her again, I swear—"

"I won't, I promise," he swore, and meant it.

Sally stared another minute and then nodded down the lane. "Cabin seven is thataway."

"Much obliged," he said, jogging off.

She watched him then turned to Roscoe and said, "I sure hope that was the right thing to do."

The two of them went into the shed to put the supplies away, Roscoe not saying anything.

Jack rounded the curve of the lane, cabin seven coming into sight. He ran to the front door about to call her name, when he heard sniffling. Approaching the door carefully he peeked inside. Bethany was sitting on an old rug, her face buried in her knees which were drawn up with her arms wrapped around them. And she was crying. A new rug, still rolled up with the store tags attached, sat beside her.

He walked inside, softly calling her name as he squatted in front of her. She jumped, her head jerking upright, tears still sliding down her cheeks. Her large, blue eyes, wide with fright, looked at him in surprise. He watched as her expression morphed into confusion.

"Jack?" She swiped her tears with the back of her hand. "What are you doing here?" Glancing down at her discarded tissue, she grabbed it off the floor and wiped her nose.

"I had to come," he explained. Then seeing her knitted brow, he continued, "I'm so sorry about your grandmother."

He watched as her face crumpled into tears again and he slid down on the floor in front of her, his legs on either side, and pulled her body into his. For a moment, he held her close as her tears continued to fall. Rocking her back and forth, he murmured words of comfort as her body relaxed into his. As the tears slowed, he knew the instance she processed what was happening.

Stiffening, she jerked back out of his arms, her face no longer holding confusion or pain, but anger. Pure anger. Standing, she said, "What are you doing here?"

He stood just as quickly, saying, "I want to talk. I want to explain."

"Explain? Oh, Jack, I think you explained very well the last time we talked. Your life doesn't include me. Period. Does that about sum it up?"

"No," he growled. "I came to tell you that I was wrong. I made a totally fucked up decision at a time when I shouldn't have been making any personal decisions. And I've regretted it ever since."

She stared, scrutinizing him carefully. Suddenly, shoulders slumping, she lifted her hand in defense. "Jack, I've got no fight left in me. Just none. I think you were right. I deserve more than someone who ran at the first sign of trouble." Giving a rude snort, she added, "You know what's crazy? I didn't even know there was trouble. I spent that week thinking about what you said on your deck. What we did. Planning for us going out. Deciding you were someone I was excited to be with. That was how I spent my week. You? You spent it planning on how to tell me to get lost!"

Skirting around him, she declared, "I have no time for this now so you can just leave." She walked out and started down the lane, yelling over her shoulder, "Close the door when you go."

He rushed out after her, slamming the cabin door before checking to make sure it locked. Jogging after her, his long legs caught up to hers almost instantly. The first drops of rain were starting to fall, so they both began walking faster.

Refusing to look at him, she wondered *Why is he doing this?* Having gone into the cabin to replace the old, worn rug with a new one that Gram had bought months ago, she suddenly felt the loss once more. Shocked when Jack walked in, she admitted it felt wonderful to have his arms wrap around her. To melt into his body and feel his strength seep into hers.

The rain was beginning to pound down on them and she broke into a jog. She could hear his footsteps right along hers but refused to look at him. Seeing the lodge ahead, she thought she would get rid of him. *But no more tears. Not over him!*

Jack was not about to be dismissed before they had a chance to talk so he jogged with her every step of the way. Running in the pouring rain was nothing to a former Special Forces soldier, but he noticed her slipping in the mud several times with her little tennis shoes.

As the lodge loomed ahead, she rounded toward the back but slipped on the wet grass. Screaming as she threw her hands out in front of her to protect her face from hitting the ground, she was scooped up in his massive arms. Giving a squeak, she instinctively wrapped her arms around his neck, holding on as he jogged up the back steps and into the lodge.

Placing her on the floor of the great room, the two stood staring at each other. Soaked to the skin, they said nothing as the water puddled at their feet.

All of the words he wanted to say flew from his mind as his gaze followed the trail of water as it dripped from her long hair onto her breasts, showcased perfectly in her t-shirt. Chilled now that they were in an air-conditioned room, her nipples had hardened to points that were straining against her bra.

She watched the drops fall from his dark hair down to his shirt that was almost translucent as it outlined each muscle in his chest and abdomen. His jeans molded to his thick thighs and she found herself unable to tear her eyes away. The loneliness of her existence bore down on her as the electricity sparked around their bodies.

Neither moved. His grey eyes did not move from her blue ones. Unspoken questions flying between them. Suddenly, they both shifted straight into each other's arms, his mouth slamming down on hers.

She jumped into his arms, wrapping her legs around his waist. One of his hands held her ass while the other enveloped her middle, his hand on the back of her head. Angling her for better access, he plunged his tongue into her warmth, swallowing her moans. Kicking the back door shut with his boot, he stalked toward the stairs, his mouth never leaving hers.

She kissed him back with as much energy as he was taking her mouth. At the top of stairs, he pulled away just enough to grunt, "Where?" and then followed where she pointed. Moving into the only bedroom that had furniture, he placed her feet on the floor, his lips still locked onto hers.

Her fingers fumbled with his buttons, but she managed to push his sopping shirt off of his shoulders while sucking on his tongue. He growled and she felt it deep inside of her, zinging straight to her core.

His hands grasped the bottom of her t-shirt and jerked it upward, their lips parting only long enough for the material to pass between them, before it landed with a wet slap on the floor next to his. She found the button on his jeans at the same time he reached around to unsnap her bra. He pulled her hands away from his pants so that he could slide the lacy material to join their other clothes.

His arms pulled her forward, her bare breasts pressed against his chest before he slid one hand upwards cupping her cheek, his mouth leading a trail from her lips down her neck. She leaned back, his lips firing a path along her skin.

He hefted her easily, turning to lay her onto the bed,

before leaning back, perusing her perfect face with her kiss-swollen lips, hooded eyes, and full breasts with rosy-tipped nipples. Unzipping her jeans, he slid them slowly down her legs, capturing her panties along the way. Finally tossing the last of her soaked clothing onto the floor, he towered over her. Her naked beauty stunned him. "Fuckin' gorgeous," he growled, his voice raspy with need.

He quickly unzipped his jeans, and jerked them down, toeing his boots off at the same time. He stood by the side of the bed, palming his erect cock.

A silver medallion hung around his neck, glistening against his tanned skin. She stared at his magnificent body, his perfect masculinity had her yearning to feel him. Touch him. Kiss him. Every inch.

"Whatever you're thinkin' baby, I assure you, I'm thinkin' the same thing."

Offering him a smile, she lifted her arms to him, beckoning his body to hers. *For only tonight, I won't care. I just want to feel him for this one time. Anything to not be so lonely and then he can leave once more.* Somewhere in the back of her mind, she knew this was a dangerous game to play. Her emotions warned her—if she felt hurt the first time he left, she would surely feel it tenfold after this.

He stood perfectly still for a moment, watching her carefully. "You understand what this means, beautiful? I want to make sure you understand exactly what we're doing."

"Jack," she begged. "Please. Just take me."

He snagged a condom out of his wallet and tossed it

on the bed beside her. Crawling over her body, he kissed her from her belly up toward her breasts. Halting just on the underside, he licked and then sucked his way to her nipples, latching onto one and pulling it deeply into his mouth.

Her body writhed, hips moving upward searching for the delicious friction that only he could provide. Lying partially on her, he slid his left hand downward through her neatly trimmed curls to the prize he was seeking. Her moist folds opened easily and his finger glided deep inside, eliciting another groan from her lips as her hips bucked up.

His mouth continued its attention on her breasts while he slid another finger into her wet core, scissoring them in a way that had her body once more undulating.

She threw her head back against the mattress, unsure of anything in her life except this man, his body, this minute in time, and her need. Her nipples were on fire as he licked, nipped, and sucked his way from one to the other. Her arms grasped around his neck, holding him in place as though he might vanish at any moment.

Jack had no plans on vanishing...ever. He thought her lips were nectar, but her breasts were divine. Sucking on her hardened buds, he could feel her sex clench tighter on his fingers. Twisting his hand once more, he knew he found the spot that would take her over the edge.

She cried out as her body bucked once more under his ministrations, the sparks flying from her core outward in every direction. Her body exploded and she could not breathe as she rode the wave of ecstasy. Drifting on her mattress cloud, her eyes closed, she did not care if she ever moved.

"Breathe, beautiful," Jack whispered.

Her eyes flew open as she sucked in a deep breath. Finding him gazing down at her as he slid his fingers into his mouth, repeating the action from his deck that morning, was mesmerizing. She watched his grey eyes focus on her and his smile pierced her sadness. *If only I could have this every morning.* But she pushed those thoughts away, focusing on the here and now.

He saw the change in her expression…from happy to guarded. He rolled onto his back, pulling her body over on top of his. She peered down in confusion until his lips latched onto hers, carrying her away with his kiss once more. One of his arms was wrapped tightly around her waist while the other cradled the back of her head.

Finally pulling back, he said, "This goes no further until I know that you understand what's happening."

She whispered, "I'm not a virgin, Jack. I know exactly what's happening."

She tried to take his lips again but found herself halted by his large hand cupping her cheek.

"Nope, you're not getting it. This," he said, giving her waist a squeeze, "means something. It's not a casual fuck. I'm not the consolation prize for your grief."

At that, her lust induced haze dissipated instantly and she jerked against his tight hold. "Let me go, you jerk. I thought this was what you were doing here.

Making me feel something besides sadness for a few minutes."

"Nope."

She glared down at him. "Nope, what?"

Suddenly, he rolled and she landed on her back with his large body covering hers. Keeping his chest from crushing her, he held himself up on his forearms while cupping her face in his hands. His hips lay on hers, his eager cock straining to have the conversation over with.

"Nope, to all the screwed up shit that's going on in your mind right now," he growled.

Her glare turned icy but before she could say anything, he continued, "I told you I messed up. I let my fears of not being able to give you what you needed take over the fact that I've never backed down from a mission in my life. Well, darlin', I'm here to tell you that my new mission is you."

At that, her glare melted...but only slightly. Seeing her questioning expression, he continued. "I don't have a job where I'm home every night but that doesn't mean that when I am home and lucky enough to have you there waiting for me, I won't make every minute count."

She blinked slowly, the iciness leaving her glare completely, but the guarded look remained. Plunging ahead, he said, "And my job has me seeing the underbelly of society, the part no one wants to know is there and sometimes living in that world can steal a man's soul. But you're in my life, then you're in my soul and there's no room left for that shit to take over. You'd be the reason I could go out every day and try my best to keep that world from ever coming into your world full of cabins and flowerbeds, and making others have a sweet vacation."

At this, her guard came down completely and she tried to lean up to kiss his lips, but he held her head fast.

"Not yet, baby, because this is what you have to take down deep. I messed up. I pussied out when I decided that I wasn't worth the risk. It was never you, beautiful. It wasn't that I didn't want you. But I gave up on me and I've never done that before and I sure as shit won't do that again."

Holding her gaze as she peered intently at him, he said, "So this is the start of you and me. My screwup caused you to be alone when you needed someone to lean on and that shit stops here and now. This," he paused to gently press his cock onto her, "is the start of us. Not casual. Not incidental. Not friends with benefits. And sure as hell, not a consolation prize."

Touching his lips to hers in a whisper soft kiss, he leaned back, seeing nothing but warmth oozing from her gaze and said, "But I gotta know that you're getting this. That you're with me. I gotta hear you say it."

His words wrapped around her heart, squeezing it until she thought it would burst. Not with the sadness and grief that had surrounded her for weeks, but with the feeling that all was finally right with the world. Sucking her lips in to quell their quivering, she fought the tears, but one escaped in spite of her efforts.

He wiped the lone, wet trail with his thumb, his heart pounding until he heard her response. Her blue eyes, now shiny with unshed tears, held him captive. "So what's it gonna be, baby?"

She nodded slowly, saying, "I was always willing to take a chance on us, Jack. That's never stopped." Sucking in a shaky breath and letting it out haltingly, "I choose you. Us. This. I know there are things we will have to work out, but from the first time I saw you… well, maybe not the first time," she smiled, remembering her fright at the huge man that captured her and held her when she was trying to get to Gram. "But as soon as I saw you so carefully taking care of Gram in the bathroom downstairs, you filled my thoughts. And dreams. And hopes."

He smiled at her, his fear receding for the first time in weeks. He pushed himself off of the bed and bent over to grab his boxers. Catching her confused expression, he said, "Not going any further today, beautiful. We're not doing this now."

She leaned up on her elbows, her glare returned as she watched him. *What now?* Her thoughts in a whirl, she opened her mouth to ask, but he bent over placing both hands on either side of her as he kissed her forehead.

"I'm taking you on a date."

"Jack, I'm confused. I'm lying here naked, and you're leaving my bed after telling me that you want this?"

Chuckling, he admitted, "Yeah. Maybe the craziest thing I've ever done and it's sure as shit the hardest." His eyes roved down her body and it took every ounce of control to keep his dick from ruling his mind. "You're no fuck, beautiful. I'm gonna take you on a real date, treat you the way you deserve to be treated. Find out what all's been going on. Work to make you realize I want to be in your life."

Continuing to rub his thumbs over her soft cheeks, he said, "There's one more thing, baby. I broke your trust when I pussied out. But no more. I promise that I'll never just give up on us. Never. And beautiful?" he peered down at her. "I never fail at a mission."

15

Jack and Bethany rose from the bed and looked down at the mass of still sopping clothes on the floor.

"Um, let me throw your things in the dryer and it won't take them too long to dry." She gave him a perplexed look, then turned and jogged into the bedroom across the hall. She returned with a pair of flannel pajama bottoms with a drawstring tie at the waist. Giving a shrug, she handed them to him, saying, "They're clean. In fact they're new, never been worn."

He lifted his eyebrow in question, wondering what man had been in her apartment. She saw his look and laughed. "It's not what you think. Gram bought these in extra-large for dad last Christmas but by then she was unable to discern sizes or anything like that. They were on sale and she was pleased. My dad is definitely not an extra-large man, but didn't want her to feel bad so I just stuffed them in a chest and forgot about them."

Mollified, he slipped the pants on, commando, as she pulled on dry underwear, yoga pants, and another t-shirt. She bent to gather the wet clothes from the floor when her arms were gently pushed away.

"Got 'em, beautiful. Where do they go?"

He followed her downstairs and she loaded them into the dryer. Suddenly nervous, she fiddled with the knobs on the machine, afraid to turn around. *What now? Talk? Eat? Does he want to hurry and get out of here?*

"I can see the wheels turning from here, babe," he chuckled as his arms wrapped around her from behind.

Smiling, she leaned back into his embrace. "Yeah?"

"Oh, yeah. You're wondering what in the hell do we do now?"

She whirled around, his arms still holding her tightly and looked up into his eyes. Meeting his returned smile, she saw the crinkles at his eyes and laughed again. Nodding slightly, she said, "Okay, busted. That's exactly what I was thinking."

He glanced around at the lodge's empty room. "Anyone can come in here?"

"Yeah. In the old days, there wasn't a TV in every cabin and people would gather here for games and conversation. Eventually Gramps had the TVs put in and then video players and then CD players, and then Wi-fi. The list keeps going! So this room is rarely used, but Gram just never changed it, so it's still a room that guests could come to if they wanted."

"Can you close it?"

She looked at him askance, saying, "Why?"

He pulled her back so he could see her expression. "I know we have a lot to talk about and I know that when my clothes are dry I'm gonna have to leave for a meeting this afternoon. But I hate the idea of you here by yourself with the door open and anyone can walk in."

She glanced at the bottom of the stairs to her apartment with its little sign warning people not to go upstairs and knew he was right. Her eyes shot back up to his in concern and he grabbed her hand and pulled her over to the sofa in front of the fireplace. He settled her on his lap, holding her face in his hands.

"What I told you upstairs was true. I want to see where this goes. I consider myself your man now and until this ends, I take that very seriously. I'll never take over your life but I'm also in the security business and this place is a disaster for a single woman. Hell, it was a disaster for you and Gram when she was here."

He glanced at the registration desk and then cut his eyes back to hers. "Placing a wall with a locking door over there would give you a large welcome area and make this room, the downstairs bathroom, and stairs secure. It would give you more of a two-story home feel and keep you safer from someone just wandering in."

Licking her lips, she said, "Jack, I like what you're saying, but I just took over. Up till now, I was just here to help out Gram. Dad has signed this place over to me and I've only been the new owner for about a week. I...I need to check on all the finances to see where we are and what I can do."

His face grew hard, knowing he could have the wall put up in one day with one phone call, but he had to make that her play. "Okay, compromise," he said. "Until that happens, you keep the front door locked unless you are letting someone in during the daytime hours."

"Okay, I should be able to take care of keeping me safe and if keeping the door locked makes me safer, then I will."

He leaned forward, touching his lips to hers, capturing them in a soft kiss. Not of passion, but one of promise.

"Jack?" she whispered, trepidation in her voice.

His eyes piercing hers, he said, "Baby, you do not ever have to fear me. You want to ask, you ask."

Nodding, she said, "I just wondered what happened that made you change your mind about us so quickly?"

Sighing deeply, he said, "Most of what I do, I can't talk about. If I can tell you, I will. But because I travel, work on cases that often involve the lowest criminals, I always thought that trying to build a relationship and deal with that, just wouldn't work. But you came along and knocked me on my ass and all I wanted to do was be the man you needed me to be."

"But…" she prodded.

"You know the Saints are working on the serial killer case. I was in on the autopsy of the last victim. The one that was just in the paper." He saw her eyes grow wide and he squeezed her hips just a little. "Tired, little sleep, bad coffee and then standing in there watching what had been a beautiful blonde, blue-eyed woman, who'd been murdered, be examined. Suddenly, I felt impotent. Felt like I couldn't separate that world from yours. And you deserve only the best. So I just gave up. Not on you…never on you. I gave up on me being able to give you what you should have."

Her expression, a mixture of understanding and

fear, tore at him. She held his gaze bravely and asked, "What about in the future? Other victims? Other cases? You say you want this but Jack, if I give my heart to you and we have our future, I don't want to live in fear that you'll decide to give up on us again."

"Your doubt cuts deep and that's on me. I created those feelings in you and I'm the only one who can take them away. I promise you that I'll work every day to make sure you know that we're in this together."

Smiling, she cupped his bearded face, pulling in his lips, this time offering more than a chaste kiss. And he was more than willing to participate.

Visiting the old homestead always made him cringe. The shutters hung askew on the windows. He glanced upward recognizing the roof needed new shingles. *Maybe it'll fall in on the old bat.* Sighing, he moved through the front door, seeing that nothing had changed, of course. The old furniture, old rug, old everything. His mother sat in her familiar chair nearest the TV as it blared an old game show re-run.

Her eyes, sharp as always, looked up. "Didn't say you were coming by," she remarked.

"No, ma. I was traveling nearby and thought I'd see how you were."

"Humph, like you care. You were probably out looking for some girl last night and couldn't get lucky so you came by here."

Gritting his teeth, he said, "Now, ma. You know I don't do that. I had business to take care of."

Her eyes looked him up and down. "Your father had business he used to take care of and don't think I didn't know he was cattin' around town."

"Well, that was dad, but not me." He sat on the sofa, pretending to watch TV with her for a few minutes, all the while fighting the urge. His hands knotted into fists, wishing for the familiar feel of his knife. *Well, dad's knife.*

He had watched his old man filet fish from the time he could first remember. The sharp blade making an easy slit through the fish's gut. A quick slice across the head. It seemed the older the knife was, the sharper it became. His dad took care of it—cleaning and oiling it when necessary. Such a delicate instrument. And so clean a slice.

Suddenly speaking again, his mom said, "If you'd followed in your dad's footsteps, you'd be here all the time to take care of me."

"Ma, you know fishing for a living wasn't what I wanted to do. Anyway, you always fussed about dad not making enough money."

"He barely made enough to keep this roof over our heads, and then went and spent it on his whores."

Her words weighed heavily on him, taking him back to a time he did not want to remember. *The first one. So pretty. I'd seen her around. Such a nice girl. Always smiled and talked to me when she saw me. One day walking into the shed on the back of their little property when his mom was at the store. The girl's naked body as his dad bucked into her. I stood and watched for a while. She had huge breasts...much bigger than mom's. Dad's bare ass kept moving as her legs lifted in the air. I tried to be quiet, keeping my hand in my pants. My cock got hard and I wanted to pound into her also. Dad had no idea I was there, but the girl turned her eyes toward me. At first, she looked surprised. Then she smiled at me and brought her hands up to her breasts, playing with them.*

He had gone back into the house and when his mother returned, she took one look and knew he was hiding something. Pursing her lips, she bit out, "Your father was with some woman, wasn't he?"

He did not answer, but she had already known. The silence stretched out between them. His mother finally, said, "I'd get rid of them if I could." Spearing him with a stony gaze, she added, "At least that'd be something you could do right."

Now, his mother, too old to do much on her own except wallow in her own misery, stood and moved to the kitchen. "Want some coffee?" she called out.

Grimacing at the thought of the bitter brew, he just said, "Sure, ma. That'd be good." Fighting the urge, he rubbed his hand over his face. *I need to find a new good girl.*

The Saints once again gathered in the command center. As soon as they entered, they could tell that something had changed with Jack.

"Boss? You're kinda scaring us," Cam commented.

Seeing Jack's raised eyebrow, he continued, "You seem sort of happy."

Jack caught the smirks of the others around the table and hung his head chuckling. "Okay, okay, have your fun." Looking back at them, he said, "If you bunch of women want your gossip then here it is. I have approached Ms. Bridwell about renewing our relationship and she agreed. There. Now are you happy?"

The men offered congratulations accompanied with head jerks in approval before they got down to business.

Luke flashed on their tablets the latest list that he had compiled from all of the data. "Let's take a look at the victims because I have finally come up with a common thread among them all."

The men eagerly looked at him, elated for the first opportunity to find a tie between the victims.

"Okay, bear with me," Luke began. "We know the victims have had virtually nothing in common, from ethnicity, socio-economic backgrounds, jobs, majors, religions, grades…nothing. But the one word that popped up in every report from their friends and relatives—good."

"Good?" Bart asked. Bart, known for believing in what he could see, hear, taste, and touch was not one for accepting things outside the measurable.

"Every single girl was described as a good girl by someone," Luke continued.

"Yeah, but don't you think that's something that anyone would say about someone who's died?" Marc asked. “You know, ‘Oh, he was a good man’, or ‘She was such a sweetie’.”

“Sure,” Luke agreed, “but take it a step further. None of the evidence supports any of these victims as partiers. None of them hung around bars, went clubbing, were in a sorority, visited frat houses. Not one.”

“Okay,” Chad said slowly. “What are you thinking?”

“From what we can gather, they were all doing something out of character,” Luke replied.

Suddenly, Blaise said, “Karen usually studied at the library—almost every night. Her roommates said you could set a clock by her with her study habits. But the night in question, she changed her routine and went to a bar with friends. What if someone had watched her and then followed her?”

“But that would take time,” Bart argued. “Time for someone to watch and then act.”

“Most serial killers take that time,” Jack said. “It would only take a few consecutive evenings watching a library to notice the same girl leaving late, giving the impression that they had been there studying. Even if they haven’t, the killer could easily make that assumption. One night they’re not and something flips his switch.”

“Or he actually follows and sees them go to a bar or somewhere that he doesn’t think fits the good girl in his mind,” Cam added.

“I’m not buying it,” Bart insisted. “It’s not logical.”

Monty quickly dialed the FBI profiler and had Luke set her up on video conference again, while Cam and Bart argued the merits of the theory.

"Shirley, thanks for joining us again," Monty greeted, effectively shutting up Cam and Bart.

She laughed and said, "I caught some of that. You have to remember what is logical to you is not necessarily going to be logical to a serial killer."

Chastised, Bart nodded, as Monty quickly explained their theory to her.

Excited, she said, "That's actually a very possible scenario. You see, if the killer is fantisizing about a good girl, he doesn't have to necessarily prove she is a good girl by watching her for long periods of time. And of course he could have his own definition of a good girl. Maybe just someone he saw. Maybe someone he has determined does not party. Who knows what his definition is? A few trips out of the library could be enough to prove to him that she is good and then a trip to a bar would make her not good, or whatever it is in his mind that gives him the urge to kill."

"What about the tie-in with a fishing filet knife?" Jack asked.

Shirley thought for a moment and said, "Well, it could simply be that he has a knife readily available to him as a weapon or it could signify something more psychological."

"Psychological?" Chad prodded.

"Yes, some trauma or experience with a fishing knife." Shirley looked down at her notes before glancing back to the computer camera. "There is the possibility he keeps the fingers as souvenirs."

"Like a kidnapper sending something that proves they have the person?" Bart queried.

"No. In the case of a kidnapper, you're right, it is for proof. In a killer, it could be that this is the keepsake, if you will, for that victim. Many serial killers like to keep a memento of the person they choose to sacrifice."

Shaking his head, Cam leaned his large frame back in his chair. "This shit just keeps getting crazier."

Thanking her, Monty disconnected and looked around the room, his eyes landing on Jack. "Now what, boss?"

Rubbing his hand over his face in frustration, Jack replied, "Keep digging. I want that photograph of the man from the bar shown around to more possible witnesses. And we need to plot out the locations again. Why did he start out in some campuses that were further out and now has localized?"

Divvying out assignments, including a few new security contracts that had come in, the men moved upstairs once more.

As soon as they hit the first floor, Jack's front gate alarm rang. Checking the panel, he saw a familiar face in an old sedan smiling at him. Pressing the controls, he allowed her entrance. Moving through his men, he opened the front door and watched as she drove into view.

Seeing him through the windshield, Bethany grinned nervously as she glanced at the other vehicles parked around. She hoped this impromptu visit would not anger Jack, but decided to test his ability to accept her into his world. *At least for cobbler.*

He met her at her door when she parked and assisted her out. She bent over and he was forced to tell his cock to obey when her jean clad ass was perched right in his line of vision. A quick glance at the front porch revealed the smiles of his men. All seven of them. One glare from him had them laughing.

Bethany shimmied back out of her car, her hands filled with another dish. "Apple cobbler this time," she declared.

He took the heavy dish from her, escorting her up his front steps. The men who had been ready to leave now headed back into the house and straight into the kitchen.

By the time he set the platter on the counter, all seven had plates and forks ready. Looking at her in mock sternness, Jack growled, "You gotta bake for me when these vultures are here?"

Laughing, she shrugged. "I had no idea who would be here so I baked enough for all."

The group dug in heartily, mummers of pleasure as well as thanks were voiced all around. Each of the men seemed to accept her in Jack's life, for which she was grateful. During their conversations, she enjoyed their commraderie and banter and began to discern the different personalities of Jack's Saints. And friends.

Jack watched her as she fit in well with his group and realized once again that he had been a fool to toss her aside for his own fear of failing. Before she left, she walked right into his arms and he escorted her to her car, he knew he would work harder than ever to give her the white-picket fence she deserved.

16

The dim lights in the little Italian restaurant in town, with the candles lit on each table, could not keep Jack from seeing the beauty sitting across from him. *How could I have ever thought of not having this in my life?*

Bethany's hair, pinned back from her face, hung in waves down her back. The candlelight cast dancing shadows over her face, but could not hide the twinkle in her blue eyes. Wearing a turquoise wrap top, parted just enough at the front to show a hint of cleavage, she had paired it with a simple maxi black skirt. He had noticed it as she had walked into the restaurant in front of him, as it cupped her ass perfectly. Even paired with heeled sandals, she only came to his chin.

The scents of bread baking, garlic, and tomatoes wafting from the kitchen made his mouth water, but the woman sitting with him made him desire more than just dinner. *Down boy,* he willed his dick.

Interrupting his thoughts, Bethany leaned forward and said, "I haven't been here in years. We rarely went out, but one summer when I was visiting, Gramps brought me here."

"He must have been a special man," Jack said, seeing the expression crossing her face at the memory.

She looked up, a smile curving the corners of her lips. "I was sixteen years old and my high school boyfriend had broken up with me. It seemed he found the…um…easy charms of Penelope Saunders to be more intriguing than me." Giving a small chuckle, she added, "At the time, I was devastated."

"Then he was a fool," he said truthfully, his hand holding hers on the top of the table.

"That's what Gramps said. He brought me here, we ordered pizza and then he told me that one day a man would come along who thought I was the most wonderful thing on earth. And I wasn't to settle for anyone less."

Rubbing his thumb across the back of her hand, he agreed. "Wise man, your grandfather." Leaning forward, he pressed his lips to hers in a gentle kiss. Whispering, he added, "Just to let you know, I think you are the most wonderful thing on earth." He saw her eyes widen before he kissed her again. This kiss gentle, but filled with all the promise he could send to her.

Lost in each other, they jumped when the waitress appeared with their food. They settled in to enjoy their meal, the conversation flowing as they learned more about the other.

"Can I ask you something personal?"

Jack looked up in surprise. "Baby, you can ask

anything in the world you want to. As long as I'm able, I'll answer."

"When you had your shirt off, I noticed a medallion around your neck. I could tell it was a Saint's medallion and it struck me that you named your business the Saints. I was curious about the significance."

His momentary silence making her suddenly unsure, she stammered, "But...um...you don't have to tell me... or anything."

His eyes sought hers and he quickly reached over to squeeze her hand once more. "No, baby," he said. "I'd love to tell you. I was just lost in thought for a moment."

Seeing her smile return, he said, "The story goes back to my name. Or maybe, it begins long before that. My grandfather was born in a little village in France. He was named Jacques Fournier. He was named, as most males in that time, for saints. St. James, or in France, St. Jacques, was his namesake. He fought in the end of World War II and when it was over, most of his village had been destroyed. He traveled to America with his bride and ended up in Baltimore. They only had one daughter, late in life, and she married my father and moved to his farm in southwest Virginia.

"They also only had one child, me, and that was late in their lives also. Named for my grandfather, I hated the name Jacques as a child. Being bigger than most, if someone tried to bully me about my name, I usually pounded them."

"Jack!" Bethany said, eyes wide. "You beat up other little kids?"

Chuckling, he replied, "Only if they deserved it."

Shaking his head slowly at the memories, he continued. "The day I left for the Army, my mother gave me the St. James medallion. She said she knew I couldn't wear it, but to keep it with me. He was the patron saint of soldiers and would keep me safe. Never knew if I believed that, but I kept it nonetheless."

Bethany sat quietly, watching the memories pass across his normally impassive face. Her heart tugged a little more…for the child who had been teased, to the man who loved his mother enough to accept her gift of faith.

"Times in the Special Forces…well, let's just say that I'm lucky to be alive even if I was on the most elite squad. Luck…or the medallion? Who knows, but I'm here and so now I wear it everyday. Kind of a tribute to my grandfather and my mom."

Reaching across the table, she grasped his hand giving it a gentle squeeze. "That's lovely, Jack. Thank you so much for sharing it with me."

"Beautiful, this goes where I expect it to go, there's nothing I won't share with you," he answered earnestly, blinded by the smile she bestowed on him.

By now, the dinner had been finished and he ordered dessert. As they sat waiting for it to arrive, she prompted, "And your company?"

"I began to think about my mom's complete faith in the protection that the Saint's medallion would provide. As much as it may seem strange to an outsider, I saw my career with the Special Forces as a protector. Protecting others…protecting our country's interests…protecting each member of my squad. When I thought of starting my own business, I knew that protecting was a large part of what I wanted to do. Somehow the Saints name fit."

"I love it, Jack," she replied honestly. Realizing he had just shared more about himself than ever before, she felt a warm glow deep inside. Nothing he had said caused her any fear or trepidation about their relationship. Instead, if possible, it renewed her desire to know all about him.

"And the men who work for you? Do they understand the significance of the name?"

Nodding, his gaze moved from the dessert that had arrived, to her face. "Yeah. They get it. Each one has the same instinct inside of them. Protection. Making life safer, not only for those who can afford our private services, but for the criminal investigations we do as well. So yeah, these men get the name." He held his thoughts for a moment and then decided to share one more bit.

"In fact," he said, capturing her rapt attention. "Each one of them have their own medallion."

Gifted with her smile, he breathed easier. He had been terrified to share anything, but instead had given her everything. So far nothing he said would ever put her in danger. *And I'd protect her with my life,* he vowed.

Finishing the dessert, they decided to walk around town a little to work off some of the meal. Placing her hand on her stomach, she complained, "I'm so full. It must be your storytelling, Jack, because I just sat there, listened and stuffed myself!"

Pulling her in closely with his arm around her

shoulders, he added, “A few pounds would not hurt you at all, babe.” With a discreet pat to her ass, he felt her giggle deep inside.

The town’s Main Street had lights in the trees that lined the sidewalk, casting a romantic glow over the pair as they strolled. Silent for several minutes, each lost in their own thoughts, they made their way back to his truck.

Looking down, he peered into her eyes, seeing trust shining back.

“Take me home, Jack?” she asked softly. Rising up on her toes, she placed a kiss on his lips. Rocking back on her heels, she continued to hold his gaze. “And stay with me?”

He cocked his head in question. “You sure, beautiful? You gotta know what this means.”

“I know. I know exactly what I’m doing. You’re not a consolation prize.”

“Damn straight,” he growled, his voice raspy with need. “It won’t be casual and sure won’t be incidental.”

Smiling once more, she nodded toward his truck. “So what’re you waiting on?”

Before she could ready herself, he swooped her up in his arms and had her ass planted in the seat and buckled. Trotting to his side, he quickly pulled himself up into the driver’s seat and was on the road.

“In a hurry, soldier?” she teased.

“You have no fuckin’ idea, baby,” he responded. Driving carefully, he pulled in front of the lodge.

By the time they made it to the lodge’s main room, they were jerking their clothes off quickly once more.

She jumped into his arms, circling his waist with her legs. Latching onto his lips, she brought him in holding onto his silky, beard covered jaw.

Making their way upstairs, he placed her on the bed. Forcing himself to slow down, he said, "We got all night, baby. I want to savor every second."

Melting at his words, she smiled giving him a little nod. He leaned over and slid her skirt down her legs, snagging her panties at the same time. Maneuvering them completely off he turned to lay them on the end of the bed. She had already lost her shirt on the way up the stairs, but he unhooked her bra and removed it as well, exposing all of her beauty to his gaze.

His shirt had also been removed and he saw her eyes drop from his face to his medallion around his neck. He started to pull the chain over his head, when she stopped him.

"Leave it, honey. It's so much a part of you."

"It could get in the way," he explained.

She shook her head. "It'll never be in the way."

Smiling, he left it on as he shucked his pants after toeing his boots off. Crawling up her body, he kissed his way from her soft feminine curls upward to her breasts, where he feasted for a few minutes. He finally pulled away from their enticement, and continued his path to her neck where he suckled at the point of her erratically beating pulse.

Making his way to her lips, he captured them, completely devouring her. Thrusting his tongue into her warmth he explored every crevice, his tongue tangling with hers.

Mindless with need, she pressed her body full frontal against his, feeling the evidence of his desire against her belly. Slipping her hand between their bodies, she grasped his cock in her hand, hearing him gasp in her mouth.

At the same time she began to slide her hand up and down his length, his fingers moved in her slick folds before he plunged them deep inside her sex, now causing her to gasp as well.

It did not take long for him to move his body away causing her to lose purchase of his dick. "When I come, I wanna come inside of you, beautiful.

His fingers continued to work their magic, lifting her higher and higher until she thought she could touch the stars. Leaning down, he grasped a nipple in his mouth, sucking it deeply.

With her head thrown back against the mattress, she knew she had reached beyond the stars. Her inner walls pulsated as they gripped his finger and with her eyes closed tightly the lights sparkled behind her eyelids.

Slowly, she came down and opened her eyes to see the medallion resting right in front of her. Jacques. Warmth flowed through her veins as she knew beyond a shadow of a doubt, this man was for her.

Lifting her gaze she watched, mesmerized, as he slid his finger into his mouth, sucking her juices off. Smiling, she pulled him closer, whispering into his ear. "Take me. Make me yours."

Jack rolled over to his back again, settling her on top of him. She eyed him curiously, but he just smiled and grabbed the condom lying on the bed beside them.

Handing it to her, he said, "First time, you're in control, baby. I'm giving that power to you."

Knowing this was huge for a man like him, she smiled. She took the condom in her hands and then placed it back on the bed. He lifted an eyebrow in question, but then she simply slid down his body and curled her fingers around his massive erection. Moving her hand up and down his silky-hard shaft, she felt the tremors move through the rest of his body. Sliding her lips over the tip, she swirled her tongue around the sensitive head.

Fuck, his mind dissolved into a lust-filled dream come true as he watched this beautiful woman with a heart of gold take him in her mouth.

Continuing to slide him deeper into her mouth, she quickly realized that she would not be able to take very much of him so she slowly pumped the base with her hand while sucking on the top with her lips. Occasionally grazing her teeth over his flesh, she heard him hiss as his hips jerked upwards.

After a minute, she was suddenly pulled up off of him as he growled, "No more. I want you." He ripped the condom wrapper, but she recovered from her surprise quickly enough to take it from him. She rolled the latex over his cock, amazed that it fit. Licking her lips, she glanced at him, not sure what he wanted.

"Baby, you do whatever you want as long as you're on top and in control. This one's all about you."

"But what about you?" she asked softly.

He chuckled as he shook his head. "You on my dick

in any position you want? Hell, girl, that's a man's dream come true."

Smiling shyly, she straddled him, placing the tip of his cock at her entrance. Slowly she lowered herself onto him, allowing her body to stretch as it fit his girth deep inside her wet channel. She was no virgin, but it had been almost a year since her last lover and she had never had anyone as well-endowed as the man underneath her right now.

It was killing him not to plunge upwards, holding himself back. He never did this…and was determined to give this gift to her. *At least this first time.*

Finally, fully seated, she glanced down at his tortured face and giggled. His eyes jerked open with a pretend glare.

"Woman, don't laugh when you're surrounding my dick," he warned.

His comment only made her giggle more. "I'm sorry, but you looked like you're in such pain."

He bucked his hips upwards and said, "Get moving, beautiful, and you can take care of my pain."

She lifted on her knees, sliding up before plunging downward quickly, eliciting a moan from her and a hiss from him. Finding her rhythm, she continued to ride him, reaching deep inside to the secret place that craved the friction only he could provide.

He watched her long, blonde hair swaying as it cascaded down her back. Her full, rosy-tipped breasts bounced as she lifted and plunged. His fingers grasped her hips, digging in so tightly that he hoped she would not bruise.

Her breathing ragged, she was tiring as she leaned forward, her hair curtaining around them, and placed her hands on his shoulders. Seeing her fatigue, he took over, pistoning upward while holding her hips in place.

He could tell she was close and as she bent forward, he captured one of her nipples in his mouth, sucking and nipping. That was the final piece of their orgasmic puzzle. She threw her head backward as the orgasm ripped through her, sending jolts to every extremity. He followed closely, plunging as deep as he could reach, continuing to thrust until every drop was poured into her.

She collapsed on top of him, panting. They lay for several minutes, sated and neither willing or able to speak. She finally became aware of his hand making soft patterns on her ass and the other hand rubbing up and down her spine. Lifting her head, she saw his face—smiling eyes gazing back at her.

"Hey," she whispered, self-consciously.

"Hey, beautiful," he replied, unable to take his eyes off of her. "You okay?"

"I'm perfect," she confessed.

"Yeah. Yeah, you are."

She allowed him to roll her to one side before he rolled to the other and moved out of bed. Disappearing into the bathroom, he quickly took care of the condom before coming back and crawling under the covers with her.

Enveloping her in his arms, cradling her head on his muscular chest, they lay for several minutes, neither saying a word but letting the blissful afterglow move across them.

Afraid to look into his face, she whispered into his chest, “So what now?”

He tipped her chin up with his fingers, forcing her to look into his eyes. “Now, beautiful? Now we’re an *us.* And the rest, we’ll figure out as we go. Agreed?”

Smiling, she nodded. “Yeah, Jack. I’m with you.”

17

Bethany headed out to the shed early to try to get some work completed before the madness began. Labor Day weekend was almost upon her and she was booked solid. Approaching the door, she found it unlocked. *I know I locked it yesterday.* Opening the door, she yelped and jumped back as Roscoe was coming out.

"Lordy, you scared me," she explained.

"Sorry, Bethany," he said, moving forward with his tool belt buckled around his waist. "I got here early so I could get started on a few repairs."

"Me too," she said. "Are you going to take down those branches over cabin six?"

"Yep, and shore up the gutters on cabin eight."

"What happened?" she said, dismay in her voice.

"Not to worry," he assured. "I just noticed after the last storm, one side was hanging a little. Won't take but a bit of banging to make it right."

He moved past her, smiling as he went. She felt his eyes on her as she went into the shed. Turning, she saw him still watching her. "Was there anything else, Roscoe?"

"I was just wonderin' if you and that neighbor man were seeing each other now? He's been around more and I noticed you skedaddling off as well."

Laughing, she said, "Yes. His name is Jack Bryant and we are seeing each other."

Roscoe nodded, then added, "Well, your grandmother would want you to be happy. You always were such a good girl."

He moved on down the path and she grabbed the dock cleaning supplies. *Time to start the day before they all come in.*

Later that afternoon, Jack made sure he came by to check on things. As he pulled up, he noticed several trucks full of men with fishing equipment at the lodge. Jaw tight, he jogged up the steps and into the room. Seeing Bethany all alone, checking them in, he moved directly behind the counter and kissed her before turning to face the men in the room. He knew it was a caveman move, but he did not care. *And from the glance to her beside him, wide eyed and jaw dropped, he'd have to explain later.*

"Gentlemen," he called out loudly. "Last time there was a group here, there was unpleasantness that required the entire group to be ejected and no refunds were given. I trust there won't be those problems with any of you."

The men quickly assured the large man standing in front of them that they were there to fish in the fishing contest at a nearby lake and promised there would be no difficulties.

"And furthermore, this lodge is locked, secured, and alarmed after eight p.m."

"Yes, sir," they hastily agreed, before signing the register and moving back to their trucks with their cabin assignments.

As the last one left, he took a deep breath and turned to face the seething woman glaring at him.

She opened her mouth, but before she could utter a word of censure, she found his fingers on her lips.

"Beautiful, I get that you're pissed, but hear me out first and then decide if you're still pissed."

She glared but kept quiet.

"Just like with children, it's better to let guests know up front what your expectations are. You've got rules on your website, posted in each cabin and there's no reason not to reinforce them."

"Yes, but—"

"And those men don't want to lose their cabin in the middle of their vacation when there's no other hotel in the area with a Labor Day opening. One of them drinks too much and even thinks about getting rowdy, the others are more likely to reign him in."

She had to admit to herself that his explanation made sense. Huffing, she said, "Okay, but what about the—"

"Same thing. Expectations, baby. No way in hell are you still leaving this door unlocked during the evening."

Okay, he's right there too.

Then her eyes narrowed, and she said, "How about the way you—"

He stepped closer, gazing down into her blue eyes, watching them widen the nearer he came. "That was because when we've been apart, I want to feel your lips on mine. Here, my place, alone, in a crowd. Wherever."

He stood directly in front of her, the toes of his boots touching the tips of her sneakers. Her head leaned way back so she could see his face.

"You don't think that was just the teeniest bit alpha caveman behavior?" she asked.

"Nope. I think it was a whole fuck-of-a-lotta alpha caveman behavior."

Seeing her jaw drop, he lifted her chin with his fingers at the same time he leaned down to place a kiss on her lips.

"Babe, this is who I am. I respect what you do here, but this is no longer the 1960's and your grandfather's not here to provide for your safety. This is a different world and I'm sure as hell going to take care of what's mine. And I don't give a damn who's around when I kiss you. Or," he said with a smile, "when you kiss me."

She could not stop the warm feeling that swirled around at his words. Lifting on her toes, she grabbed his face with her hands and kissed him back. Plunging her tongue into his mouth, she gave him everything she had to give and he took it. Then he lifted her up in his arms and took the kiss where he wanted it to go. Long. Hard. Wet.

"Ah-hm."

Bethany jerked to see who was standing there, but

her back was to the counter since Jack had turned to face the guest. She twisted to see behind her while dropping her legs to stand. Flustered, she managed to twist around and saw Horace Malinski. He looked askance at having intruded so she quickly greeted him. She saw his eyes dart continuously between Jack and her.

"Mr. Malinski, this is…um—"

"Her boyfriend, Jack Bryant," Jack said smoothly.

"Yes, um…yes," Bethany stammered.

A nervous nod was all they received and she handed him his cabin assignment and key. "Here you go. Cabin nine as usual is ready for you."

Another nod and he was out of the door.

"He always like that?" Jack asked, his eyes following the man as he hurried to his car.

"Yeah. He comes once a month and always asks for the same cabin. He's harmless enough," she added. "Always keeps to himself, hardly ever leaves the cabin." She giggled, "at least not during the day." Hearing Jack's growl, she quickly added, "Oh, he never bothers me, but I sometimes wonder if he's a vampire. You know, only coming out at night."

He glanced down at the register. Horace Malinski. *I'll check him out.* Shooting a look at Bethany, who was already greeting the next guests, he decided that he would not share with her that he was checking out her clients. *She did really well with my earlier explanations, I won't press my luck,* he thought with a smile.

He watched her for a few minutes as she smiled at the families coming in, telling them about the cabin's upgrades, the rules for swimming in the lake, and the area's amenities. He had to admit to himself that he had wondered if she would pack up and leave when Gram left...*but damn, she loves what she does.* Her smile was infectious and the guests appeared to be thrilled to be staying here. A couple of families were returning visitors that she greeted like old friends.

While she finished up, he turned to take some measurements for the wall to be erected, separating the reception area from the lodge room. *I want her in my home, in my bed, but...one step at a time. And until then, I want her safe.*

He rubbed his head, fighting the headache bearing down on him. Watching from afar, he tried to keep his eye on her. A good girl. They all start out as good girls. *Why can't they stay that way? Because they turn into sluts, that's why. Mama always said so.*

He knew the police and FBI were searching for him. The newspapers were full of stories and speculations about the Campus Killer. *Campus Killer.* Running his hand over his face again, he grimaced. *They don't understand. I'm not a killer. I make the sluts pay. That's all. I just give them their due.*

He fingered the long, slim knife again but fought the urge. It seemed to be coming faster. There was a time when he could make it go away. Ignore it.

He thought about the latest one he had seen. *Would she stay good for me? Or be a slut like the others?* He did not travel as much with his job now. Forced to stay closer to home, it was more difficult to find someone when he felt the urge.

Running his finger along the razor-sharp blade, he was careful not to cut himself. Taking a towel, he efficiently wiped the instrument off before replacing it in its hiding place. Behind it, the jar of bones sat, making him grimace.

Why do the sluts do it? Why do they have to point that finger at me when I just want to get close? He closed his eyes for a moment, seeing his mother constantly shaking her finger at either him or his dad. *Look what I've done for you, ma! What I've always done for you.*

Jack managed to be home for the entire Labor Day weekend, taking advantage of not having to travel by spending as much time as possible with Bethany. He video conferenced with the men and would see them as they rotated through security duty.

He had stayed at her place Friday and by Saturday night wanted to take her out. "You up for a trip to Chuck's for some burgers?"

Smiling huge, she agreed. "I haven't had a Chuck's burger in…wow, I don't even remember the last time I was there."

He chuckled, saying, "Well, it hasn't changed since the beginning of time. Burger's are still greasy and the beer is still cold."

"Sounds perfect!"

Fifteen minutes later, they walked into the bar, greeted by a screech.

"Oh my God, boss-man! Is this the girl that had you making moon faces weeks ago?" Trudie's voice could be heard across the room and most eyes turned toward the couple.

Bethany looked askance for a moment at the big bust, big hair, and even bigger smile on the woman behind the bar.

They made their way over to her and Jack boosted Bethany up on a barstool before moving to stand next to her, his large body pressed into hers.

Bethany could not help but smile back as Trudie made her way toward them.

"Trudie, meet Bethany. She owns Mountville Cabins up the road. And this is Trudie, bartender extraordinaire."

"Oh, don't pay him any mind, honey. I'm Trudie and I've been slinging drinks here for a long time. I remember your grandfather would come in every so often and your grandmother would run into me at the grocery store. Nice to meet the woman that grabbed this here big man."

Laughing at Trudie's running commentary, Bethany did not have a chance to respond before they were surrounded by Jack's men.

Helping Bethany off of the stool, Jack snagged her beer as well as his and ushered her to the back table where the others were sitting. He watched her walking in front of him, his eyes naturally drawn to her ass, showcased perfectly in a pair of black cords. Her light blue top dipped in the back, the color making her eyes appear even larger and bluer.

When they got to the table, she could see all seven of Jack's men were there and several had women with them as well, making for a large group.

She could not remember when she had had so much fun…at least not since she had been at Mountville. She realized how small her world had become, first taking care of Gram and then running the cabins.

Pulling her in tightly, Jack watched her closely. "You okay, babe?"

She twisted her head to look into his face, reaching her hand up to cup his bearded jaw at the same time. Absentmindedly rubbing her fingers along his cheek, she smiled. "Yeah. It's been a long time since I was out with friends, just enjoying myself."

"Wanna give you more of anything you need," Jack replied, wishing he could take the worry off of her shoulders.

"You do, honey. Just by being you."

Excusing herself to use the lady's room, she found Trudie at the sink washing her hands. Trudie's smile beamed at her once more.

"Glad to see you with Jack," the older woman said. "He and them boys of his have been coming in for the past year. All good men, every one of them. But there was always something about Jack."

Seeing Bethany's questioning gaze, Trudie continued, "Them other men? Good people, but a few of them are pretty rowdy with the women who come in here. But hey, the women know the score. Blaise, Bart, and

Marc especially are ladies' men through and through. If it's puttin' out, they're gonna tap it!"

Seeing Bethany's wide eyes, Trudie rushed on. "But Jack? Never seen a man so serious. He'd come in for a beer. Shoot the shit with Chuck, me, or his boys. But then he was all business." Trudie walked over and patted Bethany's shoulder. "He needed a good woman…and looks like he found one." With a wink, the older woman left the room, leaving Bethany to smile to herself as she washed her hands.

As she made her way back to the table, she only had eyes for Jack. But his eyes were focused behind her—and they were pissed. Before she could get to him, a leg was thrown out in front of her blocking her path. Glancing over she saw the smirk of a young, college age man as he grabbed her hand, pulling her over.

"Babe, you looking for a seat?" he said, patting his lap as his table mates laughed.

Jerking her hand back, she was about to retort when Jack charged over, moving her deftly behind him and towering over the table.

"You have a momentary lapse in judgement putting your hands on my woman and your eyes on her ass?" he asked in a growl. "And there's only one answer that I'll accept."

The one who had been openly ogling Bethany as she walked by, trying to impress his friends, now nervously looked to them to see who would back him up. They all sat numbly at the sight of the large, enraged man in front of them.

Bethany pulled on Jack's shirt. "Honey, I don't think—"

Jack whipped his head around, but before he got a word out to her, she was moved gently back a few more feet. Replacing her were the other men, all lined up with equally angry expressions. As she stared at the backs of the testosterone wall in front of her, she could feel her anger rising. *I could have taken care of this myself.*

"Sorry," mumbled the young man, embarrassed to be called out publicly, but smart enough to know that one furious mountain of a man was impossible to take on, much less eight of them.

While the men finished their *discussion* with the tableful of young men, Trudie slipped behind them and tugged on Bethany's arm. "Come on, sweetie."

Bethany allowed Trudie to pull her several feet away toward the back tables.

"Darlin', I can see you about to get mad, but you gotta let those men do what their doin'."

Her lips tight, Bethany stared into the gaze of the older woman. "Trudie, this is barbaric. I know those guys acted foolishly, but it's not like I've never been looked at in a bar before."

"Not when you were with a man like Jack," Trudie said. "Jack and those men with him are of a different breed, darlin'. They hold to tight rules about what a man should and shouldn't do. And they go into protection mode quicker than anyone I've ever seen."

"But—"

"No buts, honey. I've seen them come to the rescue of a woman they've never met before who was bein' bothered by some ass-hole. And with a woman they've claimed? Oh, lordy, they'll really go all out for someone they care about."

As the Saints returned to their table, each of them casting their eyes toward Bethany with a head jerk, she watched them warily.

"Remember girl. There's a man who'll control just for kicks and a man who'll control to make your world better. That's the kind of man Jack is."

Seeing Jack turn and walk back toward her, his face still full of anger, she whispered, "I don't know what to do with that."

Trudie flashed her huge grin and said, "Girl, you hang on for the ride and enjoy every minute. That man'll work to make sure you're safe and happy as you can be." With a pat on her arm, Trudie headed back to the bar, shouting, "All right, folks. Show's over, now get back to drinkin'!"

Bethany could not take her eyes off Jack as he approached, leaning her head back as he came closer and closer. He did not stop until his boots were directly in front of her shoes. She sucked in her lips, nervous as she wondered what she should say.

"You okay, babe?" he asked, his voice gentle considering the anger that was still pouring off of him.

She nodded.

He lifted his large hand and cupped her jaw, sliding his fingers through her hair at the back of her neck. Leaning down, he touched his lips to hers. Gentle at first and then with a little more possessiveness.

She knew he was making a statement. To the others

in the bar…and to her. And now was not the time to question his motives, not when his lips on hers had her melting into his body.

Moving back to the table, she noticed the looks of approval from the other men and wondered why. *Another thing to ask Jack when we're alone.* Deciding to put the event behind her for now, she settled back into his embrace and continued to enjoy the company.

On the drive home, she pondered how to ask the questions swirling through her mind. Before she could get a word out, Jack took over.

"Babe, whatever you're mulling over in your mind, just get it out."

Sparing a glance sideways at his strong profile in the shadows of the night and the dashboard lights, she sighed. "I…I've just never been with anyone who…um… took charge like that. It was kind of scary."

He reached his hand across the console and took hers, pulling it over to his lap. Giving her fingers a little squeeze, he said, "Not having someone put their hands on you. Not having some punk-ass do that to any unwilling woman, but sure as hell not to mine."

She nodded quietly.

He continued, "You get what being with me is like, don't you?"

He looked sideways, seeing her questioning expression, he explained, "My work, babe. My job. Career. Hell, my life. It's always been about doing whatever I have to do to keep others safe. I did that when the Army needed me and now when I'm contracted. But you gotta understand that it's not just what I do. It's who I am.

And any man that puts his hands on an unwilling woman, especially my unwilling woman, is not going to be tolerated."

Seeing her turn in her seat to face him, her face concentrating on his, gave him the encouragement to continue. "I know you're the most independent woman I've ever met, other than my mom. You get out and tackle whatever needs to be done and don't worry about breaking a nail or messing up your clothes." Chuckling, he said, "And gotta tell you, that's a real turn on for me. I've always known I couldn't deal with a woman that couldn't do for themselves or whined every time I didn't get something done when they wanted.

"But," he emphasized, "that doesn't mean that you aren't mine to care for and protect. And babe, I'll do that in any way I see fit. I can tell you didn't think that punk-ass college kid was too serious, but I'm a man and I'll tell you straight up, any man that manhandles an unwilling woman will not think anything about continuing to do that…to you or anyone else. My response to him was immediate and may have seemed over the top, but I'll tell you right now, he'll think twice before trying that with someone else."

Understanding, she nodded as she gave his hand a return squeeze. "Thank you, Jack," she whispered, her words hitting him both in the heart and the dick.

"Damn, girl."

"But don't you think as big and bad as you are, you made your point? Why did the others join in?" she asked.

"Someone move you backward?" he asked.

"Um, yeah. Chad moved me back away from you all."

"He did that 'cause he knew my attention was on the punks in front and my men wanted you out of the way in case things got ugly."

"Ugly?"

"Yeah, babe. He didn't give me the response I was looking for, I'd a taken him outside and we woulda had a *Come to Jesus Meeting*, where my fist would have made him see the error of his ways."

At Jack's description, a giggle erupted from Bethany's lips.

"And in all things, my men have my back, just like I have theirs. And now that includes you. Protecting you is now a priority of theirs as well."

Parking in front of the lodge, he pulled her hand from his lap up to his lips and asked, "We straight?"

Nodding, she smiled. "Yeah," she whispered as he tugged her closer.

His lips latched onto hers, hard, wet, and possessive. A moment later he leaned back, grinning as she mewled at the loss of his heat.

"Come on, baby. Let's get inside. Wanna fuck you hard and fast first then take my time and make love to you nice and slow. Okay?"

"Yeah," she whispered once more.

Hours later, as he tucked her into his side while she drifted off to sleep, she felt his lips against her forehead. "Love you, baby girl."

A smile curved the corners of her lips as his words settled deep.

18

The next day was her day off and she declared it Jack's time. Sally and Roscoe were at Mountville all day and Jack intended to give Bethany her own mini-vacation.

Sunday morning he arrived early and whisked her off, declaring it Bethany's Non-Labor Day. She laughed as he tossed her overnight bag in the back seat and lifted her into his SUV. Buckling her in, he saw her cocked eyebrow.

"Know you can do things yourself, beautiful, but don't deny me a chance to get near you like this." He leered at her breasts which were directly in front of his face before capturing her smile with his lips in a kiss that promised everything.

Pulling through his security gate and driving toward his house, she turned and said, "So, how come we get this time?"

He glanced to the side, seeing genuine interest and not pouting because of his work hours, he responded, "Don't have to travel all of the time, babe. A lot of what we do is in the field and, depending on the contract, can involve going to about anywhere. For now, I'm keeping my contracts in either North or South America. Eventually, we could move worldwide, but I don't have the manpower now to do that."

She listened carefully, amazed at what he had accomplished.

He continued, "And a lot of what we can do is research, taking what others have gathered in the field and well…uh…let's just say that my men can find things out in unconventional ways."

"I see," she replied, although truthfully she had no idea what he meant. "Does unconventional equate to… um…illegal?"

He smiled but did not answer and she found that she really did not want to know. *Maybe the less I know, the better off I am!*

"I don't want to spend our Non-Labor Day holiday talking about work, but let's just say I've got good men working for me. Luke runs most of our software programs and he is my data-mining guru, but as far as the other six? Every one of them loves working in the field, so…I'm learning I can investigate from here perhaps more than I had in the past."

"Oh?" she smiled to herself. "Is there something here that keeps your interest?"

By then they had pulled around to the back to his garage entrance and parked inside. He twisted his body toward hers and answered, "Oh, beautiful, just the thought of being here with you has not only my interest, but my dick twitching."

Seeing her blush, he chuckled. "Come on, let me show you around."

The tour of the living space of the house had Bethany's mouth watering. In Richmond, her apartment's kitchen was a decent size, but since making her home at Mountville, she had to get used to a miniscule kitchen. *But Jack's? Oh my God.* She had seen it when dropping off the cobbler but had not really taken a look around. Huge space, loads of countertops, cabinets galore, stainless-steel appliances. She whirled around gleefully and declared, "I want to cook you dinner here tonight."

His brow furrowed as he answered, "I was gonna take you out tonight, babe."

"No, please," she begged. "Let me cook here. I haven't had a chance to cook in a kitchen this big in soooo long."

The smile on her face convinced him that she was telling the truth, so he acquiesced. He tagged her hand and, since she had seen the living room and deck, he led her toward the back of the house. "I've got an office here for non-secure work, a guest bathroom, and the laundry room leads to the garage."

She nodded as she perused his home, alternating between admiration of the beauty and neatness of his house and the feel of his fingers linked with hers. They stopped at the bottom of the stairs and she looked up quickly as he suddenly turned and met her gaze.

"Gonna leave this decision up to you, beautiful." He saw her quizzical expression and continued. "I show you the upstairs now, no way can I see you in my bedroom for the first time and not take your sweet body. I've got other things for us to do today, including taking you out wheeling over my property. So I'll leave it up to you. Sightsee now and fuck later, or we head up the stairs now."

He watched her carefully, but she never hesitated. Standing on her tiptoes, with one hand balancing against his heartbeat, she whispered, "Let's fuck."

Grinning, he scooped her up into his arms and took the stairs two at a time. Stripping her slowly he peeled away each layer, savoring the gift that lay underneath. Her breasts spilled over the tops of her demi-bra, their luscious mounds with the hidden rosy-tips beckoning. Slipping her bra off, his lips found their way to the hardened buds and he suckled deeply.

While his mouth worked its magic on her breasts, he hooked his fingers into her panties at her hips and slid them down as well. Now, completely bare for his perusal, his dick was straining at his zipper.

He shed his shirt and she stared at the bare-chested magnificence. Massive pecs and rippled abs. Her fingers traced the muscles along his front, downward to the delicious V pointing straight into his pants. She unzipped his jeans and pushed them down his hips, snagging his boxers, freeing his engorged cock. As much as she loved his mouth on her tits, she gently pushed him back, allowing her body the room to sink to the floor on her knees at his feet. Taking him into her mouth, she began working her own brand of magic.

His hands found their way into her hair, cradling her head without pushing, as he allowed her to suck his cock at her own pace. Looking down, the sight of her beautiful mouth taking him in almost undid him. *What the hell did I do to deserve this?*

Her pace increased and he knew he was close. He reached down to pluck her up from the floor, but she glared and shook her head slightly while still sucking.

"Baby," he growled, but she just shook her head again. She was holding on to his hips tightly. Spreading his legs slightly to open his stance, he allowed her, and his own body, to take over. He felt his balls tighten and, throwing his head back with a roar, he came, his hot semen pouring out of his jerking body and into her waiting mouth.

Thrusting through his orgasm, he felt the jolt all the way down to his toes and lowered his head to see her swallowing until every last drop was gone. *She's so beautiful.* He realized that with past blow-jobs, he never had the desire to watch the woman take him. *Just got lost in how it felt for me.* But this time, with someone he cared about...watching her take him while he emptied himself...*fuckin' amazing.*

He staggered, trying to get the feeling back into his legs, then scooped her up and gave her a little toss onto the bed. She giggled as she bounced, but he did not give her time to think. Grabbing her ankles, he pulled her forward until her ass was resting right on the edge of the mattress and her legs were in the air, opening herself for him.

He dropped to the floor and gently pulled her legs up onto his shoulders. Her folds glistened with moisture and he licked his lips before diving in. She tasted better than he could have imagined as he licked, nipped and sucked his way around her folds, finally latching himself onto her clit.

She screamed out his name as the sensations poured over her body from her core outwards. Bucking her hips upward, she felt his large hand press down on her stomach, holding her in place. The exquisite torture continued as she felt his tongue move inside her sex and as he moaned, she felt it vibrate inside. His beard scratched her sensitive skin as her body wound tight, racing toward the finish line, the goal just outside of view.

He moved back toward her clit, sucking it into his mouth while his hand slid up from her stomach to her breast and rolled her nipple between his fingers.

That was all it took for Bethany to hurl across the finish line, her hips bucking once more as the orgasm vibrated deep inside, spreading outwards.

Jack kept licking, feeling her juices spread over his tongue. *Better than anything, baby.* Opening his mouth wide, he felt her vibrations throughout, wanting them to last forever. They slowly subsided and he raised up, seeing her head back on the mattress, her eyes closed… and a smile on her face. He wanted to roar...*I put that fuckin' smile on her face!*

Standing with her legs still raised up high, his cock was at her entrance. He watched as her eyes opened when the crinkle of the condom wrapper broke into her sated orgasm coma.

Realizing that he was going to take her in this position, she smiled again, already licking her lips in anticipation.

"I see my baby wants it hard," he chuckled.

"Hard, fast, blow my mind...oh yeah," she said, watching his eyes darken with desire. Her gaze caught the condom and she said, "Jack?" He stilled, his gaze latching onto hers. "Um, are you um...you know? I'm on the pill, and I'm clean. So if yo—"

"Babe, get checked out every six months for the job. Haven't been with a woman since before that. I'm clean."

She did not have time to process the realization that he had actually been without sex for that long before he interrupted her thoughts.

"You sure?"

She nodded, smiling once again. Then she did not have time to process anything other than to hang on for the ride of her life.

In one swift movement, he plunged inside her wet channel to the hilt. Her body quickly adjusted to his girth as he touched her womb.

"Oh, my God," she breathed, as he began pistoning in and out, hard and fast. At this angle, it felt as though he was touching her very soul.

He leaned over the edge of the bed, his hands on either side of her hips, watching her breasts as they bounced in rhythm to his thrusts. Unable to keep from touching them, he reached up, palming their firmness, before tweaking her nipples once more. Giving them a slight tug elicited a groan from deep inside of her that shot straight to his dick.

He lifted his gaze to her face and saw she was looking down to where there were joined. *Hot as hell. Jesus, she's gonna kill me.* His cock, slick with her juices, continued to find a tempo all its own, pounding inside her grasping sex.

"You close, baby?" he growled, his voice like gravel.

Her eyes squinted shut as her fingers clutched his hips. "Yes," she panted.

"Eyes. I want your eyes on me," he ordered.

She heard his words through the haze of sensations bombarding her, but they did not obey. Suddenly, his hand came down on her ass with a sharp slap, the sting immediately causing her eyes to snap open. Before she could protest, he smoothed his palm over her red globe, soothing the sting away.

"Want your eyes on me when we come, beautiful." He chuckled as he saw her eyes widen first with indignation and then hood with lust. "Yeah, my baby likes that," he said, giving her ass another little pat.

With her eyes trained on his, he tweaked her nipple at the same time as using his thumb to press on her clit while his cock continued its assault. He watched as she flew apart underneath him, her orgasm grabbing his dick as it began to pour itself deep inside of her.

Never went gloveless. Never wanted to until now. Fuck me, I'll never be able to go back to a sheath again, he admitted as the indescribable feeling of coming while buried bareback inside of her hit him. His legs, weak with strain, buckled and he fell on top of her, rolling to the side at the last second before crushing her. Wrapping his arms around her, he pulled her to his side, her cheek resting on his chest. *I want this. I want her. Everyday.*

As the post-orgasmic coma descended, they both lay quietly. She wondered what he was thinking. And she had to admit that she was already falling for this man—the one who works so hard to fight injustice when there will never be any glory in the success. She lay in his arms, luxuriating in the power of his embrace.

An hour later, after one more round of shower sex, a new experience for her and one that she could fully enjoy in his humongous tiled shower enclosure with the multi-head faucet raining water down upon them, they finally went back outside.

She squealed with delight as he handed her a helmet and proceeded to back an ATV out of the garage.

"You ever been on one?" he asked. Seeing her shake her head, he added, "Jump on and wrap your arms around my waist. Hang on and I'll show you my property."

In a few minutes, they were following the trails that covered the outskirts of his twenty-six acres. The back of his land rose steadily as it climbed the base of the closest mountain. When they slowed down, she was able to discern the fencing that divided his property from the park. Stopping at the peak of his acreage, he twisted and assisted her as he took her helmet off. He watched with pleasure as she turned and gazed down over the land.

"Oh Jack, it's beautiful!" she exclaimed.

Her blonde hair had partially escaped its ponytail and the breeze blew it around her flawless face. Her wide, sky-blue eyes took in everything as she viewed the trees, meadow below, and in the distance, his home.

"Yeah," he said, staring at her, "It's beautiful."

They sat in silence for a while, the late summer sun warming them on its descent. He sat on the ground at her back, his long legs stretched out on either side of hers.

"This is going to be beautiful in the fall when the leaves change colors," she added after a while.

"I wasn't here often last fall, so this'll be my first time to see it." Catching her smile as she twisted around to look at him, he added, "And being able to experience it for the first time with you will make it even better, baby."

As she leaned her head back onto his shoulder, he kissed her once more. Soft. Gentle. With the promise of good things to come.

By the time they returned home, it was almost dinnertime and she insisted on cooking. He offered to help, but mostly just stayed out of her way. She flitted around the kitchen, discovering where he kept items and utensils. Soon, the smell of homemade tomato, basil, and garlic pasta sauce was simmering, hand-rolled meatballs were cooking, and garlic toast was baking.

Sitting down at his table for their dinner, the conversation flowed, just as it always had. She learned more about his business, what he could tell her, and she regaled him with tales of life at the cabins.

He managed to convince her to let him have the wall built this week for her protection. After dinner, they settled on the deck swing, her legs stretched out in the seat with her ass in his lap. Sipping wine while watching the sunset over the mountains in the distance was the perfect end to a perfect day. Or so she thought.

It was actually when she fell asleep, her head on his chest with their legs tangled and his arm protectively around her middle after another round of sensational sex. Then it was the perfect end to the perfect day.

19

The next weekend, Jack was gone once more so Bethany took a drive to visit her grandmother. The facility was a long, one-story, red-brick building with stately columns in the front. The flower gardens and lawn were meticulously manicured.

Walking through the lobby, she waved at the receptionist and headed to the main room. Gram was sitting at a table with other women as they worked on a puzzle. She looked up as Bethany came in and her smile spread across her face.

"Helen!" Gram called out. She turned to the other women at the table and said, "My sister has come for a chat."

The other women looked up at Bethany, all with expectant smiles on their faces. She greeted each one as Gram stood and moved over, linking arms with her.

"Come on," Gram said conspiratorially. "I can work puzzles anytime, but I want to hear the gossip!"

Walking a short distance they sat on a small, but

sturdy, setee. "So," Gram began. "Are you still seeing Charlie?"

Bethany had no idea if Gram was referring to Jack, or if she was really thinking about Helen and Charlie from sixty years ago. *It doesn't matter. Either makes her happy.*

"Yeah, Gram. I'm still seeing Charlie."

They chatted for a few minutes, more like old friends than in the here and now, but Bethany was learning to accept the changes. A few nurses walked by smiling at the two of them and, occasionally, stopping by to speak.

As Bethany was getting ready to leave, a nursing aide came over. "Oh Mrs. Bridwell, I see your granddaughter came to see you."

Bethany saw the confusion pass through Gram's eyes as she turned and stared at her. Linking her arm with hers, she said, "Come walk with me, Gram."

They said nothing as they made their way back toward the front of the beautiful building. As she turned to hug her grandmother, Gram spoke softly, "You're not Helen are you?"

Licking her lips nervously, wanting to say whatever would give her grandmother the most peace, she confessed, "No. I'm Bethany. Your granddaughter."

Gram stood peering into her eyes and then smiled. "You're so pretty, just like my sister was."

Bethany hugged her tightly and whispered, "I love you, Gram."

Tears sprung to her eyes when she heard whispered back, "I love you too, pretty girl."

The weekend after Labor Day found Mountville almost deserted, so Jack took advantage of the lull. Having made arrangements ahead of time with Sally, who had agreed to stay, he whisked Bethany off early Saturday morning.

"Where are we going?" she asked, as he made his way to Hwy 81 heading south.

"Gotta surprise for you, but I think you'll like it," he replied, flipping on the radio to a country music station. Pleased to discover that she was a fan, they sat in comfortable silence for a while as the tunes lulled her to sleep.

He glanced over when they were near their destination and saw her head leaning against the window. *She works too fuckin' hard.* Turning off the highway and then again off of the main road, he noticed her head bump against the glass as he hit a pothole.

"Babe. Babe, wake up," he cajoled, gently shaking her shoulder.

She blinked several times before rubbing her eyes. "Mmm, are we almost there?" she asked, her voice groggy.

"Yeah, we should be there in about ten minutes. I was afraid the potholes in the road were going to slam your head against the glass too much."

"Oh, that's okay. I needed to wake up." She flipped the visor down to fix her light makeup and smooth her hair back. Looking around, she saw farmlands on either side of the road before he turned down a long gravel drive.

Whipping her head around to him, she said with excitement, "Jack, is this your farm? Your mom's place?"

"I thought we'd take a trip here so I can check in on my mom and introduce you to her," he said smoothly, belying the trepidation he felt. This was a big step and he knew he was ready. *But is she?*

He need not have worried. One look at her and the smile returned to his face. Her eyes were darting everywhere, excitement pouring off of her.

"All of this land was in my family. When my dad died, mom ran the farm for a while, but it was more than she could handle. She and I talked and, since I had no desire to come back and work the farm, we sold most of the acreage, rent the rest and she keeps the house and three acres that surround it."

Just then, passing the tall corn stalks, they came to a clearing and a white, two-story house came into view. Jack pulled the truck to a stop as a woman walked out onto the front porch. Wearing a simple button-up dress with an apron tied around her waist, she lifted a hand in greeting and offered a smile.

Assisting Bethany out of the truck, he noted her smoothing her hands down her pants nervously. Leaning in, he whispered, "You're gorgeous. Don't worry, she'll love you."

She only had time to spare him a glance before they walked up the front porch steps. He let go of her long enough to envelope his mom in a huge hug before turning to introduce Bethany.

Jack's mother was tall and slim, with shoulder-length gray hair pulled back from her face.

"Oh, my dear, welcome. Please call me Jeanette." The two women hugged and then Jack gently settled Bethany back into his embrace as they walked into the house.

The entrance foyer held an antique coat rack and mirror and then, a few steps in, she could see the living room to the left and the dining room to the right. Ushered into the living room, they sat on a comfortable sofa and Bethany's gaze tried to take in the whole room. Antique frames held pictures that appeared to be a hundred years old. Some were of couples and others of whole families. The mantle held newer ones, most of Jack and his parents in his early years.

Flowered curtains were pulled back allowing the noon-day sun to stream through, making the room feel light and airy.

After a few minutes of Jeanette explaining some of the pictures that she had seen Bethany peruse, she stood saying, "I'm just finishing lunch. Jack, why don't you show Bethany where the powder room is and I'll have lunch on the table in a bit."

Coming out of the small bathroom into the laundry room behind the kitchen, she could hear Jack and his mother talking low.

"All these years and you've never once brought a woman into this house, Jack. Does this mean what I think it does?"

She could not see, but she could imagine Jack's grin as he answered, "Yeah, mom. I met her and everything I thought about how my life was going to go just changed. Almost fu—I mean messed it up, but found my way back to her and she was right there giving me what I needed."

"Well, good, son. I like her."

Bethany made a bit of noise closing the bathroom door behind her so that her presence would be noted. As she stepped into the large eat-in kitchen, with its table already loaded with food, she smiled warmly as Jack moved toward her. She walked straight into his arms and felt his lips on the top of her head. Tipping her head back, she gifted him with her smile before turning to Jeannette, offering to help.

"Oh, it's ready," Jeannette called out. "I hope you don't mind if we eat in the kitchen. It's usually just me so I eat in here and this seems more cozy."

"I don't mind at all," Bethany replied truthfully. The room had strawberry print curtains on the windows next to the table and over the sink. From her seat at the table, she could see out of the window over the farmland that extended as far as she could see.

"All of this was your land?" she asked. "Your father farmed all of this?"

Nodding, Jack answered, "Yeah. Dad had some hired help back then and I would work after school and in the summers."

As though to answer Bethany's unasked question, Jeannette said, "It was never Jack's destiny to be a farmer. His father knew that. He was so proud of Jack joining the military."

Bethany caught the loving gaze passing between

mother and son and, if possible, her heart warmed even more.

After lunch, they sat and looked at photographs of Jack throughout his childhood. When they came to the pictures that he had sent home from his time in Afghanistan, Bethany stared at the group of men, so similar to the men he had working for him now.

"That's Tony Alvarez, our captain," Jack pointed out. "He and I do some business together now. And these crazies work for him. That's Gabe, his twin Vinny, and Jobe," he said. Shaking his head, he looked down at her quizzical gaze. "Sorry, babe, it's just that every one of them are settled down and married now. When I knew them back in the wild days, settling was the last thing on their minds."

"And you?" she asked with a grin. "How wild and crazy were you back then?"

Jack had the good grace to blush slightly, but only said, "Not nearly as much as them, and now it looks as though I've found my one as well."

As the afternoon sun began to descend into the west, they said their goodbyes with Jack's mom, with promises to visit again soon. Driving away, Bethany settled back into the seat of his truck, a contented expression on her face.

"Happy, beautiful?"

"Absolutely," she replied. "I love your mom and it was really nice to see the two of you together. Now that she doesn't run the farm, has she ever considered moving closer to you?"

He shook his head and said, "We've talked about it. I

know your family did really well planning with Ann's needs and I hope to be able to take care of mom as well. For now, she's happy in the old family house, but said that in a few years she'd consent to moving."

With one more surprise up his sleeve, Jack continued past Mountville toward Richmond. On the outskirts, he turned off the highway and within a few blocks pulled into the parking lot a large, luxury hotel.

She whipped her head around, looking at him in confusion. "What are we doing here? Dinner?"

"You'll see," he said, coming around to assist her down. Opening the back of his truck, he snagged two overnight bags. One, she recognized immediately.

"That's mine! How did you get mine?" she asked, incredulously. Then it dawned on her. "Oh that sneak. You got Sally to pack, didn't you?"

Throwing his arm across her shoulders, he pulled her in tightly. "Babe, you work so hard to take care of all of your guests. So tonight, you get to be the guest. And let them pamper you."

Staring from his smiling face upward to the high-rise, she said, "My guests never get this treatment."

Hours later, after a dinner in the upscale restaurant, drinks in the bar first listening to music and then holding each other closely on the dance floor, a long bath in the oversized whirlpool tub complete with candles and wine, Bethany found out just how pampered she could get.

As Jack toweled her off, taking his time over every inch of her body, he carried her to the king-sized bed, the soft sheets beckoning them.

The sight of her long hair laying across the pillows, her body glistening in the moonlight streaming through the their fourteenth floor window, had him eager and ready.

She lifted her arms, but he planned on taking the night slow. Leaning over, his bare chest brushing against her breasts, he kissed her. Long. Wet. Loving.

Sliding her arms around his neck, she tangled her hands in his dark hair, her fingers running through the almost-needs-a-haircut length, loving the feel of it.

His hands found their way skimming down her body, stopping to pay attention to her breasts before moving across her belly to the prize he was seeking. Then his kiss became longer. Wetter. And a helluva lot more loving.

And for the rest of the night, she discovered just how pampered she could be.

20

Jack sat in the bar, where Karen Solter was last seen, talking to the bartender and one of the waitresses. They were the two who noticed Karen had indeed been talking to the man in the picture.

"They were just standing there," the bartender said. "The only reason I noticed them at all was because the man had on a coat and it was ninety degrees outside and probably over a hundred degrees in here with all the bodies."

"Did you see them talking?" Jack prodded.

"No. I glanced up and saw this guy with a coat on and thought 'what an idiot' and the only reason I noticed her was because she was standing on the step below and, swear to God, this dude was leaning over looking down her shirt."

Turning to the waitress, who had been eyeballing him since he walked in, Jack asked her the same questions.

"Well," she said, leaning forward, "I only noticed him

'cause he'd been standing around not ordering any drinks and when I tried to get him to order, he glared at me. Seriously? Me? Like he could scrape me off of his shoe."

"Did you see the two of them talking at all?"

"Never saw them talking, but he got what he deserved," she groused.

Cocking his head to the side, he asked, "How so?"

"He must have said something to her because I saw her turn around and poke him right in the chest like she was trying to get him to stop doing whatever it was he was doing."

"Do you remember which hand she was using?"

The waitress' face scrunched up in thought before brightening. "Yeah, it was her right hand."

That night he worked in the command center alone, knowing Bethany had her hands full with renters. She said she had been working on a new business plan but did not want to talk to him about it until she had done more research. But she swore it could bring in more money during the off season.

Shaking his head to clear his mind of Bethany, he refocused on the files in front of him. He stared at the faces of the victims. Pale in death, their vibrancy snuffed out, bright futures taken away. Bethany was working right now on the future of Mountville. *Can her work include me?* He stood up quickly, cursing at his thoughts straying from the case. *Jesus, I can't concentrate for thinking about her. How is this ever going to work?*

He paced the floor for just a moment, the burden of the job he needed to do warring with the desire to simply be with Bethany crowded his mind. The gate alarm sounded and, irritated at the intrusion, he went to the monitor. Then stopped. And smiled. Her face, peeking out of the old car she drove, was grinning at the camera.

Buzzing her in, he jogged up the stairs and through the house to the front door. She must have flown down the driveway because she was out of the car and hurling herself toward him by the time he made it down the front steps.

He caught her in mid-air as she jumped up, wrapping her legs around his waist. Throwing her arms around his neck, she kissed him.

Finally coming up for air, she beamed at him and, seeing the questioning look on his face, said simply, "I missed you."

Throwing his head back in laughter that she felt rumble against her chest, she tightened her grip, knowing she had done the right thing. As his eyes, still lit with pleasure, came back to hers, she said, "I know you're busy. I…I just wanted to see you."

"Oh, beautiful. I couldn't concentrate for thinking about you," he confessed.

"Can we talk for a few minutes?" she asked, shyly. "Then I promise I'll leave and let you get back to work."

"Abso-fuckin'-lutey," he answered. "Can't think of anything I'd rather do." He paused on the top step, leered at her and quickly amended, "Well, yeah I can."

Giggling, she said, "Not now, big boy." Placing a kiss on the side of his neck, she whispered, "But hopefully later."

He carried her inside and sat on the sofa with her in his lap. "So, what's up darlin'?" Staring at her face beaming up at him, he was filled with the realization that he did not mind the interruption. Just having her here gave him a sense of peace. Of rightness.

"You know I've been thinking of ways to bring in more business during the off seasons and using my marketing degree at the same time." Seeing him nod, she continued, "But I just couldn't think of the right angle. One that fit for me. So, I was sitting the other day going through Gram's old photo albums and came across the ones from when they were first married. And there was one where they were standing in front of the second cabin they had built and…" she paused for effect. "It had a **Welcome Honeymooners** sign in front. See, when they first started building, they advertised Mountville as a perfect getaway retreat for honeymooners."

Seeing the interested look on his face, she said, "That wouldn't work anymore because couples go to exotic places for their honeymoons nowadays, but…what if Mountville was advertised as a wedding venue?"

He caught her excitement, but hesitated. "Um, I can tell you're excited, but I gotta confess I don't have a clue what the hell a wedding venue is."

"It's where an outdoor wedding can be held. You know the grove on the west side of the lake, where the mountains in the background can be seen? It would be a gorgeous place for an outdoor wedding. The cabins would be perfect for the wedding party to rent since most have to be there the day before the wedding."

His mind wandered to the place she was referring to.

Green grass in an open field, the lake to the side and the Blue Ridge Mountains rising behind the tree line. *Beautiful. Hell, if we got married, that's where I would want it to be.* The idea jolted him. *Married?* Suddenly, the rightness of the idea settled deep inside, sending a calm throughout him that he had not had in months. He realized that, no matter what happened with his business, he wanted this woman in his life. In his home. In his bed. With his name.

"So what do you think?" she asked excitedly. "I've been doing research and other places that offer a similar campaign do really well."

Jolted out of his personal musing, he smiled, saying, "Beautiful, I think it sounds amazing…just like you. Whatever you want to do with Mountville is fine with me, as long as you're *with me*."

Her enthusiastic smile morphed into one focused directly on him. "I want that too, Jack."

He slid one hand up her back, across her neck and into her thick hair, cupping her head as he brought her mouth to his. Taking her lips, he moved over them slowly. Feeling. Tasting. Savoring. Capturing her groan, he took the kiss deeper. For once, they did not take it further. Both just satisfied to let their lips do the exploring, they melded into each other.

Finally, pulling apart, she said, "I know you've got to work and I've got to get back. I've got another group to check in this afternoon."

Hating to let go, he slowly acquiesced. "More families?"

"Yeah, everyone is trying to get in their last vacations. I'm going to be doing some checking into the wedding venue idea, so I'll talk to you later." Rising on her tiptoes, she grinned. "Well, hopefully, the next time I'm here I can give you other ideas that don't involve work." She poked him in the chest with her finger for emphasis. "Got that, big boy?" she teased.

Glancing down at her small, right index finger, he knew. The Saints were right. The girls had used their forefinger to poke the killer, probably for trying to come on to them. And it enraged the killer. Enough to cut off their fingers.

Bethany saw the strange expression crossing his face and said, "Okay, I get the hint. Your brain is on work. And honey?"

He looked down at her guiltily.

"That's perfectly fine. Go solve crimes, Jack. I'll be here when you're finished." With one last kiss, she headed to her car, giving him a goofy wave as she drove away.

Another month passed without the Campus Killer striking again. Most college campuses in Virginia, while still vigilant, were celebrating homecomings, football season, and the students were preparing for midterms.

Jack's Saints were still on the job but were more diversified in their work. Taking on a personal case for their friend Jobe Delaro who worked for Tony's security business had sent Cam out of the country. Jobe and Jack had been brothers in the Special Forces and he would have taken the case himself, but it fit Cam's specialty so he received the assignment.

Mountville's successful Labor Day weekend helped Bethany financially through the fall that was typically slimmer. Guests would still come out for the weekends, but until Thanksgiving, she would not have full cabins. She was hoping the holidays would be good so that the steady income kept coming in. As usual, Roscoe would come and go, sometimes working for a construction crew in town, but always showing up when she needed some work done that was too hard for her. During the non-peak seasons, Sally only helped on weekends, leaving Bethany to wash the linens and cleaning which was not time consuming since the rentals were not used as often.

She spent some of her downtime planning for her new venture. Already lining up a wedding planner who loved the idea and would help promote, she met with a local vineyard that had a building large enough to hold receptions.

Jack had someone come in to install the wall and, in two days, it was finished. She had to admit her worries were for naught—it looked great. Now when guests came in to register, they had a large area to sign in, pick up brochures of area attractions, a small bookshelf holding paperbacks to borrow, and behind the registration desk was still the small office. But behind the bookshelf was now a wall, dark paneling to match the original wood keeping the guests from wandering back to what was now Bethany's area. She gave away the old table and chairs that had sat unused for so long and replaced them with a new, comfortable sofa facing the fireplace. Plans to expand the kitchen upstairs since the small living room up there was no longer needed had been discussed, but she wanted to wait to see how much money the wedding venue would bring in.

She and Jack, initially deciding to see where the relationship would go, had now decided that they were definitely a couple. Settling into a routine, he spent his evenings at Mountville when she could not get away or, when she could, she headed to his place.

The Saints were used to seeing her old sedan sitting in Jack's driveway and that was fine with them. They all liked her and could see that she was perfect for their boss. And she baked kick-ass desserts, always making enough for the whole group.

The fall leaves were coloring the Blue Ridge Mountains when the Saints gathered again for a meeting in the command center. Cam was still away and Marc was with him, but the others were opening their tablets with the latest reports. After discussing the various cases they were working on, the topic always came back to the Campus Killer.

"Luke has been narrowing down the field for us to take a look at and we now have, while it is still large list, it is at least more manageable for you to divvy up," Jack announced.

Luke began, "The last time we talked with Ms. Kerstig, she said something that stuck with me. It had to do with the knife and how he kills. She said his knife is an extension of himself, not just any weapon that a murderer might grab in an unpremeditated crime of passion."

Bart queried, "So the knife means something to him and isn't just a knife that he has lying around?"

"Right. And the cuts are very precise like. Jack's reviewed the coroners' reports and they all say the wounds are deliberate, not random stabbings."

"So…?" Chad prompted.

Luke said, "Commercial fishermen have the most handlings with a fish filet knife, but they usually work all year and wouldn't have opportunities for being on college campuses. Butchers or ones working with preparing fish would have a better chance at moving around. Possibly." He sighed before adding, "But I still don't consider them to have jobs that allow them be able to travel much."

"It could just be a sportsman, a man who enjoys fishing and is used to fileting his own catch," Blaise added.

"I've gone back to see if there were any unsolved murders involving these kinds of cuts and changed the search to remove college campuses. Every serial killer has a first time. A first time when they kill and subsequent events may follow different patterns. His first time may not have involved a college student."

Monty leaned in closer, his eyes alight. "So what'd you find?"

Jack smiled and said, "Maybe the next clue for us to investigate."

"Almost thirty years ago," Luke continued, "a young woman was found near the James River. Charlene

Polaski. Her body was partially decomposed, but the coroner's report included that she had been sexually assaulted, and her torso was cut with a very sharp knife. There was no pattern to the cuts, but her neck was also sliced. This was the first murder that I can find like this."

"Shit," Marc said, looking at the information on his tablet. "It's not exactly the same, but it's sure as shit close."

Jack agreed, "I'm wondering if she was not the first. She wasn't a college student and there's not much about her background other than she'd just graduated from high school and was working for her dad's company. Which was," he paused and looked at them, "working for the diesel gas pumps for the commercial fishermen in the area."

"You want us heading there?" Blaise asked.

Jack nodded, "Yeah. I'm going and I'll take three of you with me. I'd like us to spread out and gather as much information on that old murder as possible. See if there is a tie into the ones now. Luke, you manage what we send back. Monty, see what you can dig up on the old murder with your Bureau buds. Bart, Blaise, and Chad, that means you go with me."

Meeting back in the hotel room that night, the four Saints went over their findings. Bart, still grinning from his break-in, had managed to get the victim's school records as well as her medical records.

"What'd you find out?" Jack queried.

"Well, I found out she terminated a pregnancy a month before she was murdered," he replied. "Something that was never in the medical examiner's report."

Chad said, "That never came up in talking to her former friends who are still in the area either. In fact, once again, the common phrase I heard over and over was what a good girl she was. How sweet she was. Same thing as now."

Blaise jumped in, "Except for Todd Cramer." The others looked at him, so he continued. "I talked to a Todd Cramer, a former classmate of hers, who said the same thing at first. Nice girl. But then he said he noticed a change her senior year. She was working for her dad down at the docks and seemed to get really chummy with a few of the fishermen."

"Yeah?" Jack prompted.

"He said she was a real looker and started wearing new clothes that were a lot more revealing. He also said he overheard someone mention she had a sugar daddy who would give her things."

"And he never mentioned this to the police?" Bart growled.

"Didn't you notice?" Blaise asked. "This community gets most of its money from the docks. You think they're gonna turn on each other?"

"What else did he say? Did he have any idea who she might have been seeing?"

"No, but he did imply perhaps that was because no one ever saw her around town with anyone."

The four men looked at each other before all saying, "Married," at the same time.

Jack, eager for the pieces of the puzzle to begin falling into place, said, "Okay, lets surmise Charlene started working for her dad's gas business on the docks and that brought her into daily contact with a bunch of the fishermen. We know she was pretty and had a figure that would make men look. So she catches the eye of someone who's married and begins an affair. She's just eighteen so that's another reason for keeping it a secret. She gets pregnant but has to get rid of it."

"Think that's who we're looking for? Her old lover?" Chad asked, but then quickly worked out the ages. "That'd make the man in the mustache not fit the age."

Jack agreed, "Unless he was real young. But, then he probably wouldn't be able to buy her things at that age. The wife may have found out but then again, she doesn't fit the profile and the age isn't right, either."

"What about her family members? Younger brothers? A jilted high school boyfriend?" Blaise added.

Rubbing his hand over his face, Jack said, "Tomorrow, keep digging. I'll talk to her family and you divide up the friends some more. Look into anyone who was male, probably teen years, and probably had experience with a fishing filet knife."

Jack sat the next day in a tiny office cluttered with papers, receipts, an old computer in one corner with a newer laptop balancing precariously on a sheaf of files in another. He studied the man in front of him who seemed agitated and defensive. Charlene's brother, Isaac Polaski, now the owner of his father's dock gasoline business, sat behind his desk, glowering.

"What I don't understand is why after all this time the police are draggin' up Charlene again. Hell, didn't seem like we could get anyone interested when it happened."

"Do you know why that was, Mr. Polaski?" Jack asked.

Shaking his head derisively, he replied, "Charlene was a good girl, hard worker, real sweet to everyone. But no one in this community wanted to believe that it could have been someone from here. So the sheriff developed a quick theory that she must have been at the wrong place at the wrong time and some outside drifter got hold of her." The silence hung for a moment as he continued his thoughts. "Fuckin' moron. Jesus, I was glad to see him get booted out of office several years afterwards and don't mind tellin' you, I spat on his grave about five years ago when the old coot finally died."

Jack sat quietly, knowing people usually kept talking to fill the silence and he wanted Charlene's brother to talk.

Isaac continued, "Sweet girl. God, I swear she'd believe anything that anyone told her." He chuckled at the memory. "I used to say she was the most gullible girl around."

"Anyone in particular she was interested in?"

Isaac made a face, "Not from here, I don't think, but

hell, you couldn't keep the men away. I thought dad was an idiot for letting her work down here." He looked at Jack, an embarrassed expression on his face. "My sister was…um…well, bluntly put, Mr. Bryant, my sister had rather large breasts. My dad was an okay guy, but he wasn't against using her to get what he wanted."

Jack continued to sit, waiting for the explanation.

"There was another man who worked the docks who also sold gasoline. There was plenty of business for both, but dad wanted to have the edge. He had Charlene work once she turned eighteen and, well, he encouraged her to wear low cut shirts. It had the desired effect. Our business grew and the other man's didn't. I was sixteen and hated how he exploited her, but she seemed to like the attention."

"Any of the fishermen pay close notice to her? Ask her out? Spend money on her?"

Isaac shook his head. "I don't know. I was still in high school so I wouldn't have seen anything during the day."

"Do you remember any of the names of the fishermen who worked around here from that time? Any records?"

Isaac said, "I only took over about ten years ago and just finally got the business online." He glanced around the office and said ruefully, "My wife's been trying to get a lot of the old stuff organized. That's why it looks like this." His eyes lit up, "But she did at least get a bunch of old receipts in files by year. You can look at that if you want."

Jack thanked him and sent a text to Blaise and Chad

to meet him there. Isaac left the office, returning to the dockside to work. As soon as the other two joined him, they began combing old records.

That night, Bart made a clandestine visit to the competing business, gathering the information that Jack had sent him for. Once again, they met to go over their findings. *Finally,* Jack thought, *the noose is tightening.*

21

Jack had been gone for three days and Bethany missed him more each day. They talked on the phone, but it just was not the same. He was due in today, but said he needed to meet with his group first. Leaning with one elbow on the counter, her head in her hand, she watched as the weekend guests arrived.

Roscoe moved across her line of vision heading back from working on one of the cabins. He walked around to the back, assumingly to the shed. *I'll have to check to make sure he locks up after he's through. Years of no lock on the door left him in the habit of leaving it open.*

"Mr. Malinski," she greeted Horace as he came in. "I was surprised to see you reserve a cabin this weekend. You usually wait longer between visits."

"Needed to...um...work," he said with his typical nervous demeanor.

"I don't have your usual cabin available since you booked so late, but I do have another one."

His expression contorted and, for the first time, she

saw emotion on his face. And it was not pleasant. "I'm sure it will be fine, Mr. Malinski. It looks exactly like the other one you're usually in."

He finished the registration process wordlessly and she found herself breathing a sigh of relief when he left the lodge. *What a weirdo,* she could not help but think.

She continued to check her guests in while taking phone calls from the wedding planner who was booking a full cabin rental for a weekend one month from now. It seemed that a popular wedding venue had overbooked and a desperate bride was looking for anyone who could handle her needs. It was certainly more than she had hoped for, but was ready for the challenge. The wedding planner assured her that she would send a contract over—the only thing Bethany needed to do was supply the cabins and the nearby vineyard would handle the wedding and reception.

"This is a great way to dip your toes in the business," the planner enthused.

Bethany could not agree more, mentally calculating the profits from a full weekend, all cabin's rental agreement in a month when she normally had few visitors. Grinning to herself, she could not wait to tell Jack.

Looking up, she was pulled from her musings as another group of fishermen came in to register.

Jack started the meeting quickly, much to the grins of the men around. Each knew he wanted to get over to the woman that now was claiming his heart.

"We did a cross check of the fishermen who used one of the competing gas services, or both, and then went to exclusively using the Polaski's service after Charlene showed up. Interestingly, the most satisfied customers of the Polaski's competition stayed with them and, upon interviewing some that were still around, it was found that some of the men hated the way old man Polaski was exploiting his daughter. Bart hung around a bar that was close to the docks and found some old salts who were willing to talk with a few beers under their belts."

"Good to know those years of boozing at your frat parties did you some good, bro," Luke joked. The others joined in as Bart shook his head in mock embarrassment.

"Seems most of the men who used to fish had to eventually sell to corporate fishing companies. Their sons moved on, went to college, or just weren't interested. A few passed down their boats and businesses, but they all remembered the days of Charlene Polaski's murder. Most said they agreed at the time with the Sheriff's idea that she went off with some drifter and got killed. But a few..." he glanced down at his report, "said that they always felt it was someone there."

Bart continued, "I got two men to talk to me privately for a few bucks, and they told me that, while most of the fishermen would flirt with Charlene and may even ask her out, there were only a couple that seemed to be really interested. One was Zeke Barnham and the other was Jeff Jefferson."

The double name elicited chuckles from around the table.

"Really? Jeff Jefferson?" Blaise asked.

Smiling, Bart nodded. "So, I went to talk to Zeke and he admitted he tried to get in her pants, as he said, but she never gave in. He even admitted to offering to pay her for sex or even a blow job, but she refused. Said it didn't bother him too much because she was a good girl and, that back then he was young and cocky. Said he'd just given it a shot but wasn't upset when she didn't go for it."

"Fuck, there's that 'good girl' phrase again," Monty growled.

Continuing, Bart said, "But then he noticed Jeff Jefferson seemed to be gettin' some, as he called it. Said he went around to Jeff's house one day and his wife was in a foul mood and told him to go look in the shed. So he walked around back and sure enough he heard noises. A glance through the dirty window showed a rutting Jeff on top of what looked to be Charlene. He didn't go any further—but was disgusted and left. Said he was disgusted 'cause Jeff was married and because his wife seemed to know what was going on."

"What the hell was happening in that town when this girl turned up dead? No one said anything?" Chad bit out.

"I asked him that very question. He looked me in the eye and said it wasn't any of his business," Bart said.

Luke, adding all of the information into his computer databases, continued to peck away as the others broke out in discussion.

Jack took over the reporting. "I went to visit Jeff Jefferson, but he's dead. Appears that he died of natural causes about ten years ago."

"So he isn't our killer," Monty noted under his breath.

"I talked to his widow," Jack said, "and this is where it gets interesting. Seems that she's just as unpleasant now as reported thirty years ago. She grumbled about the corporations taking over the fishing. About how her husband never could hang on to his money. You name it, she griped. I asked her about Charlene and her demeanor changed immediately. If I thought she was nasty before...she turned even nastier. Called her a whore. Said everyone thought she was nice but she knew she was a scheming whore. And a few other choice words."

"Did she admit that she knew her husband was having an affair?" Jack asked.

"No, not directly. But then she said, 'Everyone gets what's coming to them and she certainly did.' I asked her if she knew anything about the murder and she wouldn't respond."

"So another dead end?"

Jack grinned. "While she was puttering around in the kitchen when I first got there, I saw a family picture on the mantle. It was her, a man I assumed to be Jeff... and a boy. A teenage boy."

Monty picked up on this quickly, turning to his computer to get into the FBI files. "We need to find Jeff Jefferson's son."

"I asked her about him," Jack replied, "but she grimaced and said he was dead."

"Fuck!" Monty cursed, about to slam his tablet down.

"Hold on," Luke cut in. "Jack had me look. His name was Stan Jefferson, but there's no death certificate on record for him. He disappeared after his high school graduation and dropped out of sight."

Bart shook his head, "No one disappears. He's gotta be somewhere."

"If the dad was banging Charlene in the shed on their property and the wife knew, then perhaps the son saw it as well."

Monty, thinking out loud, said, "Teen boy sees his dad screwing a girl he knew. He's excited. Maybe gets his rocks off or at least fantasizes. He hears his mom complaining about his dad's whores, so he equates this girl with whores. If dad's a fisherman, he'd have grown up around the knives used in the trade."

Jack nodded, "Gotta tell you, I wouldn't put it past Mrs. Jefferson to actually tell her son to get rid of the girl. Or, if she knew her son had killed Charlene, she certainly wouldn't tell anyone."

"That would put the kid at about forty to forty-five years old now, which would be the right age for the photograph from the bar with Karen Solter."

"So why now?" Chad asked. "And why the college girls?"

"There's no death record of Stan Jefferson and the people I asked about him all said they remembered he left town because he didn't want to have anything to do with his father's business. What if he went to college? False name, everything. And maybe killed there for the first time."

"Tries to get into some girl's pants, she shoots him down, pokes him with her finger and he goes off again. He's killed once, why not again?"

"We gotta find Stan Jefferson," Jack stated. "Bart and Chad acquired his dental records while we were there." This statement elicited several grins from the other men. "Luke, see what you can come up with. Monty, get the Bureau on this and see what they can find. Gentlemen? I have a feeling we may be getting close."

With renewed enthusiasm, the men got to work.

Why is she sleeping around? She was such a good girl. Just like all the others. Tramps. Whores. Stealing men with their wicked ways. He watched carefully as the light went out after the man entered the room. The urges were coming more often.

He grimaced, palming his cock. His head was pounding, the headaches coming more frequently. Stepping back into the shadows, he unzipped his pants and worked his cock until he came against the building. Looking around to make sure no one had witnessed, he tucked himself back in. Glancing down at his watch, he knew if he did not get back soon, he would be missed.

Slipping deeper into the shadows, he turned and hurried away.

The morning sun peeked through the curtains covering the windows in Bethany's bedroom, sending shards of light shining down on the couple in bed. Jack gazed at the woman in his arms as she stirred awake, her eyelids fluttering open. He leaned over capturing her lips in a kiss, the memory of the previous night's lovemaking on his mind.

"Morning," she mumbled against his lips just before he plunged his tongue deep inside her mouth. She expected a chaste morning kiss, but the white-hot, all-in Jack morning kiss sent a zing straight to her core. Meeting his tongue thrust for thrust, she could tell her panties were already wet. *Wait, I'm not wearing panties!* Rubbing her thighs together, she could feel the moisture pooling between her legs.

That was the last conscious thought she had before he took over, sending her senses into hyperspace.

His fingers found their way through her slick folds, deep into her sex, tweaking the places that he learned made her writhe, moan, and ultimately come on his command. And he was in total command.

"Dump your shirt, beautiful," he ordered softly and she gladly jerked her t-shirt over her head tossing it to the side. Her breasts bounced with the motion and he grasped one distended nipple in his mouth as his fingers continued to work their magic. It did not take long before she was hurling toward her orgasm. Pressing on her clit with his thumb, she screamed her release and he felt her inner walls grab his fingers as he nipped her breasts.

Sliding down her body, kissing as he went, he slipped between her legs lifting each one over his shoulders. She leaned up, saw his eyes twinkling at hers before he clasped his mouth over her dripping folds, lapping loudly.

"Oh, my God. Are you trying to kill me? Death by orgasm?" she breathed.

He lifted his head just long enough to growl, "In the mood to eat you then fuck you, baby. Is that okay with you?"

"Oh hell, yeah, Jack. Go for it," she moaned, throwing her head back onto the pillow. His tongue now worked the magic that his fingers had previously accomplished, and her core once again tightened. Moving her hands to her sensitive breasts, she gently tugged on her nipples immediately feeling the zing throughout her body.

Suddenly the desire to have him fill her with his cock was overwhelming. She slid her hands down to his head and gave his hair a little tug. "Jack, I've got to have you in me now," she gasped between pants.

Chuckling, he gave one last lap before moving up over her body, pressing his engorged dick at her entrance. Pushing in barely an inch, he asked, "How much do you want me?"

Her only answer was a moan. He slid back out, causing her to mewl in protest.

Sliding the head in again, he repeated, "How much do you want me?"

"Jack," she groaned, glaring up at him when he pulled back.

"Come on, beautiful," he coaxed. "How much do you want me?"

"I want all of you. Now!" she cried out, then gasped as he filled her completely in one thrust.

He began to piston in and out as she grasped his shoulders with her fingers. Running her hands down his back, she felt his muscles cord and bunch underneath her fingers. She felt his power as much as experienced it as her hands made their way down to his firm ass.

Just as she was beginning to fly again, he suddenly pulled out. Her eyes jerked open and a threat to his manhood was on the tip of her tongue, when he flipped her over on her stomach, pulling her hips up.

"Ass up, beautiful," he ordered gently, giving her bottom a playful slap. She felt him enter her from behind in one swift plunge, hitting a place that sent shivers from her core throughout her body.

"I can feel you grab me every time," he panted. "Are you close?"

"Yes," she managed to say as she looked to the side and saw their reflection in the dresser mirror. Having never watched herself, she was amazed at how titillating it was. Her breasts swung with each forceful thrust as his fingers dug into her hips.

"Spank me again," she whispered.

Jack wasn't sure he heard her. "What did you say?"

"Spank me, please," she begged.

Smiling, he nodded and she watched as he slapped

her ass several times, the pain of the sting making her wetter than ever. He smoothed the reddened skin between spanks.

His thrusts increased and he leaned over her body, sliding his hand from her hips to her breasts. Palming the full mounds, his fingers tweaked her nipples, finally giving them a hard tug and she screamed out her orgasm.

Her tight walls milked his cock as he powered through several more thrusts until the last drop was emptied deep inside of her body.

They crashed on the bed together, his massive body lying on top of hers, crushing her into the mattress. She did not have the energy to ask him to move but instead found his weight comforting. After a few seconds, he managed to slide to the side, pulling her with him. She rolled over, facing him, and placed a whisper soft kiss on his chest.

"Beautiful?" he called, his voice as soft as her kiss.

"Um hm?" she answered, gazing up at him.

He palmed her cheek, rubbing his rough thumb over her silky skin. "Want you to know that I love you, baby."

Her breath caught in her throat, tears stinging the back of her eyes. Beaming her smile on him, she cupped his beard covered cheek and wiggled upward just enough to place a kiss on his lips. Pulling back, she said, "I love you too, Jack."

"I want to wake up every morning I can, staring at your beautiful face," he confessed. "Don't have a clue how we're going to manage that, but that's my goal."

Warmth slid over her, melting the lonely corners, as

his words wrapped themselves around her heart just as his arms enveloped her body. "You're not afraid anymore? About us and your business?"

"I was a fool, willing to throw away a chance at what we have here outta my fear that I couldn't concentrate on the business and have you in my life. I know now that, no matter how we work this, I want you."

He captured her lips, nipping them gently before moving his lips over hers in soft whisper kisses. Then, tucking her head against his chest with his hand holding the back of her head, he said, "But babe, I want you in my bed every night as soon as we can work it out."

Running her fingers over his broad chest, she traced patterns along his muscles. "Jack?" she called out tentatively.

"Right here, beautiful."

"I've actually already been thinking. About us, I mean. You know? In case?"

Lifting her chin with his fingers, he peered into her eyes again. "Gotta speak plain, baby. So far, you're not telling me anything."

"Well, I've been thinking, but I didn't want to say anything. In case you didn't want this. But since you do, then I've already kind of got a plan."

His eyes blinked as his chest rumbled with a groan. "Spit it out, girl."

Huffing, she said, "It's just embarrassing to admit that I've already been planning on how to make this work before you actually said you wanted it to work."

Lifting one eyebrow in question, he stayed silent, so she plunged forward.

"Jack, my grandparents built this lodge to be their home. That's what they wanted. And living right there allowed them to take care of the guests. They were living their dream." She stopped, holding his gaze as she continued. "But that's not my dream."

He moved his fingers from her chin and slowly slid his large hand over her cheek, cupping it closely while rubbing his thumb over her soft skin. "What's your dream, beautiful?"

"You," she breathed out. "You're my dream."

He closed his eyes for a moment, allowing the emotion to wash over him, carrying away the doubt, the concern, the hesitation. Opening them once more, he smiled, seeing her still staring up at him as though he truly was her dream.

Before he could speak, she continued. "Since I didn't know if you felt the same, it's kind of embarrassing to admit that I've got it all figured out. But since you do love me, do you want to hear my plan?"

"Abso-fuckin-lutely, beautiful," he admitted, his ego bursting with the knowledge that she wanted to be in his life and in his home. *Their home.*

"I can still own and work at Mountville. I can be here during the day, manage it, run, it, and keep doing what I do now. But like a day job. Then I can be with you every night. And if you're gone on business, I can take care of your place as well. All I need is to find someone, or a family, who wants to live in the lodge and be there for the occasional need at night. And if I find that the wedding business goes well, then I could build a large reception hall on the east side of the lake where the small meadow is now. And—"

Before she could finish her thoughts, he latched onto her lips. This time the kiss was anything but gentle. It was a scorching, white-hot, tongue-tangling assault as she melted under him. It was another hour before they managed to get out of bed.

22

Standing in Jack's kitchen later in the day, Bethany washed the dishes from lunch. "Honey, I've got to get back. There're at least two more groups coming in this afternoon and that'll fill up my last three cabins for the weekend."

"I didn't think the fall was that busy once Labor Day was over," he commented, coming up behind her placing a hand on either side of her at the sink, entrapping her in his embrace. Nibbling on her neck, he knew she needed to go and he was expecting his men at any time. But the soft skin over her pulse was calling to him.

Giggling, she playfully slapped at his arm while unable to contain the moan that escaped. "Later, I promise."

Walking her to her car parked in the front of the house, he saw several vehicles approaching. As some of the Saints came in, they all greeted each other. Marc was still with Cam on an assignment somewhere else, but the other five were there. Chad and Blaise smiled, seeing the ease with which Bethany fit into their camaraderie, while Monty and Luke noticed their boss' apparent happiness.

"I've got to get out of here," Bethany called out once more, standing on her tiptoes to place a quick kiss on Jack's lips. "Those fishermen have got to get checked in so they can head to the lake."

"More fishermen?" Bart asked.

"Yeah. Well, I call them fishermen. They're not professional fishermen. They just love fishing and they travel all over the state to these fishing competitions that the various parks and lakes have. You know? Whoever catches the biggest fish, wins the prize. These men and women are dedicated to this sport."

Fishing. Travel. Different lakes and rivers. Jack's mind began to whirl as Bethany hopped into her car and headed back to Mountville. The men stared at each other for a few seconds before rushing inside to the command center.

"Pull up a list of the contests," he barked to Blaise. Turning to Chad, he ordered, "Get a list of what bodies of water are near the campuses where the victims have been." To Luke, he said, "Dig into the college records from about twenty-eight years ago."

"What am I looking for?" Luke asked.

"White male, discipline records. Personal not academic. Can you get that?" Jack asked.

Luke appeared hurt. "Boss, you want it, I can hack into it."

"Good. We might just be closer to finding our mysterious Stan Jefferson."

"You thinking he may be one of the hobby fishing sportsmen?"

"Don't know, but if we can get a name, then we can cross reference it to the lists of contests for the past few years."

While the others were busy with their computers, Monty surmised out loud. "So this Stan, in order to please mom, kills the girl he sees his dad banging, or to act out his own fantasy. Or maybe he liked her first and she'd turned him down. Manages to not get caught. If mom knows, she sure as shit isn't saying. If dad knows, he's not about to say anything or he'd have to admit he got the girl pregnant. Stan graduates from high school, gets outta town and completely changes his identity. Goes to college to be a new person."

Bart looks up from his computer and says, "Yeah, but the urge to kill is still there?"

Jack nodded. "Yeah, we know from the profiler that the urges may have always been there, but until Charlene they were never acted on."

"So what do you figure?" Chad asked. "He gets shot down by some girl and kills her, using the same method he used on Charlene?"

Jack slowly nodded. "Gotta be a good girl. Someone he liked. Someone who may have been nice to him. He makes a move or sees her doing something that doesn't fit his ideal of her. He presses, she pokes him in the chest to make her point and he kills her."

"Why are you looking for disciplinary records?"

"Hoping, just hoping that someone may have made a

complaint about him. If he got kicked out or warned, that could have taken him over the edge."

Working quickly, the men set about their tasks.

Bethany walked through the lodge after checking out the last of the fishermen that had stayed. A bit flirty, but overall, a decent group this time. She looked back at the wall Jack had built. With its strong door and lock. *Wow, how did Gram and I live here all alone for so long without any trouble?* Stepping out of the back door, she turned to head to the shed. The door was open again, but as she stepped inside, she was pleased to see Roscoe bent over in the back, digging around in several boxes.

"Hey, what're you looking for?" she asked.

He stood, quickly twisting his body to face her. "Oh," he mumbled. "Startled me." He stepped in front of the box he had been searching, saying, "Thought you were over at your man's house."

Glancing down at the box he seemed to be hiding, she replied, "I was, but I needed to be back here to get some work done this afternoon. Were you looking for something in particular?"

"Nah. Well, Mr. Malinski said there was some strange rattling coming from his bathroom. Figured it was a squirrel he heard, but he's been saying that he never had that problem in cabin nine where he normally stays."

Rolling her eyes, she nodded. "He always stays in cabin nine, at the back side of the pond, but he made his reservation so late that it was already reserved. I told him it was now clean and he could move his stuff in there as soon as he wanted."

"You want me to go check out the vents in cabin seven?" Roscoe asked.

"That's okay. I'll do it, although the Taylors were just there again and they didn't complain. They always stay in that cabin because it's close to the trails where their kids can play, but I guess Mr. Malinski just wanted to complain so that he could move. Why don't you check the dock and see if the paddle boats are all tied up? I saw the Taylor boys out there yesterday."

Nodding, Roscoe hesitated to leave so she turned and walked out ahead of him. *First chance I get, I'm looking in that box!*

Having grabbed her tool belt, she headed down the lane toward the offending cabin, still shaking her head at the thought of a rodent getting into creepy Mr. Molinski's bathroom. Waving to a few of the guests, she got to cabin seven and knocked. She noticed his car was gone, so she let herself in. *Hmm, so the vampire does go out during the day. At least to get himself moved to the cabin he prefers. Funny how guests often request the same cabin each time.*

"Got a hit, boss," Luke called out. The Saints' eyes darted to the screen on the wall as Luke projected his findings.

"Twenty-six years ago, Stan Jefferson registered for classes at college. His name pops up in a campus police report which never made it to the town's police, hence no official record. A girl, Josie Simpkins reported that he stalked her and then kept asking her out. He never touched her so the campus police just filed it and forgot it. The college has no record of him coming back after the first semester."

"That's awfully circumstantial," Bart commented.

"Yeah, but get this. Josie Simpkins finished out the second semester and then did not come back either. She was from North Carolina and when I did a search on her…nothing. It was right at the end of the school year so the campus police weren't involved."

"So where is he now?" Chad asked.

Monty, using his FBI information, cursed, "Fuck. Stan Jefferson just disappeared. Not using his social security number, no taxes, no employment."

"Go with his middle name, any variation. Check his mom's bank account and see if anyone has been putting money in it."

The tension in the room grew with each minute that the men furiously tapped on their keyboards. Each focused soley on finding the killer before his urge came again.

"Got it," Luke declared triumphantly. "Son of a bitch dropped his last name and is using his middle name as his last name."

"Get everything. His address, where he works. Get into his bank account. I want to know where the hell he is right now," Jack growled.

As soon as Bethany entered the bathroom of cabin seven, she could hear the sound. *What is that?* Listening carefully, it seemed to be a rattling in the air duct, as though there was a loose object inside. Tossing her tool belt to the toilet seat, she pulled out a screwdriver and, standing on her tiptoes, she unscrewed the four screws holding the metal plate in place. Once it was down, she realized she was too short to see inside. Huffing, she walked back into the kitchen and picked up a chair, carrying it back into the bathroom.

As she climbed up onto the chair, she heard the front door close. "I'm back here, Roscoe," she yelled. "In the bathroom."

Turning toward the vent, she peered in. *What on earth is that?* "Roscoe, come here. I can't tell what I'm looking at."

Reaching her hand in, she pulled out a long, thin, slightly curved knife. She recognized what she was holding, having seen the fishermen washing their filet knives off when they came in from fishing. She stared at the pristine instrument in her hand, the fluorescent lights shining off of its stainless surface.

But how did it get here? Her mind was still pondering that question when she looked back into the vent, seeing a glass jar further back. Squatting, she lay the knife down on the toilet seat along with her tool belt and then stood to stick her hand deep into the cavity. Grasping the glass jar, she pulled it forward.

Her hand shook as her mind tried to understand what she was holding. Little bones. "What the hell?" she said out loud to herself. *Bones?* A queasy feeling started in her belly and slid upward toward her throat, threatening to choke her.

"They were all good girls," someone said behind her.

Whirling in fright, the jar slipped out of her hand smashing onto the bathroom floor scattering the small bones amongst the glass shards.

She stared into his smiling face, incomprehension flooding her expression before she dropped her gaze to his hand. Holding a rag.

"Wh…why…?" she stammered.

"They were all good girls," he repeated.

Looking down at the mess on the floor, she began to shake as dawning slowly descended. Jerking her eyes back to his, she gasped, "You? Oh, Jesus, you?"

Blaise delved into the bank accounts, quickly scanning the information. "Seems he makes regular deposits to his mom."

The rest of the suspect's bio flashed up on the whiteboard on their wall while Monty sent the information to his FBI contact so they had it at the same time. "This is our man," Monty shouted into his phone.

Jack's gaze scanned the information hurriedly as more and more of the suspect's bio fell into place. There was only one word out of the multitude of words on the screen that grabbed his attention, squeezing his lungs until he was not certain he would be able to breathe.

The last place the suspect's credit card was used…**Mountville Cabins**.

With a roar, he bolted out of his seat, shouting directions to the others as he pounded up the stairs. The Saints, only a few seconds behind him in seeing the words, fully understood that this changed this case from detached and professional to intensely personal; each jumped to their duty.

Monty informed the FBI, who would helicopter their Richmond agents immediately. "Tell your boss not to do anything stupid," Monty's contact yelled. Monty watched the retreating back of his employer…and friend. "Too late," he said, disconnecting his phone and charging after him.

Gravel flying behind the SUV, Jack jumped out before it came to a stop. Taking the lodge steps two at a time, he slammed through the door, screaming, "Bethany!" No response.

With Chad and Bart on his heels, he flew through the connecting door into the private area and toward the back door, continuing to scream her name. His heart pounding faster than his footsteps, he turned to the left seeing Roscoe coming out of the shed.

"Bethany, where's Bethany?" he yelled.

Roscoe looked up in surprise, his expression a mixture of shock and guilt. Wiping his mouth, he answered hastily. "Cabin seven. A guest was complaining about a noise so she moved him and went to investigate."

Jack turned to begin running up the lane toward the

right of the pond, pulling his weapon out, yelling instructions over his shoulder to his men.

Chad changed direction, heading back to the SUV, to grab his Kevlar and other weapons, making sure their radios were activated. Bart followed Jack, catching up to him as they approached the cabin.

"Jack," Bart growled, seeing Jack's recklessness. "Keep your mind in the fuckin' game."

The trio spread out around the cabin, as Jack stalked in toward the open front door. Weapon raised, he entered. Other than a missing kitchen chair, he moved through the house, not seeing anything out of the ordinary. "Living room clear. Bedroom one clear."

Entering the bathroom, his heart stopped. His eyes took in the small room, immediately categorizing the scene. Bart shoved him aside, stepping in. The missing kitchen chair was next to the wall where the vent cover was off, leaving a gaping hole where the duct work was. A tool belt was on the toilet seat and on the floor... *fuck...a shattered glass jar with bones scattered everywhere.*

Bethany's eyes blinked, the sickly sweet smell still lingering as she slowly regained consciousness. Her foggy mind tried to make sense of her surroundings, but only bits and pieces would fit together, the whole picture staying just out of her reach.

The hard floor came into focus. Realizing that she was sitting on concrete, her gaze moved upward, seeing cinderblock walls. Trying to push herself up, the rattling of chains sounded in her ears, the noise scraping against the wall. Blinking several more times, she saw a ring in the wall above her head with a chain leading down from it to a metal cuff around her wrist.

Managing to lean her back against the wall, she gazed around the rest of the enclosure. A metal table sat in the middle of the room, dark rust stains all over the legs and the concrete floor underneath. Her head lolled to the side as she took in the wall to her left. Covered in wallpaper...a very busy wallpaper print with lots of pictures on it. As her eyes focused a little more, she could see it was not wallpaper. But photographs. She had to strain to see what they were.

Oh, shit. Oh, my God! The photographs were all of naked women. Tied to the table. Sliced. Some eyes wide in fright. Some eyes wide in death.

Her gaze shot back to the table in the middle of the room. *That's not rust. It's blood.* The gruesome realization mixed with the lagging effects of the chloroform that was in her system had her pitching forward, vomiting what little contents were in her stomach.

Shaking, she jerked her arm against the metal restraint, hoping her small wrist would come loose. No such luck. All she managed to do was tear the skin and bruise her hand more.

How could the Campus Killer be him? I've talked to him. Joked with him. Laughed with him. And his family!

The metal door opened with a loud screech and she jumped at the noise. As she turned her eyes toward the offending sound, Stan Taylor walked through, his usual smile gone, replaced by a pained expression. She watched him warily, pressing her back against the rough cinderblock wall.

Muttering to himself, she managed to catch, "Not right. Not how it's done. Not the right time."

His gaze came to hers and he said, "Why did you meddle? You've been a good girl. It didn't have to come to this."

Not understanding what he was talking about, she croaked, "Mr. Taylor?" Her tongue felt large in her mouth, but she was desperate. "Let me go. We can get help."

"You don't know," he bit out, his face contorting in pain. "I don't need help. They did. Good girls on the outside, but really sluts. Just sluts." His eyes lifted to the wall of photographs, darting over them, searching. His breathing slowed as he perused his handiwork, finding comfort in his wall.

"I need to get you ready," he added as he moved toward her, a cloth in his hand, the familiar sickly odor emanating.

Nooooo, her mind screamed and she could not be sure if her mouth said the word at the same time. A flash of Jack's face flew through her thoughts. *Find me. Please find me,* as she steeled herself.

23

While Jack was gone out of the command center on his way to Mountville, Luke, Monty, and Blaise immediately went to work collating the data gathered.

"Find their property," Monty shouted, as Luke responded, "On it."

Within a minute, Luke displayed three properties that Stanley Taylor Jefferson owned. Monty called it into the FBI who was on route to the main residence, where the family was, in the suburbs of Richmond. They would be there shortly.

"Got two others besides his mom's place," Luke called out. "One is property he owns about halfway between here and Richmond. No house, but could be outbuildings. Chad, get a visual. The other is a piece of land on the far side of Richmond."

Within a minute, Chad brought up satellite images of the property. Monty immediately sent the information to the FBI, cursing that they had no idea which one Stan would use.

Blaise turned around, catching the eyes of the others while listening to the radio earpiece. "Roger that," he called out, then lifted his eyes to Luke. "Jack's on his way back. The cabin's empty. No sign of Taylor or Bethany. And a shattered glass of bones was on the floor."

"Fuckin' hell!" Luke shouted out in frustration.

Within ten minutes Jack, Bart, and Blaise charged back into the command center.

"Give me everything you've got," Jack growled, panting, his expression ravaged.

Monty started to report but was interrupted as Luke jerked around, pinning Jack with his gaze. "We've got her," he said, drawing all eyes to him. "Ann's tracker bracelet. It's at the closest property that Stan owns. He's taken her there."

"She's wearing the bracelet?" Bart asked, disbelieving her location could be identified so easily.

"Jesus," Jack said. "She started putting it in her pocket each day. She said it gave her comfort and I sure as shit forgot about it." Pivoting quickly, he barked out, "Suit up. We're going in."

The men grabbed their tactical equipment and headed back out of the door. Filling four SUVs they spun gravel behind them once more, this time knowing exactly where they were going and what they were going to do when they got there.

Please God, don't let it be too late.

As Stan moved closer to Bethany, she cowered against the wall, the fear making her limbs quiver and her stomach lurch. He seemed distracted as he continued to mutter, "I'm not ready. This isn't the right time." He gazed at her, saying, "I heard Roscoe tell you there was a noise. I didn't know what to do. I thought it was a good hiding place. I couldn't keep my trophies at my house. But when we would come visit you, it was easy to add to my collection. No one would think to look there. But you did."

She stared, not knowing what to say to his explanation…not even sure if he expected a response.

Rubbing his hand over his forehead, he grimaced as though in pain. "But you were such a good girl, taking care of your grandmother." He shook his head back and forth several times, continuing to mutter. "You have to go away now that you found out. But…it's not right." He paced the floor before stopping right in front of the wall of photographs.

He turned slowly, his eyes boring into hers. "You slept with that man. You're just a slut like the rest of them." Nodding now, he seemed to have come to a conclusion. "Yes, yes. I have to take care of you too."

Fear overrode her numbness and she struggled to get away, only managing to snap her wrist held in captivity. The pain sliced through her arm, causing the nausea to fill her mouth once again.

As he bent toward her, the offensive cloth in his hand, he added, "You can't stop what has to happen. I'll make it work."

Her mind finally coming unglued, she reacted

immediately, taking the only move she knew how to make—she rolled her face away from him on her back while bringing her feet up and kicked him in the groin as hard as she could.

Howling, he went down on the floor, dropping the chloroformed rag and grabbing his crotch with both hands. Tears streaming out of his tightly closed eyes, he was unable to speak. Rising to a kneeling position, she wanted to search his pockets for the key to the metal lock but realized his hands were in the way.

In a panic, she grabbed the cloth with one hand and twisted her face away to keep the odor from affecting her. Slapping the wet fabric over his face, his cries stilled and his body stopped writhing on the floor. She stuck her good hand into his pants pocket and found a keyring.

Trying several of them, she discovered the correct one and, with her hands shaking with fright and adrenaline, she opened the metal cuff. She could not tell if her wrist was broken, but she used her good hand to push herself up. Holding on to the wall as she hauled herself upward, she then stumbled toward the door, pulling it open. The monstrous smells of the death room fell behind her as she made her way outside, gulping the fresh air deep into her lungs as she pitched forward onto her knees on the gravel drive.

The sun was slicing through the tree foliage and she could see his car parked to the left. Staggering to his vehicle, she discovered the car keys were not in her hand. Too afraid to go back inside to search for them, she attempted to run, although the lingering effects of the chloroform made her unsteady on her legs.

The trees on either side of the road became flashes of fall colors all swimming in front of her eyes. The sunlight beating down seemed too bright, causing her to squint. *Got to get away. Just keep going,* her muddled mind screamed.

A sound ahead had her stopping in the middle of the drive. Hearing the noise of an automobile, she froze, her disoriented mind unable to ascertain from which direction it came. Turning too quickly, she slid down the gravel drive's edge, rolling and tumbling into a small ravine. Thorns and underbrush tore at her clothing, scraping her limbs until she finally came to a stop at the bottom. Covered in leaves and dirt, she lay exhausted, praying that she was hidden from whatever terrors might come.

Making the thirty-minute drive in only fifteen minutes, the men coordinated their assignments while en route. Jack drew on his Special Forces training to slow his heart rate and focus on the mission at hand, but found the task almost impossible.

Monty's voice came through the earpieces, "ETA for FBI is ten more minutes."

"Not waiting," Jack growled, his body moving with the speeding vehicle driven by Bart as they took the country curves at a speed much too fast for ordinary drivers.

Pulling to a stop just down the drive from the property's windowless structure deep in the woods, they alighted, immediately circling. The car sitting outside curled Jack's stomach. *Fuck, I saw that car driving around whenever Taylor's family was at Mountville. I was so close to the killer and never fuckin' knew it.*

"Boss," Blaise said, causing Jack to jerk his head toward the left. "Get it outta your head. Not gonna help her now."

Sucking in a huge breath to clear his mind, Jack nodded. *Time to go down, asshole.*

Approaching the door, Chad was prepared to blast it open when they saw that it was slightly ajar, allowing Jack and Bart to storm in first. Jack's gaze looked for Bethany, his stomach lurching as he saw the blood-stained table and gruesome photographs on the wall. But no Bethany.

Bart ran to Stanley, beginning to stir on the floor near chains connected to the wall. Seeing the chloroform rag next his face, he barked out, "She must have turned this on him. She's out."

Blaise and Chad entered as Jack stomped over to Stanley and picked him up with one arm. "Where the hell is she?" he roared.

Just then the area was swarming with FBI as Monty led them to the hideaway of death. Chad caught Jack's arm as it was swinging toward Stan's face.

"The knife," Chad yelled, catching Jack's attention. "There's no blood on it. Swear to God, Jack, I think she escaped."

Blaise quickly said into his radio, "Luke, find her

with the tracer. We're at the location. Got Stan but Bethany's not here."

Luke's answer had Jack and the Saints pounding out of the structure, leaving it to the FBI as they ran back down the drive. Looking side to side as he ran, Jack noticed broken branches in the gorse. "Here," he shouted.

Moving off of the gravel drive, he fought his way past the brambles, seeing a torn piece of cloth clinging to a thorn bush. He heard another Saint behind him and called out, "She's been here," knowing his men would be following.

Pushing past the last of the brambles along the steep slope, he saw movement in the underbrush down by the ravine. Just as he slid to a stop, shouting her name, Bethany's scratched face peeked out from the brambles. Dazed and confused...*but fuckin' beautiful.*

Charging into the ditch, he slid down beside her, pulling her into his arms. "Jesus, Jesus, thank Jesus," he said over and over, his chest near to bursting.

"Jack?" her weak voice said, as she buried her face in his neck, her good arm clawing to find its way around him as she held her injured arm close to her body.

"I'm here, beautiful. I've got you."

Hearing noises beside them, he did not have to look to know his men were circling around to assist. Feeling hands help them up, he turned as Blaise said, "Jack, get her up to the road and let me check her out."

Nodding, Jack stood with her in his arms, allowing the men to get them to the road. Kneeling with her in his embrace, he realized his body was shaking. Not knowing what horrors she had faced before escaping, he warred with wanting to talk to her and simply wanting her to never think of it again.

Bethany's slightly dilated eyes took in the men around her as Jack held her tightly. "I'm…I'm okay," she stammered.

Blaise gently wiped her scratched face and arms, noting her clothing was intact and there were only slight bruises on her neck. Her wrist seemed to have suffered the most injury as it was swollen, abraded and bleeding from the metal cuff.

Blaise opened his backpack and pulled out the makings for an emergency splint, quickly binding her wrist.

His eyes met Jack's and he gave an imperceptible nod, Jack's breath letting out slowly. Monty came running down the drive, having informed the FBI of her whereabouts.

Several ambulances pulled into the drive, one stopping at the group. Jack placed Bethany on the stretcher against her protests.

"Babe, not taking a chance. I want you seen," Jack ordered gently.

Still clutching at his shoulders, she peered into his face, fear written on her expression. "Don't leave me!"

Touching his lips to her forehead, he nodded. "I'll be with you always, beautiful."

One week later, the Saints gathered at Jack's house, not heading down to the command center but piling up in the living room instead, surrounding Jack who was sitting on the sofa with Bethany tucked into his side. Each leaned over, kissing Bethany's head or offering a hug as they entered. Jack caught her nervous smile as her eyes sought his and he winked his encouragement. Wrapping his arms around her, he pulled her more tightly into his embrace.

"You okay, babe?" he whispered.

Biting her lip, she breathed, "Yeah."

He kept his arm around her as the men took their seats and settled in. Engaged in small talk, the group avoided discussing the Campus Killer.

Jack's mind wandered back to the events of the past week.

Sitting in the hospital ER bay with her while she was checked out, he began to shake as the adrenaline wore off. With antibiotic salve on her scratches and her bruised and injured wrist wrapped in a cast, she was ready to be discharged.

It was afterward that took him over the edge. Monty came in to let them know an FBI investigator needed to question her. "Would you be more comfortable doing this at home?" Monty asked, concern on his face.

Shaking her head fiercely, she cried, "No! I can't go there!" The idea of seeing her cabins was terrifying.

Jack squeezed her, saying, "She's coming to my place."

"No!" Bethany cried. She glanced up at him, seeing his concerned expression, and explained, "I don't want it there. I don't want to relive it there." Her gaze begged him to understand. "I want to get it out and then leave it. I don't want it to stay with me."

Jack and Monty shared a glance, both knowing that she was not going to be able to talk about it without dealing with the after effects. Monty nodded and said, "They'll meet us in the local sheriff's office and do the interview there."

Two hours later, sitting with Jack at her side and the Saints listening in as well, she recounted her tale. All of her encounters with Stan and his family. How he always asked for the same cabin when they came to stay and no, she did not think that was weird. And then, the events of the day.

She maintained her composure until describing the wall of photographs. Her voice faltered as her eyes filled with tears. Face pale, she began to shake. Jack wrapped his arms around her in an attempt to share his body heat with hers, but her mind had completely taken over her body. Haltingly, she talked of finding the jar of bones. Finding the knife. Having him rush at her and placing a rag over her mouth. Waking up in the room, shackled by chains to the wall. Seeing what she thought was a rusty table, before realizing it was blood. Then the photographs.

"Do you need a break, Ms. Bridwell?" the investigator asked.

She did not hear him. All she could hear in her mind were the screams of the women on the wall.

"Enough!" Jack growled, starting to stand.

"No," she whispered, her tearful eyes imploring his. "I need to do this for them."

"These investigators will get their information from the evidence. They don't have to have you relive this fuckin' nightmare."

"No," she whispered again, her small hand on his arm. "I have to do it. For them. For the women."

He searched her eyes, seeing fear mixed with strength. Then, sighing, he nodded as he settled back down, pulling her into his side. His eyes met the investigators, daring them to keep their mouths shut as she talked.

She finished her tale of terror, recounting his unstable ramblings, explained her attack on him and subsequent escape. "I think the only reason I had a chance was that he kept saying 'this wasn't how it was supposed to be'."

"Most serial killers have a routine they're comfortable with. You didn't fit that profile, nor was he expecting to have to kill at that time, so your situation threw him off of his norm."

Finishing the interview, she suddenly turned to Jack and said, "Take me home." The investigator informed her that Mountville had been barricaded from the public and the cabin had been sealed off for the investigation.

"Oh, Jack, what about my guests?"

Assured that Roscoe and Sally had taken care of them all, she leaned heavily against him. He took her weight wordlessly, with another squeeze around her shoulders. "I'll have to close Mountville," she said, bringing her hands up to her face. Twisting around to face him, she moaned, "The publicity will kill me."

Now it was a week later and the gathering in Jack's living room kept the conversation lively, no one wanting to upset her. Neither she nor Jack had brought up the events, each dancing around the subject.

Finally, not able to stand it any longer, she blurted, "I need to know."

Jack gave her shoulder a quick squeeze and the others stared. First at her. Then at Jack. Then at each other.

"Babe, there's no need to—"

"Jack," she interrupted, twisting around to look up into his scowling face. "I'm fine. Don't you get it? I'm fine. Yes, what happened sucked and I'll have nightmares about that horrible room and wall for years. But honey," she said, bringing her face in close while cupping his jaw, "I got out. I'm safe."

"If I live to be a hundred, I'll never forget how fuckin' scared I was," he confessed. Leaning forward, touching his forehead to hers, he forced his heart rate to return to normal, giving a little nod.

With a nod from Jack, Monty began, "When all the pieces of the puzzle fell into place, it appears that Stan began killing when he saw his father bang—uh...having sex with a young woman that he knew. Whether his mom asked him to get rid of her or he did it on his own out of spite to his father, who knows."

Luke added, "We assume that started his journey

into killing. He thought of her as a good girl and was upset that she was being…well, in his mind…being a slut."

"But he was married! He had kids!" Bethany exploded. "And he seemed so nice!"

"It's a myth that most serial killers are loners and completely antisocial," Luke continued. "From what we can tell, he had to leave college after stalking a woman who spurned him."

"He worked for a marketing company selling advertising and would continue to go to campuses, try to pick up women he had watched and determined were good girls. Maybe he wanted sex with them, and if they turned him down, that's when he would go after them. We have no idea how many he may have watched, but when he would come across one who changed their patterns, like going dancing or to bars, or one-night-stands. He would kidnap them, and then…um…"

Chad had taken over the explanations but hesitated at this part of the story. His eyes darted to hers and his voice faltered.

"He would rape them, torture them, and kill them," Bethany finished for him. "What about what I found? In the bathroom?"

Bart replied, "It appears those were souvenirs. He would…um…" he stumbled over his choice of words, looking to Jack for guidance when he saw Bethany's wide eyes.

Jack, hating the conversation, squeezed her shoulders. Sucking in a deep breath, he said, "Babe, you'll go over all of this with your counselor, but I'm trying to get these images outta your head. So this is the last of it. Some killers keep something to remind them of what they've done. For memories, for a power trip, for the hell of it."

"But why here? Why not at his house? Or that… that…place?"

"Don't know, but if I had to guess, it was because he felt safe at the cabins. He always asked for the same one. Figured no one would find them. If they were found, it wouldn't be tied to him since you have lots of guests who stay there. It was…safe."

The room grew quiet, each to their own thoughts while attuned to the young woman, so close to the same fate, that had come to mean so much to their boss…and to them.

After a few minutes of reflection, she said, "While I never thought it was one of my guests, I would have assumed Horace over Stan."

"The writer?" Blaise asked.

"The who?" Bethany asked, in surprise.

Chuckling, Blaise continued. "Yeah, when he was checked out by the FBI, he was indignant he had to leave his cabin. Seems he lives in a very noisy building so he would come to Mountville at least once a month for the quiet and solitude to write his mystery novels under a pen name."

Before Bethany could respond to that, Jack interrupted her thoughts and said, "You're also gonna have to talk to Roscoe."

Jerking her gaze to his, her brow furrowed in question. "Huh?"

"He's been keeping some hooch stashed in the tool shed," Bart laughed.

"Hootch?"

"Uh, moonshine," he explained. "He's been buying some locally distilled whiskey and found the storage shed to be a good place to keep it."

The idea that one of her favorite guests was a serial killer, one of her unusual guests was a mystery writer, and her handyman was storing his bootleg whisky in her shed had her falling back against Jack's body.

"So much for my idea of a wedding venue," she mumbled. "So far the press hasn't come around, but I know they will and I'll be ruined."

"It'll be fine, baby," Jack murmured against her hair.

Monty shook his head slightly, saying, "Bethany, don't worry. The FBI is keeping Mountville out of the press."

Jack's eyes darted to his friend as she jerked her gaze toward Monty.

"How?" she asked incredulously.

Chuckling, Monty looked down for a few seconds before lifting his gaze back to hers. Softening his tone, he just replied, "Called in a few favors. Racked up quite a few while I was with the Bureau so it was time for a little payback. Press gets the story, but Mountville is kept out."

Her throat clogged with emotion as she mouthed her appreciation to him. *Thank you so much.*

Monty smiled in return, offering a simple nod to both her and Jack.

"It's a good thing you were wearing your grandmother's tracer," Bart said.

She smiled as she nodded. "When Gram moved to the memory-care facility, I felt so alone. She never wore jewelry or I probably would've worn that. But since her tracker bracelet was the only thing I had, I kept it in my pocket and whenever my fingers would happen across it, I felt as though she were right here with me." She looked into Jack's face, "Kind of like my own personal Saint."

Looking down at her face, Jack said gruffly, "We done?" his voice belying his need to take away her fears.

"Yeah, sweetie," she said, knowing he hated talking about what had happened, "We're done." She smiled remembering what he told her last night. *"You need to talk, beautiful, we'll talk. You need to see a counselor to get over the nightmares, we'll do that too. Whatever you need... that's what I'll give to you."* She then smiled wider, remembering what she needed last night...his powerful body rocking into hers, the moonlight streaming through the windows, two major earth-shattering orgasms, and then cuddling.

Yeah, whatever she needed...he gave to her.

24

SEVEN MONTHS LATER

A new gazebo sat near the pond on the west side of Mountville, the Blue Ridge Mountains in the background. Decorated with white, billowy sheers and sprigs of early spring flowers, Jack stood underneath its covering. Looking out into the small gathering, he grinned at his former Special Forces brothers-in-arms, Tony, Gabe, Vinny, and Jobe with their beautiful wives.

He had come to the area for privacy, but found friendship and love along the way. Behind him, on either side, stood his seven Saints, all friends as well as employees.

Two months after her ordeal, he took Bethany riding back up to the scenic overlook on his property where they picnicked on a blanket and watched the sun begin to set. Watching her mesmorized by the brilliant evening sky, he pulled out a princess-cut diamond ring and held it up in front of her. The sunset colors flashed off of the gem and her eyes grew wide. She turned quickly, gasping in disbelief.

"I told you before," he said. "I want you in my home, in my bed, and in my life...permanently." He watched carefully as her expression morphed into joy as he slipped the ring onto her finger.

It was a rush to put together a wedding in only five months, but the vineyard next door was thrilled to help with the occasion. The wedding coordinator volunteered her services since Bethany would be promoting her as Mountville's wedding guru.

His gaze wandered to the back, wondering when things would get going. Just then the music began and he lifted his eyes to see his bride walking between the chairs, her ivory dress fitting tightly at the bodice, then floating behind in layers of lace. It was her tribute to Gram even though she could not be there. She had a seamstress re-work Ann's wedding dress, which had been much simpler, and incorporate it into the vision in front of him right now. Her hair, pulled back in the front with a crown of flowers, flowed down her back in waves. Her eyes never left his and the smile on her face pierced his heart as it always did.

How did a cuss like me get so fuckin' lucky? he wondered. Smiling as she made her way toward him, her hand on her father's arm, he stepped forward as they neared the gazebo.

The ceremony did not last long, but the vows spoke of everything that was in their hearts. Bethany smiled up at the man holding her hand as he promised to chase away all of her dragons while allowing her to follow her dreams.

Mountville had been her dream and Jack had made

sure it still was. She never stayed overnight there after the kidnapping. From that moment, she shared his home…and his bed. They demolished cabin seven, planting a beautiful flower garden there. A myriad of seasonal flowers with a bench in the middle would be all anyone would see.

Encouraged by Jack, she continued to pursue her dream of turning Mountville into a wedding venue, while still allowing rentals when a wedding wasn't taking place. Building the gazebo was a start and their wedding was the first to take place there.

She now worked with several local wedding coordinators and had weddings scheduled for the next year. The vineyard nearby was thrilled to work with her and, in fact, was hosting her reception later that day.

Mountville had been her grandparents' dream and Bethany was determined to keep it going…just her way now.

As the vows were completed and the rings exchanged, Jack encircled her in his arms as she lifted herself on her toes to meet his lips in a chaste kiss. Jack leaned back and to her surprise, reached into his coat pocket and pulled out a silver chain with a beautiful silver medallion dangling on the end—Saint Ann. Slipping it over her head and settling the Saint medallion against her breasts, he leaned down and whispered, "There's a tracker attached to the medallion. Keep it on at all times and then me…and Gram will always know where you are."

With her eyes wide, shining with unshed tears, he leaned down again, capturing her lips in a not so chaste kiss, pouring his soul into hers, now knowing that he could have his business and get the girl. He had it all. Or so he thought.

One year later

Coming home from an investigation, having been gone for two nights, Jack pulled into the garage and grabbed his bag. Moving quietly through the laundry room toward the kitchen, he toed off his boots so that he would make as little noise as possible.

Entering the living room, he saw Bethany on the sofa, a nursing baby at her breast, her Saint medallion resting next to his son's face. Her eyes lifted and then sparkled in greeting as he walked over, sitting carefully next to her. Young Peter had almost nursed himself to sleep as his mouth went slack and a little milk drooled down his chin. Shifting slightly, she tucked her breast into her bra and slipped her shirt back into place.

He smoothed his son's cheek with his rough finger, amazed at the silky softness of his skin. Throwing his other arm around his wife, he tucked them both in tightly to his side. As Peter slept, Jack and Bethany sat watching the sun set behind the Blue Ridge Mountains out of the large picture windows.

The back yard was now surrounded by a white picket fence, perfect for when Pete and subsequent children could run and play safely. The fence glowed against the darkening evening sky.

She twisted her head around so she could kiss Jack. He gave her a chaste kiss, then chuckled as he saw her pout. Cupping her face in his hand, he took the kiss deeper. Wetter. More passionate. Pulling back, he smiled at her hooded gaze. "That better?" he rumbled.

"Um hmm," she mumbled. "I'll put him down in a few minutes and we should have time for a little fun before he wakes up again."

Good with her plan, Jack leaned back once more, his wife and baby son tucked into his side as the brilliant sunset colored the evening sky.

And he knew he had it all.

Don't miss the next Saint… Cam's story!
Healing Love

ALSO BY MARYANN JORDAN

Don't miss other Maryann Jordan books!

Lots more Baytown stories to enjoy and more to come!

Baytown Boys (small town, military romantic suspense)

Coming Home

Just One More Chance

Clues of the Heart

Finding Peace

Picking Up the Pieces

Sunset Flames

Waiting for Sunrise

Hear My Heart

Guarding Your Heart

Sweet Rose

Our Time

Count On Me

Shielding You

To Love Someone

Sea Glass Hearts

For all of Miss Ethel's boys:

Heroes at Heart (Military Romance)

Zander

Rafe

Cael

Jaxon

Jayden

Asher

Zeke

Cas

Lighthouse Security Investigations

Mace

Rank

Walker

Drew

Blake

Tate

Levi

Clay

Cobb

Hope City (romantic suspense series co-developed with Kris Michaels

Brock book 1

Sean book 2

Carter book 3

Brody book 4

Kyle book 5

Ryker book 6

Rory book 7

Killian book 8

Torin book 9

Saints Protection & Investigations

(an elite group, assigned to the cases no one else wants…or can solve)

Serial Love

Healing Love

Revealing Love

Seeing Love

Honor Love

Sacrifice Love

Protecting Love

Remember Love

Discover Love

Surviving Love

Celebrating Love

Searching Love

Follow the exciting spin-off series:

Alvarez Security (military romantic suspense)

Gabe

Tony

Vinny

Jobe

SEALs

Thin Ice (Sleeper SEAL)

SEAL Together (Silver SEAL)

Undercover Groom (Hot SEAL)

Also for a Hope City Crossover Novel / Hot SEAL...

A Forever Dad by Maryann Jordan

Letters From Home (military romance)

Class of Love

Freedom of Love

Bond of Love

The Love's Series (detectives)

Love's Taming

Love's Tempting

Love's Trusting

The Fairfield Series (small town detectives)

Emma's Home

Laurie's Time

Carol's Image

Fireworks Over Fairfield

Please take the time to leave a review of this book. Feel free to contact me, especially if you enjoyed my book. I love to hear from readers!

Facebook

Email

Website

ABOUT THE AUTHOR

I am an avid reader of romance novels, often joking that I cut my teeth on the historical romances. I have been reading and reviewing for years. In 2013, I finally gave into the characters in my head, screaming for their story to be told. From these musings, my first novel, Emma's Home, The Fairfield Series was born.

I was a high school counselor having worked in education for thirty years. I live in Virginia, having also lived in four states and two foreign countries. I have been married to a wonderfully patient man for thirty-five years. When writing, my dog or one of my four cats can generally be found in the same room if not on my lap.

Please take the time to leave a review of this book. Feel free to contact me, especially if you enjoyed my book. I love to hear from readers!

Facebook

Email

Website

Made in United States
North Haven, CT
28 September 2022